COWBOY STRONG

He parked her car in his driveway and let the engine idle. "So you're not coming up?" He said it as if he was disappointed.

"Not today," she said. "Why, you afraid you'll miss me?"

He cut the motor and rubbed the bristle on his chin. "Maybe," he said. "One thing I'll say about you is that you're entertaining."

She turned in her seat to face him. "And my food. Don't forget you'll miss my cooking when I go, even if it is making you fat." She took a slow turn down his T-shirt–covered torso, pausing on his abs. Nope, not an inch of fat on him.

"I guess I could always buy your frozen entrées. Try to choke 'em down." The light in his blue eyes sparkled. He was enjoying teasing her.

"Then you'll have your kitchen back."

"Yep. Can't wait." He reached across the console and took off her sunglasses. Next came her hat.

She suddenly felt naked without them. Especially as he sat there, gazing at her face. She started to finger-comb her hair, but he pushed her hand away and held it in his much larger one. Then, he did something completely unexpected.

He leaned in, covered her mouth with his, and kissed her.

For a hard man, his lips were soft. And exquisitely pliant as they moved over hers, roaming until his tongue was licking into her mouth. She opened for him, letting him take the kiss deeper. He tasted good, like heat and desire, and she practically climbed over the center divider for more of him...

Books by Stacy Finz

The Nugget Series
GOING HOME
FINDING HOPE
SECOND CHANCES
STARTING OVER
GETTING LUCKY
BORROWING TROUBLE
HEATING UP
RIDING HIGH
FALLING HARD
HOPE FOR CHRISTMAS
TEMPTING FATE

The Garner Brothers
NEED YOU
WANT YOU
LOVE YOU

Dry Creek Ranch
COWBOY UP
COWBOY TOUGH
COWBOY STRONG

Published by Kensington Publishing Corporation

Cowboy Strong

Stacy Finz

LYRICAL SHINE
Kensington Publishing Corp.
www.kensingtonbooks.com

LYRICAL SHINE BOOKS are published by

Kensington Publishing Corp.
119 West 40th Street
New York, NY 10018

All Kensington titles, imprints, and distributed lines are available at special quantity discounts for bulk purchases for sales promotion, premiums, fund-raising, educational, or institutional use.

Special book excerpts or customized printings can also be created to fit specific needs. For details, write or phone the office of the Kensington Sales Manager: Kensington Publishing Corp., 119 West 40th Street, New York, NY 10018. Attn. Sales Department. Phone: 1-800-221-2647.

Lyrical Shine and Lyrical Shine logo Reg. U.S. Pat. & TM Off.

First Electronic Edition: July 2020
ISBN-13: 978-1-5161-0928-9 (ebook)
ISBN-10: 1-5161-0928-7 (ebook)

First Print Edition: July 2020
ISBN-13: 978-1-5161-0929-6
ISBN-10: 1-5161-0929-5

Printed in the United States of America

To the food crew at 49 Mary. I miss our times in the kitchen.

Acknowledgments

A special shout out to Bill Addison and Amanda Gold for all the cooking expertise. I couldn't have done it without you. Any mistakes made are my own. Thanks to the entire staff at Kensington. John Scognamiglio, Alex Nicolajsen, Jane Nutter and the rest of the crew, you've been my writing family for the last six years and for that I'm so grateful. And always thanks to my non-writing family who endure my crazy schedule, my plot panic attacks and all the other eccentricities that go with being a writer. You too, Rebecca Hunter. I'm so thankful for your friendship.

Chapter 1

It was midday and Sawyer Dalton desperately needed a shower and eight hours of uninterrupted sleep. He'd caught a red-eye from Heathrow to Sacramento after a four-day journalism conference where he'd spent his nights drinking and telling war stories into the wee hours of the morning.

As he pulled past the ranch gate, his chest gave a little kick, like it always did. Five hundred acres of the most pristine land in the Sierra foothills. Okay, he was biased. But Dry Creek Ranch, a working cow-calf operation, had been in his family for four generations.

On a clear day, you could see all the way to Banner Mountain. And the green, grassy hills rippled through the valley like a storybook version of the countryside. A series of gable barns, worn and weathered, dotted the landscape, their rooflines often hidden in the tall pines.

Now, the ranch belonged to Sawyer and his two cousins, Jace and Cash, an inheritance from his late grandfather. And while the ranch had fallen into disrepair, Sawyer and his cousins had big plans to someday restore the place to its former glory.

They just had to keep from losing it first.

He didn't bother with the garage, just parked his Range Rover in his driveway. Slinging his duffel strap over his arm, he climbed the stairs to his apartment. It had once been the hayloft of an old livestock barn. He'd hired a San Francisco architect to convert it into 2000 square feet of kick-ass, mostly open, living space with lots of windows, open-beam ceilings, and modern amenities. The bottom had been turned into a garage and workspace, while still preserving the barn's rustic charm.

When he wasn't traveling for work—which was all the time—the ranch and the loft were home sweet home.

He made it to the top of the stairs and tripped over a pile of luggage on the landing. Louis Vuitton. Not his—he'd be the laughing stock of the press corps—and sure the hell not his cousins'. None of them owned anything remotely designerish, unless you counted Levi's and Stetson. Besides, Cash and Jace both had their own homes on the ranch.

"Hello?" He craned his neck around the corner to find the house empty. Someone, however, had left a pile of dishes in the sink and cooking accoutrements all over the counter. It wasn't like Cash or Jace, or their women, to lend out Sawyer's house without permission.

Yet, there were people camping here and they weren't cleaning up after themselves.

He supposed the mystery would soon solve itself when whoever it was returned to claim the luggage.

Unable to keep his eyes open, he headed to his bedroom, dropping his duffel on the floor. On his way to the bathroom, he dragged his T-shirt over his head, tossing it somewhere in the vicinity of the hamper. Next, he went to work on his belt, looking forward to cranking up all six jets in his walk-in shower. The water pressure in his London hotel had sucked.

"Who are you?"

He jumped at the voice, then whipped his head around to find a woman sitting in his bed with her legs drawn up and a laptop perched on her knees. She looked vaguely familiar, but not familiar enough to be in his bedroom.

Yep, apparently he'd missed the memo that his home had been turned into an Airbnb in his absence.

"I'll ask you the same," he said. "And since this is my house, you go first."

She flicked her gaze at his bare chest, then went back to studying her laptop. "You must be Wendy's son," she said, distracted by whatever was on her screen. "She's been trying to reach you."

Ah, his mother.

Why she'd sent a complete stranger to his apartment was beyond anyone's guess. "I've been on an airplane for the last fourteen hours."

"That's probably why she couldn't reach you." She tapped the space bar on her keyboard, completely absorbed in whatever she was looking at. "She said you'd be gone awhile and it would be okay if I stayed here."

"She did, did she? Well, I'm home now, so that obviously won't work."

"I don't know what to tell you. That's what she said. I saw a big house on my way in. Can't you stay there?"

The question threw him for a second. "Uh, no, because I live here." What part of that was she having trouble understanding?

"Okay, then I'll stay in the big house."

Wow. He shook his head.

"Yeah, I don't think so. My cousin and his two kids and fiancée live in the big house. Last I heard, they weren't taking in boarders. Why don't we start with you telling me who you are?" He'd take up the rest of this freak show with his mother.

"Son of a bitch!" She slammed her laptop closed, scrambled off the bed, and swiped a smartphone off his dresser—which was now covered with women's lingerie—punched in a number and started yelling at someone.

He listened in because he was nosy and because she made it difficult not too. People on the other side of the continent could hear her, she was that loud. From her side of the conversation he extrapolated that it was a business situation. Someone was pulling out of a deal and she was going apeshit over it.

He searched his duffel for his own phone and took it into the living room. Sure enough, there were four missed calls from his mother and a CALL ME ASAP text.

He took a long, calming breath and dialed.

She answered on the first ring. "How's London, darling?"

"The trip was great until I got home." He leaned against the wall and cradled the phone to his ear with his shoulder. "Who is she and why is she here?"

"Oh, boy." Long pause. "You said you'd be overseas until August."

"I got all my interviews done for the piece I'm writing and came home a week early. Who is she, Mom, and why have you foisted her on Dry Creek Ranch?"

"You didn't recognize her?" His mother was pacing now; Sawyer could hear her high heels clicking on the marble floor in her office. "I guess that's good. She's Gina DeRose."

"That FoodFlicks chick?" Sawyer had caught her food show a few times. Not because he liked to cook, but because Gina DeRose was hot. At least on television. It was amazing what makeup and good lighting could do.

"Not just FoodFlicks. She owns an entire culinary empire. Cookbooks, kitchenware, pots and pans, her own line of seasonings, cake mixes, and packaged frozen foods."

He moved to the kitchen and rummaged through the fridge, looking for a bottle of water. They seemed to have all disappeared.

"What did she do, murder someone?" If Sawyer's parents were representing DeRose, she had to be dealing with a professional crisis of significant proportions. Dalton and Associates wasn't your garden-variety

publicity firm. His parents' company specialized in making career-killing mistakes go away for anyone rich enough to afford its services.

"She's accused of having an affair."

"People still care about that?" Call him jaded, but show him a celebrity, politician, or sports figure who hadn't been caught with their pants down. He wasn't condoning it, but society seemed immune, especially in the Hollywood-type world Gina DeRose ran in.

His mother sighed. "She broke up Candace and Danny Clay's marriage. There are pictures circulating all over the internet."

Sawyer knew the Clays also had a cooking show, kind of a Lucy and Ricky bit. He'd caught fleeting minutes of the program while channel surfing.

"It's a mess," his mother continued. "Candace's fans, of which there are legions, called for a boycott of Gina's show. When sponsors started pulling ads, FoodFlicks canceled the rest of the show's season, including reruns, and suspended negotiations for next season. Investors are talking about walking away from the retail end: the cookware, the prepared meals, and all the rest of it. And—"

"Okay, okay." He was too tired to hear anymore. "What do you want me to do?"

"Let her stay on the ranch. Everywhere she goes, she's chased by paparazzi. Your father and I just want her to lie low while we manage the bad press and stop the bleeding. And a hotel or a resort…she's too recognizable. I know I should've gotten your permission first. But we were desperate. She can't even leave her house without being ambushed. And Jace said it would be okay."

"When did you talk to Jace?"

"When I couldn't reach you. He let her in…gave her his spare key."

Sawyer rubbed his hands down his face. "I'll find her something," he said, though he didn't know what. "But she can't stay in my place." Besides the fact that he only had one bedroom, the apartment was also his office and writing cave. Then there was the fact that he'd never been good with sharing his space.

"Somewhere on the ranch, please." When he muttered that he would, she said, "Thank you, Sawyer. You're a good son."

"You mean I'm a sucker. Bye, Mom."

Gina came into the kitchen, looking like a bird had nested in her blond hair. She had bags under her eyes and the cleavage she was famous for was hidden underneath an oversized T-shirt. Either that or she wore a really good push-up bra on her television show.

"How'd you get here?" he asked, suddenly realizing he hadn't seen a car.

"To the kitchen? Or here to Timbuktu?"

He rolled his eyes and stifled a pithy comeback. The sooner he got her settled, the sooner he could sleep. "Did you drive and if so, where's your vehicle?" He said it slowly, enunciating each word.

"In the garage or barn, or whatever is below us." She pointed at the floor. "We'll need to keep the door closed at all times. I don't want the vultures to know where I am."

"And who would the vultures be?"

"Reporters. Bloodsuckers, every last one of them."

He reached into his back pocket, held his press pass in front of her face, and hitched a brow. "Don't worry, I only cover real news. Let's go."

For a second, she looked afraid, like he might root through her garbage or snap pictures of her naked. Then she must've realized that his mother—her crisis manager—wouldn't have sent her to the lion's den, and she went back to copping an attitude.

"Where?" She folded her arms over her chest.

"To your new safe house."

She perked up. "I hope it has a pool. It's hot here."

He was pretty sure that was her lame attempt at sarcasm.

"Yep. Five-star accommodations," he tossed back. "Pack up your stuff."

He got a fresh shirt from his closet, sent the rest of her luggage down in the hay elevator— one of the things he'd kept before the redo—and met her at the bottom of the stairs. She scrolled through her phone while he loaded her baggage into the back of his Range Rover.

"Careful with that," she said as he hefted one of her suiters. "My laundry service pressed everything and I doubt there's a good dry cleaner's anywhere around here." She stared out over the pastureland and shuddered as if she were stuck in a hellhole.

He held his tongue, looking forward to being rid of her. Never mind that the ranch was his lifeblood, everything that mattered.

"Hop in," he said, blasted the AC, and got on a rutted dirt road that followed the creek through a copse of trees that opened up to a clearing of green-colored fields. In the distance, the Sierra mountain range, covered in Ponderosa pines, loomed large. And green. It had been a wet winter.

Not a mile away, he cut the engine in front of a small cottage. The now-vacant log cabin used to be his cousin Cash's and every time Sawyer saw the broken steps, the sagging porch and the screen door that hung on one hinge, he hummed a few bars of "Dueling Banjos."

"Welcome home." He reached across her lap and swung open the passenger-seat door.

"You're kidding?" She squirmed. "You're punking me for calling you a bloodsucker, aren't you?"

"I'm not that petty." The heat hit him the second he jumped down from the cab. Hopefully, Cash had left the old swamp cooler in the cabin when he and his daughter, Ellie, moved across the creek.

"Watch your step, now." He waited for her to trail him up the rickety stairs, found the key under the mat, and held the door open for her.

"Uh-uh, I'm not going in there first." She waved her hand over the threshold for him to take the lead.

He went inside and flicked on a light. To air the place out—it stunk of dead animals—he opened a few windows.

There wasn't much to the cabin. Just one large space that made up the living room, kitchen, and eating nook. Off a narrow hallway there were two bedrooms and a bathroom. The smaller of the two bedrooms had been decorated in pink and white stripes when Ellie had come to live with Cash. The rest of the cabin was a depressing beige, although some of the walls were made from rough-hewn logs.

"Can't beat the views," he said and gazed out the window. "You can fish right off the front porch."

"Or die."

Even if the porch appeared to be held together with a piece of chewing gum, it was safe. "It's been here for a hundred years; it's not going anywhere."

She lifted her chin and locked eyes with him. "Sotheby's called and said to tell you you're fired."

Sawyer ignored her. "It's also furnished." He motioned at a dun-colored sofa that he was pretty sure Cash had found on the side of the road somewhere.

"Restoration Hardware or Pottery Barn?" She folded her arms over her chest and clenched her jaw so tight Sawyer thought she might crack a molar. "I can't possibly stay here."

The cabin might not be the Palace of Versailles, but it was certainly livable. Cash and his now thirteen-year-old had managed here just fine. All it needed was a good scrubbing and, depending on how long she planned to stay, Ms. FoodFlicks Star with the stick up her ass could afford to buy herself some decent furniture on the internet.

He brushed by her and hauled her luggage inside. "Well, I'll leave you to unpack and get settled. Just holler if you need anything."

He was making his way down the front-porch stairs when a Louis Vuitton cosmetic bag sailed past his head and landed in the dirt. "You cannot leave me here. This place...this dump...it should be condemned."

He pointed across the creek to another cabin. Unlike Gina's, that cabin had graced the pages of *Sunset Magazine* and *Country Living*. "My cousin and his wife and kid live there. Aubrey's an interior decorator. For the right price, she'll hook you up." Sawyer kept walking.

"Why do you hate me?"

He stopped and turned around to face her. "I don't hate you, I don't even know you. But to be real honest, you haven't made the best impression. You seem pretty damn self-entitled, if you ask me. This isn't a resort: It's a working cattle ranch. And I'm not your servant. The only reason you're still here is because I love my mother. She's a pain in the ass, but there's nothing I wouldn't do for her."

She started to respond and he held up his hands. "I haven't slept in three days. I'm going home now. If you need your car—which, by the way, prevents me from parking in my own garage—just follow the dirt road we took to get here. There's a grocery store and a coffee shop in Dry Creek, thirteen miles from here off the highway, when you get hungry."

He got in his Range Rover, discovered he'd hit that point where he was too exhausted to sleep, and headed to Jace's ranch house instead. Sawyer was greeted with a snout in his crotch by Sherpa, Jace's Australian shepherd. Scout, the other mutt, rolled on his back for a belly scratch. Sawyer obliged, then let himself in the back door.

"Anyone home?" The house was unusually quiet.

"In here," Jace called from his study.

Sawyer found him behind his desk, staring at a spreadsheet. He sank into the sofa. "Where is everyone? And what are you working on?"

"Ranch expenses." Jace looked up from his paperwork and rubbed his hand down his face. "Charlie's with Aubrey at a flea market. Travis and Grady are at friends. How was your trip?"

"Good, until I got home."

Jace laughed. "Your mom called. I know all about your houseguest. I never heard of her, but Charlie and Aubrey went nuts. They say she's a big deal. Has a cooking show, huh?"

"Yep, or rather she had a cooking show."

Jace nodded. "Though your ma didn't get into too many details, it was clear this DeRose woman is on the tabloids' shit list."

"She's probably on everyone's shit list. Have you met her yet?"

Jace jerked his head in surprise. "Last night for a few minutes, after I gave her the key to your place. She seemed more than pleasant. Friendly, self-deprecating. Likes dogs."

Sawyer didn't think they were talking about the same person. "That must've been her nicer twin. I moved her to Cash's old cabin. Hope you're okay with that."

"It's vacant." Jace hitched his shoulders. "Better her than varmints."

Sawyer leaned back on the couch. "I'm not so sure about that. Unlike you, I had a different experience. Only thirty minutes in her presence and I already can't stand her."

Jace chuckled. "How long is she staying?"

"I've got no idea. I guess until her troubles blow over and there's a new celebrity scandal for the public to obsess over. As long as she keeps out of my way, I don't care."

Sawyer bobbed his head at Jace's spreadsheet. "You figure out how to pay for this place yet?"

The Daltons had always been cattle ranchers. But when the drought came, Grandpa Dalton had been forced to cull the herd. Now, Sawyer and his two cousins ran about a hundred head. The income it generated wasn't enough to cover the expenses of the taxes, insurance, and upkeep on 500 acres. Their goal this summer was to find sustainable ways the ranch could bring in more money.

"Working on it," Jace said. "A lot will depend on how well Charlie and Aubrey's home goods store and design studio does. If the business takes off and brings traffic to the ranch, we'll have a better chance of leasing out space to other shops."

Sawyer wasn't thrilled with the idea. He didn't want a business park on the unspoiled land that had been in the Dalton family for four generations. But he supposed it was better than developing the property and turning it into a gated community of mini-mansions, swimming pools, and clubhouses. Or even worse: A Sam's Club with a giant parking lot.

"Let's make sure these shops have an agritourism vibe and not an outlet center feel."

"You think Cash and I would do that? Give me a break, Sawyer. We're looking at Harris Ranch as a model."

Besides producing something like 150 million pounds of beef a year, the Harris family had turned their San Joaquin Valley cattle ranch and feedlot into an attraction for motorists traveling between Southern and Northern California. They offered luxury lodging, dining, and a gift shop. The whole setup had become a California institution, as well as a license to mint money.

"A bit of a tall order, don't you think?" Sawyer stretched out, hanging his boots off the edge of the couch. "What makes Harris Ranch work is that

it's halfway between San Francisco and Los Angeles and there's nothing else for miles. Dry Creek isn't on the way to anywhere."

Jace wadded up a piece of paper and threw it at Sawyer. "Whatever happened to your standard 'Go big, or go home'? We're on the route to Reno. Best ski resorts in California are only an hour away. But you don't have to be so literal about it. I'm using Harris Ranch in theory. We're not talking about building a one-hundred-fifty-room inn or a steak house. Just businesses that subscribe to the ranching way of life that'll attract tourists and locals."

"Like what?"

"Hell, I don't know. That's what we're trying to figure out."

"Maybe we could become a halfway house for disgraced celebrity chefs."

Jace's lips twitched at Sawyer's sneer. "She really got under your skin, didn't she?"

"She's a piece of work. Threw a bag at me because she didn't like her accommodations. The woman's lucky I didn't throw her out in the street and drop a dime to a food blogger friend of mine at *Eater*."

"I don't think your folks would be too thrilled with that. But we have some horse stalls that need mucking if you want her to earn her keep."

The idea appealed to Sawyer. Nothing like shoveling horse shit to bring a person down to earth. "Hopefully, she won't be here long. My gut tells me after a few days in the heat without air-conditioning, she'll pack up and book herself into a Ritz-Carlton somewhere."

Sawyer's stomach growled. Besides some nuts and pretzels on the plane, he hadn't had a real meal since leaving the UK. "You got anything to eat?"

"I think there's some leftover meat loaf in the fridge. Help yourself."

Sawyer got to his feet and wandered into the kitchen. It was the best room in the house, which was saying a lot, because the log rancher was a showstopper. His grandfather had spared no expense on the house, with its thirty-five-foot high ceilings, enormous stone fireplaces, rough-hewn log walls, and enough windows to take in views of the foothills on four sides.

Jace had grown up in the ranch house and had been raised by their grandparents after his mother, father, and baby brother had been killed by a drunken driver on Highway 49.

Although Sawyer had grown up in Los Angeles, he'd spent much of his youth sitting at the massive center island in this room, sneaking his grandmother's home-baked cookies from the pantry before dinner, and eating countless pancake breakfasts with his cousins. As kids, he and his sister, Angela, spent every holiday and summer at the ranch.

Dry Creek had always felt more like home than his parents' sprawling Beverly Hills compound.

He found the meat loaf and a bowl of leftover mashed potatoes, fixed a plate, and heated it in the microwave. While waiting, he nursed a bottle of beer. It looked like his afternoon nap was on hold. Probably better to stay awake until his regular bedtime to fight his jet lag anyway.

"You get a lot out of the conference?" Jace joined him at the island.

Sawyer shrugged. "It was mostly a bunch of journalists drinking and networking. At least while I was there, I did a few interviews for a piece I'm working on for *Forbes* about globalization." He was happy to be back in the swing of things. For the last year, he'd been chained to a desk, writing a book about the war in Afghanistan.

The microwave dinged and Sawyer took his food to the breakfast table. "You on call today?"

"I'm always on call; the joy of being sheriff. So far, though, it's been a slow Saturday."

"Nice," Sawyer said around a mouthful. "What's Cash up to?"

"Dunno. Probably with Ellie. She might've had a horse show today. Have you seen her jump? The kid's good. We might have an Olympian on our hands."

"Sounds like she takes after Angie, huh?" Unlike the rest of them—and much to their grandfather's horror—Sawyer's sister had preferred English riding to Western. Grandpa Dalton had given her no end of grief about her preference.

Sawyer would do anything to be able to tease her about it again.

He ate the last of his meat loaf and potatoes and polished off the rest of his beer. A second wave of exhaustion hit him and he considered taking a dip in the creek to wake himself up.

"Thanks for the meat loaf." He cleared his plate. "We grilling tomorrow?" It was a Sunday tradition Jace had started last summer. They gathered in his backyard around the outdoor kitchen for suppertime and ended the evening with the kids roasting marshmallows over the firepit.

"Yep," Jace said. "Bring beer. None of that weird shit."

Sawyer rolled his eyes. Jace's taste was as pedestrian as anyone's. Cash's wasn't much better. "Sure, something from 7-Eleven, preferably in a can. While I'm at it, I'll get some boxed wine." He headed out, calling behind him, "See you tomorrow."

When he got home there were four missed calls on his phone. All from his mother.

Chapter 2

Gina walked around the cabin, trying to decide whether to find the nearest hotel or haul ass back to Los Angeles. Ultimately, the prospect of the paparazzi chasing her down Interstate 5 convinced her to stay put. *But this place.*

She held her nose and spent the next ten minutes wheeling her suitcases into what served as the master bedroom. With an old dish towel from the kitchen, she dusted down the closet and bureau before unpacking. Terry cloth wasn't enough to clean the bathroom. A gallon of gasoline and a match might be the only way to save it.

Nevertheless, she found a can of scouring powder and some steel wool under the kitchen sink and went to work on the tub, then the toilet and sink. It didn't sparkle when she finished, but at least she was no longer afraid of contracting a disease.

The white tile floor was next on her agenda and she went in search of a mop. At home, in Malibu, she had people to scrub her floors and do just about anything else she didn't have time for, including cooking.

Which was ironic.

But she was too busy running a multimillion-dollar company and taping thirteen episodes a season of her show, *Now That's Italian!*, for FoodFlicks. Even her cookbooks were written by someone else now. Sometimes she wondered if she even remembered how to make scrambled eggs.

Stop whining.

She reminded herself that she'd achieved the dream. Not the cooking so much, which had been her escape, her joy, the one thing that made her feel loved. No, her kitchen skills had never started out as part of the master plan. But being rich and famous…yeah, that had always been the goal.

And now she stood a good chance of losing it all.

There wasn't a mop anywhere. Not in the pantry or the laundry room, or in the hallway linen closet. But she did find soap, a bucket, and a scrub brush. On her hands and knees, she cleaned the floor, which wasn't as dirty as it looked. Just old and chipped and faded.

And the physical labor did her good, even in the ninety-degree weather. It helped work off her nervous energy.

Her T-shirt stuck to her like a second skin. Outside, she could hear the creek flowing and for a rash second considered going in. Sawyer had said something about fishing off the porch and Gina didn't swim where she ate.

Sawyer…ugh…what a jerk. She was trying to escape the press, not shack up next door to it.

After he'd dumped her off here, Gina had called Wendy to give her a piece of her mind. Wendy had used that calming voice of hers to talk her off a ledge. She trusted Wendy's judgment; she really did. Dalton and Associates was the best in the business when it came to quelling a crisis and Gina's situation had morphed into full-blown catastrophe. But she was out of her depth in Dry Creek Ranch. Raised in Beverly Hills, dirt roads and cattle crossings gave her hives.

At least Sawyer's apartment had been modern and rather gorgeous, though it pained her to admit it. This place, though, didn't even have a decent stove. It was freaking electric and not even induction. And a Mr. Coffee? Who even used those anymore? She planned to remedy that as soon as possible and hoped to God UPS, FedEx, or the US Postal Service delivered here in the middle of nowhere.

She tugged off her sticky T-shirt and slipped off her shorts for a quick shower, letting a stream of cool water sluice over her. After twenty minutes, she got out of the tub, feeling human again.

She rummaged through her newly-hung clothes, trying to find something that wouldn't draw attention to herself. Gina finally settled on a lightweight peasant dress she'd bought at Fred Segal ages ago because she'd liked the way the blue fabric had matched her eyes. The dress still had the tags on it. Slipping on a pair of sandals, she grabbed her purse and hiked to Sawyer's garage to fetch her car.

His Range Rover was still parked in the driveway. She stared up at the barn loft, but couldn't make out any signs of life through the big picture windows, not that she cared. How hard could it be to find the coffee shop he'd told her about? That's what GPS was for.

She pushed her oversized sunglasses up on her nose, adjusted her floppy hat, and opened the garage door. There was probably a switch that did it automatically, but she had no idea where it was.

She backed her BMW out. Instead of taking the dirt road again, she used the same blacktop driveway she'd taken the night before and followed it to the gate. There, she set her GPS for the center of Dry Creek.

Ten minutes later, she was hopelessly lost on a back road. The highway was nowhere in sight and nothing looked familiar. Just a lot of barns, cows, goats, and an occasional house. She couldn't deny that the scenery was picturesque. It kind of reminded her of the Tuscan countryside where her father had grown up.

But hunger and frustration killed any chance of enjoying the view.

There hadn't been much food in Sawyer's house. Just a jar of beluga caviar, a heel of Manchego cheese, and some stale crackers. She'd helped herself to all of it, as well as to Sawyer's excellent wine collection. The man had good taste, she'd give him that.

"What the hell is wrong with you?" she yelled at her GPS, which had the good grace not to yell back. She'd managed to navigate Los Angeles's labyrinth of freeways just fine. But a tiny backwater…She threw up her hands, then hung a U-turn.

"Recalculating," the damned GPS whined.

She drove for what seemed like miles. But this time, judging by the Dry Creek sign—Welcome to the best cowtown in America—the fickle piece of equipment had come through. She cruised Mother Lode Road, peering through her window at the sights. Or rather the lack of them. Sawyer's coffee shop, which didn't appear to have a name. The obligatory supermarket, a seamstress shop with the cutesy name of Sew What, and a mishmash of other stores.

She hung a right on Main Street and was equally disappointed. A construction company, some kind of county office complex, a Greyhound bus station, and as Main came to the end of the road, a high school and a park.

Nothing to see here, folks.

She pulled into a gas station, flipped around, and drove back to the coffee shop. Parking was definitely not a problem in this town. Gina pulled her hat down lower over her forehead and made her way to the restaurant. From the sidewalk it looked like a greasy spoon. There was a menu taped to the front door and she stood there a while perusing the offerings. Basic truck stop fare with a Southern flavor, which done right could take you to heaven.

Gina had no illusions that this little diner would take her anywhere other than to heartburn hell. But starvation trumped standards.

She let herself in and a bell hanging from the door jangled. The restaurant was unexpectedly crowded, but it was dinnertime after all. The hostess, a sturdy middle-aged woman wearing an apron, pointed to a sign-up sheet and shouted something into the kitchen. Gina scrawled *Linda Jackson* on the page. It was her business manager's name and generic enough not to arouse suspicion.

She sat on the bench, an old wagon seat, and waited for her name to be called. The place was just as unimpressive on the inside as it had been on the outside. A cash register that looked as old as Gina, scarred wooden tables and chairs, and lots of photographs of cattle. The pastry case was cleaned out, typically a good sign this time of day. There was a cake display fridge that was filled with pies and other desserts that looked decent. Gina wondered if they were made in-house.

The hostess walked over, giving Gina a thorough once-over. She must've looked ridiculous wearing her sunglasses inside the restaurant, not to mention the floppy hat. But it was better than being recognized.

"There's a space at the counter if you're interested."

"I'll wait for a table."

"Suit yourself," she said like she thought Gina was being high-maintenance and walked away to greet a couple who'd just come in.

By the time a table came available, Gina had come close to leaving and hitting up the grocery store for something she could eat in her car. This town needed another restaurant. There probably wasn't anything else for hundreds of miles, though she remembered driving through a good-sized town only thirty minutes from the ranch.

Maybe it was Taco Tuesday on Saturday here at the greasy spoon. At this point she didn't care as long as she got fed. Miss Congeniality led her to a table.

"What wines do you have by the glass?" As soon as the words left her mouth she realized the ridiculousness of it. "Never mind, I'll just have a San Pellegrino. You do have that, right?"

"All day long," the hostess said in a saccharine voice that was blatantly sarcastic. "I'll give you time to look over the menu." The hostess, who apparently seconded as a server, moved on to another table, then back to the kitchen.

She returned a short time later with Gina's San Pellegrino and a tall, frosty glass of something else. "My husband told me to tell you this is on the house."

Her husband? Gina craned her neck around the large woman to see if there was a man behind her.

"In the kitchen," the woman said and rolled her eyes. "It's our homemade sarsaparilla."

Aha, she was the owner. Gina was about to thank her for the drink when someone at the table next door beckoned the woman over. Laney, they called her.

Gina was used to getting comped at restaurants. Everyone wanted something from a FoodFlicks star. A feature spot on the show, product placement, or just to rub elbows with a celebrity. But here, in her disguise, no one knew her from Adam.

Gina took a sip, not expecting much. And then *pow!* It was amazingly good. Better than any wannabe sarsaparillas she'd ever tasted, which had mostly been root beer with a hint of licorice. This, though, had notes of vanilla and caramel and a touch of wintergreen. No artificial flavors were used, according to her taste buds, which were usually right on the mark. Just real sarsaparilla root. There was a nice even balance between bitter and sweet.

She took a few more sips to make sure the heat and thirst hadn't tricked her into believing the homemade concoction was better than it truly was. But after draining half her glass she came to the same conclusion: the sarsaparilla was a home run.

And smart.

It was the perfect drink for a Southern-style diner with a decidedly cowboy vibe. She hadn't been in the food biz for more than a decade to not recognize the marketing genius of it, especially if the restaurant catered to tourists. And judging from the crowd, it did.

Complimentary sarsaparillas for everyone who walks in the door to set the mood and a little hole-in-the-wall coffee shop becomes a destination restaurant.

Laney returned. "What'll you have?"

"What's the house specialty?"

"Everything here is special, but we're most famous for our chicken and waffles."

"I'll have that and a side of collard greens. The sarsaparilla was amazing, by the way."

Laney didn't bother to write down the order in her notebook; she was too busy giving Gina side-eye. "If you think those sunglasses and hat are working, you're crazy in the head. I knew you were Gina DeRose the minute you walked in, though you're skinnier in real life. I guess what

they say about the camera adding ten pounds is true." Her eyes skimmed Gina's chest and she tsk-tsked. "You check yourself into that rehab facility down the road or are you staying with the Dalton boys?"

Boys? If Laney was referring to Sawyer, he was no boy. Not even close. She took in a deep breath and slowly glanced around the restaurant, worried that everyone in the place had also made her. "Shush," she told Laney and motioned for her to sit down. "Rehab? What in heavens for?"

Laney arched one dark brow. "Sex addiction."

"Give me a break. Does everyone know who I am?"

"Jimmy Ray didn't believe me when I told him, but I can't speak for everyone else. Did Dan and Wendy send you here to hide?"

Dan must've been Dry Creek's success story. According to Wendy, he grew up in this godforsaken town. It stood to reason that everyone here knew him.

She gave a slight nod. "Are you planning to rat me out?" Tabloid reporters would pay Laney good money for Gina's location.

"Not if you give me your recipe for that strawberry shortcake you're famous for."

The cake mix was one of Gina's top-selling items. It was 100 percent organic and just required eggs, milk instead of water (a trick to add density, fat, and flavor) and, of course, strawberries. Last year, they'd cut a deal with Whole Foods to double the grocer's order. The secret was putting mascarpone in the cream frosting (sold separately) and flavoring the berries with a bottle of Gina DeRose basil syrup. Everyone from Martha Stewart to two first ladies had begged her for the recipe to make the cake from scratch.

"You're blackmailing me?" Gina continued to peer around the dining room to see if anyone else had identified her yet. What was she thinking coming out in public? That was her problem: She let her impulsiveness be her guide.

From now on she vowed to stay on the ranch and order everything she needed from the internet.

"You bet I am," Laney said.

"I'll trade you for the sarsaparilla recipe." At least Gina could do something with that.

"Not on your life, sugar." Laney got to her feet. "I'll put in your order."

Gina deliberated on whether to cancel dinner and hightail it back to the log shack from hell. In the end, she decided she was too hungry to drive. Besides, the smell of fried chicken had hypnotized her.

While waiting, she took in the crowd. Definitely not a Saturday-night scene in Los Angeles. No designer clothes, just a lot of cowboy hats and boots. If she had to guess, the tourists up for a weekend in Gold Country were the diners in shorts and T-shirts.

Occasionally, a man in a chef's jacket popped his head through the window separating the kitchen from the dining room to call something to Laney. He must've been Jimmy Ray.

Let's see what you got, Jimmy.

If the food was as good as the sarsaparilla, the trip to town wouldn't be a total loss. But Gina had her doubts.

Laney finally brought her meal, which was large enough to feed Los Angeles. At first, she thought she was getting special treatment because… uh, Gina DeRose. But it was the same portion size everyone else in the joint got.

"Enjoy," Laney said. "You can leave the cake recipe with the check."

"You'd really sell me out?" Gina had been observing Laney for most of the evening. She wasn't the hard-ass she pretended to be. In fact, Gina could tell which diners were local and which were visiting based on who Laney hugged.

"Faster than a hot knife through butter."

"Whatever." Gina stifled an eye roll. She'd give her the damn recipe and leave out the two extra egg yolks she threw in to make the cake moister, like she'd done with everyone else.

"Jimmy Ray wants to know what you think." Laney's gaze dropped to the heaping plate of chicken and waffles and greens. "Holler when you're done."

As soon as Laney left, Gina layered her fork with a crispy piece of chicken and slice of fluffy sweet-potato waffle and took a bite, letting the flavors—sweet from the cane syrup and a little spicy from the Tabasco—meld on her tongue.

Holy mother of God, was it good. So good she wanted to cry. She dipped into the collard greens and closed her eyes to savor the salty, pungent flavor. Everything down to the bits of smoky bacon was sublime.

How the hell did she not know about this place?

She continued stuffing her face while searching Google on her phone with one finger. Besides a smattering of Yelp reviews, there was nothing about a coffee shop in Dry Creek, California. No writeups or reviews in *Zagat, Eater,* TripAdvisor, *Michelin Guide,* or anything else.

Laney returned to find that Gina had cleaned her plate. "For a skinny girl, you sure can pack it away. I brought you a slice of my chess pie."

"Laney, I don't think I can eat another bite."

"Just a little taste. You can bring the rest home with ya." Laney put her hands on her hips and stayed rooted in her spot.

No didn't appear to be an option.

Besides, Gina wanted to know if it was as good as everything else she'd eaten. She took a small bite, then another one, and before she knew it had devoured half the slice. Laney watched, a smug smile playing on her lips.

"Oh my God," Gina said around another bite. "I'm going to explode, but can't stop." She pointed at the pie with her fork. "You guys should wholesale this."

Laney grabbed Gina's arm. "Tell that to Jimmy Ray." She dragged Gina through the dining room.

Jimmy Ray was holding down the line by himself.

"Come meet Gina DeRose," Laney said to him and Gina shushed her again. "No one can hear us out there."

Jimmy Ray dropped a few battered chicken pieces into a skillet, took off his plastic gloves, and shook Gina's hand. "Pleased to meet you. How was your supper?"

"So good that I think you guys should franchise."

"Nah," he said, but grinned with pride. "We like the coffee shop just the way it is, don't we, Laney?"

Laney pulled a face. "I wouldn't mind being rich for a change."

Jimmy Ray kissed his wife on the head and said to Gina, "I hear you're staying at Dry Creek Ranch."

The word was certainly out. Gina gave it twenty-four hours before the paparazzi came knocking on her Unabomber cabin.

"Your wife promised not to tell anyone as long as I gave her my strawberry shortcake recipe." Gina locked eyes with Laney and squinted in challenge.

Jimmy Ray laughed. "She's joshing you. She won't tell a soul, will you, Laney?"

"We made a deal" was her response. The woman drove a hard bargain.

Gina paid her bill and scribbled the recipe on a page in Laney's order pad. On her way out of town, she stopped at the Dry Creek Market, deciding to risk detection for a few days' worth of provisions.

The grocery store wasn't the Santa Monica farmers' market, but it didn't completely suck. Gina left with a shopping cart full of grocery bags.

By the time she got home and put everything away, she was exhausted. She would've sat outside on what passed for a porch, but there were bugs everywhere and there wasn't any outdoor furniture to speak of, just an old wine barrel turned upside down.

She poured herself a glass of wine, took it to the monstrosity of a couch, and scrolled through her emails on her phone. Her manager had sent a couple of invoices for her to sign off on; her agent and lawyer notified her that they were still fighting with FoodFlicks over the public morals clause in her contract; and Gayle King from *CBS This Morning* wanted an interview. Blah, blah, blah.

She switched to her fan email account, which had been taken over by Candace Clay devotees, threatening to boycott Gina's show and her products. One person hoped she died and another offered to help her find Jesus.

Why are you reading these?

She put the phone down on the coffee table. It had a layer of dust as thick as Candace's mascara. She went in search of a rag or the terry-cloth towel she'd used earlier, but got her laptop instead. Back on the couch, she flipped it open, turned it on, and did a search under her and Danny Clay's names.

It was stupid, but she couldn't help herself.

She clicked on the picture she'd been looking for and blew it up on the screen. There they were, barely clothed, on a sandy beach together. Danny with an ear-to-ear smile on his face. Gina's breasts on display, looking even perkier than they did on her TV show.

She stared at the photo a long time, like she'd done a million times since the picture had hit the internet and had ruined her perfect life, then quickly slapped down the cover of her laptop.

Chapter 3

Something smelled fantastic and for a few cloudy seconds Sawyer thought he was still at the Park Plaza and room service had just been delivered. He rolled over, squinted at the clock on his nightstand, and tried to go back to sleep.

But there were sounds coming from his kitchen. Water running. Pots banging. The beeping noise his refrigerator made when the door remained open for too long.

He tossed his head against the pillow, let out a groan, and swung his legs over the side of his bed. Slipping on a clean pair of jeans, he ducked inside the bathroom to brush his teeth and strode into the kitchen in his bare feet.

"I thought we were clear on the fact that I live here and you don't," he said to Gina DeRose's ass. She was bending over to put something in his oven.

"Ow." She hit her head on the counter. "Don't sneak up on me like that."

He started to tell her that she was the one sneaking around his kitchen, uninvited, but got distracted by the smell again. Whatever it was, it was making his mouth water. He sat at the breakfast bar and watched her work.

She was dicing onions with a utility knife. Not his. His were Henckels and hers didn't have a brand or a logo. There was an efficiency and grace to the way she sliced. Like a choreographed dance with her hands.

"Pass me those carrots, would you?" She nudged her head at a colander filled with vegetables.

He slid it across the granite countertop. "What are you making?"

"Spinach and cheese soufflé for breakfast and chicken stock to freeze." She lifted her gaze and stared at his chest. "Do you ever wear a shirt?"

"Not if I can help it. What's wrong with your kitchen?"

She snorted again. "You're kidding me, right? Hand me that, please." She pointed with her chin because her hands were full of chicken.

He reached across the counter and handed her a box of kosher salt. There was fresh coffee and he got up to pour himself a cup. She had a knack for making herself at home. Since he planned to get a meal out of it, he wasn't about to complain. But she couldn't just come and go as she pleased in his apartment.

"Why are you looking at me like that? Collecting information for your next exposé?"

He laughed. "You're a little obsessed with yourself. I write exposés about totalitarian governments that starve their people, drug cartels that rule entire countries, contaminated water supplies that kill children—not about fallen celebrity chefs."

She had the good sense not to respond.

He continued to watch her over the rim of his cup. She looked better today than she had yesterday. The dark circles under her eyes were mostly gone and she'd combed her hair and tied it back into a smooth ponytail. Her shorts were white and her legs Coppertone bronze. Sawyer suspected it was either a spray-on tan or Gina had a standing appointment at a tanning salon. She had on a low-cut tank top. But the spectacular rack that had made her a household name with men who couldn't care less about cooking was missing in action.

Then again, so was that breezy, charming personality that had netted her a couple of Emmys. The moral of the story was don't believe everything you see on television.

But if someone was holding a gun to his head, he'd be forced to admit that Gina DeRose was a beautiful woman. Blond, blue-eyed with a mouth that was slightly too large for her heart-shaped face. It was sexy as hell and made her stand out from all the other beautiful blondes he'd known in his lifetime.

"The soufflé will take another twenty minutes if you want to get dressed." She zeroed in on his chest again.

"My body too distracting for you?"

She snorted. "Right."

He went back to his bedroom, took a ten-minute shower, and dressed. By the time he wandered into the kitchen, she had his large stockpot on the range top with her chicken broth simmering. He wasn't crazy about soup, especially in summer, but the fragrant smell was driving him crazy.

She gave him a sideways glance. "You have a lot of nice equipment."

"That's what I've been told." He flashed a salacious grin.

She shook her head and, yeah, it had been a cheesy line. "Why do you have all this stuff?" She eyed his pot rack. "You don't even own a bottle of olive oil, yet you have enough All-Clad to open a Williams Sonoma store. Why?"

"I got it in the divorce." He'd never been married and the expiration date on most of his relationships was two months. His job didn't leave a lot of time for romance and so far, he hadn't met a woman who'd made him want to slow down. "I like good food. Someday, I plan to spend more time on the culinary arts."

She quirked a brow, like she wasn't buying it. "When were you divorced?"

"Never, I was joking. The pots and pans were a gift from my mother, a not-so subtle hint that I eat like shit."

"Did she get you the knives too?" She perused his block of Henckels.

"I got those, figuring I'd look like a poseur with top-of-the-line pots and pans and only crappy knives." He bobbed his head at the soft case on the counter. "I assume those are yours. What's the brand?" He didn't recognize the logo, not that he was into that kind of stuff.

"Gina DeRose. But ChefAid actually makes them. I'm ChefAid's brand ambassador...or at least was. We're...in talks about my contract."

"Ahh." From his mom, it sounded like most of her talks weren't going too well. "May I?" He lifted the chef's knife to feel the weight of the handle in his hand. "Light, but it's got heft. Nice."

"Accessible to a home cook, right?"

"Seems like, yeah. Is that who you're targeting?" The black faux leather case seemed a little fancy for Suzy or Sam homemaker. But what the hell did he know?

"Uh-huh, but the experienced home cook. Someone who spends a lot of time in the kitchen."

Sawyer nodded. It sounded like she had done a full demographic workup, though he wouldn't have expected anything less. According to his mother, Gina had built quite a franchise, which meant she had to be a savvy businesswoman.

"I didn't know ChefAid made knives, just appliances." Refrigerators, ovens, microwaves, range tops, mixers, food processors, and built-in coffee makers. Half the shit in Sawyer's loft.

"They don't. We rolled them out a couple of years ago as part of a marketing campaign to announce that I'm the new face of ChefAid." She paused, then quickly amended, "I'm not sure if it's still working out for me."

"For you?" He cocked his head and suppressed a laugh. Never bullshit an investigative reporter. "You mean your relationship is no longer working for ChefAid, right?"

She stalled and finally said, "I'll win them back."

"How?" As long as she was mired in controversy, Sawyer didn't see it. Then again, look at Martha Stewart. A stint in the joint for insider trading hadn't tarnished her silver star.

Gina shrugged. "I'm meeting with them in September to discuss our five-year contract." She emphasized *five years* as if that meant ChefAid was locked in.

Sawyer knew most endorsement contracts could be nullified if the personal life of the company's representative embarrassed the shit out of said company. That gave Gina less than six weeks to brush up her image.

"Please don't tell me that's how long you're staying?" He tried to sound as if he were joking, but he wasn't.

The oven timer dinged and Gina gingerly pulled out her soufflé. It was impressive. Puffy and a pale shade of yellow.

She examined the egg dish and pulled a face.

"What?" he asked. It looked perfect to him.

"It could've risen more and it's sinking too fast. Floppy egg whites and I left it in a tad too long." She turned it slightly, examined it some more, and then, as if to herself, said, "I'm so damned out of practice."

"Why's that? Don't you have to do it every day as part of your job?"

She let out a bark of laughter. "You mean for my show? Here's a little secret for your exposé. I have twenty assistants. By the time I walk onto the set, everything is done for me."

He wasn't surprised and since they were being honest was tempted to ask if she had a body double for the cleavage shots. But decided against it, fearing that the soufflé would wind up in his face.

"It looks pretty good to me," he said. "You think we can eat it any time soon?"

She reached into one of the top cabinets for two plates and dished them each a serving. He took one bite and thought maybe they could be friends after all. Because if this was what "out of practice" tasted like, he wanted to be around when she got her groove back.

"It sucks," she said. "Dry and overpowered by the basil."

Dry? He'd thought it was quite moist. And the basil…well, he'd only caught a hint. He thought it was just right. Better than right. Superb.

"Don't be so hard on yourself." He forked up another bite. "I'm managing to choke it down."

She shot him a dirty look. "You also just admitted that you'll eat anything."

That wasn't exactly what he'd said. He ate like shit, no question about it. But he'd also dined all over the world in Michelin-starred restaurants, at nearly all of Michael Bauer's top 100 restaurants in San Francisco and anything the late Jonathan Gold or the living Bill Addison, of the *Los Angeles Times*, liked. Some would even call him a foodie.

"Okay, you're right, it sucks. You should redeem yourself by making something I can bring to my cousin's barbecue this evening."

She perked up. "What kind of barbecue?"

Wasn't there only one kind? "It's a thing here in…I think you called it Timbuktu. We light up a grill, put meat on it, drink a couple of beers, and eat. People do it all over the country, especially in summer."

She shot him another one of her looks and he was mesmerized by her blue eyes. They were like topaz.

And before he could stop himself he said, "You're invited if you want to come."

That seemed to fluster her. "Today? I've got a thing."

A thing? He hitched his brows but withheld comment. What the hell did he care whether she came? "Okay. It's over at the big ranch house if you change your mind. Can I have more of the soufflé?" He'd cleaned his plate.

She pushed the crock toward him and stirred her pot on the stove. "Knock yourself out."

"What's the soup for?"

"It's not soup, it's stock. It's good to have as a base." She put her spoon down and came back to the breakfast bar. "How come you live here instead of LA?"

"Like it here better," he said as he wolfed down his second piece of soufflé.

She took a visual stroll down his Levi's to his cowboy boots. "Why? You seem more sophisticated than your average cowpoke."

"You know a lot of ranchers, then? Because beef is a two-and-a-half-billion-dollar industry in California. We cowpokes are pretty damned sophisticated."

"If it's so lucrative, why do you have to moonlight as a journalist?"

Because he loved being a journalist and because Dry Creek Ranch took every resource they had just to keep the lights on. "Someone's gotta make the world a better place."

She crossed her arms over her chest. "A little high on yourself, aren't you?"

Her stock bubbled over and she hustled over to the stove to turn the flame down. "Is there a kitchen store around here?"

"There's Tess' in Grass Valley. Why? What do you need?"

"Just wondering," she said. "Are there any good gourmet markets?"

"There's a number of farmers' markets in the area. But as far as a Dean and DeLuca, you'd have to go to St. Helena for that. But there's the internet. They do deliver out here—*in Timbuktu.*"

She blew out a breath and sank into one of the barstools. "I'm trying to cut the cord with the World Wide Web these days."

"My mother said something about pictures."

A splotch of pink crept up her neck until it reached her cheeks. "Did you see it?"

"I didn't look." Though he'd thought about it a few times. He found a roll of cellophane he didn't know he had, wrapped up the rest of the soufflé, and put it in his fridge. A little presumptuous, but the price of using his kitchen without his permission was excellent leftovers. "Don't you have people who can get you the things you need?"

"Your mother told me not to tell anyone where I am. My staff all signed NDAs but…you know how that goes."

He nodded, because he did. People liked to talk for all kinds of reasons, including for money, which the tabloids would pay. Handsomely. "How long are you planning to stay in hiding?"

She hitched her shoulders. "Your mom thinks I need to lay low and stay out of the spotlight at least until the meeting with ChefAid." Staying out of sight might quell some of the chatter.

And that's what he was afraid of. Because it meant she'd be here for thirty-eight more days. Even if her soufflé was out of this world, he didn't want to like her. Besides making herself too at home in his loft, she hadn't shown the least bit of remorse for screwing around with someone else's husband. She was just sorry she got caught.

That told him a lot about her character and character was everything to Sawyer. His grandfather used to say, "A man without character is a man without a soul."

"How much do you have riding on the ChefAid gig?" It had to be a lucrative deal. But according to his mother, Gina had a large portfolio. Maybe a few days from now, she'd come to the conclusion that living in the sticks wasn't worth it and crawl back to wherever she came from.

She sighed, deliberated for a moment, and finally said, "A nice piece of my net worth, especially now that my show might get canceled for good and I have investors pulling out left and right."

Well, there went that theory.

Her handbag began to chirp and she stuck a spoon in his hand. "Stir that." She fished her phone out of her purse and took it inside his bedroom, leaving him alone with her chicken stock.

A short time later she appeared, her lips pressed in a grim line. "I've got to go."

Before he could ask her if everything was all right, she jogged down the stairs and let the screen door slam. From his window, he watched her BMW jackknife on the dirt road, leaving a cloud of dust behind her.

He turned the stock to simmer. One look around the kitchen and it didn't take long for him to realize that she'd stuck him with all the dishes.

* * * *

That evening Sawyer drove the half mile to Jace's. He would've walked, but he had a case of beer and a few bottles of wine. The gang was out back where Jace had the grill fired up. Sawyer stowed the beverages in the outdoor fridge and uncorked a bottle of Napa Cabernet to let it breathe.

Charlie and Aubrey would appreciate the wine. Jace and Cash, on the other hand, would drink swill from a paper cup.

Once his hands were empty, Ellie and Grady tackled him. They liked to stand on his feet while he walked like a robot. Jace's oldest boy stood back. At fourteen, Travis was too cool to be demonstrative. He bobbed his chin at Sawyer, instead.

Sawyer broke away from the little ones and put Travis in a headlock. "How you doin', pardner?"

"Good. Dad says a movie star lives here now."

"Not a movie star. She's on TV, though. And she's only here temporarily." Hopefully more temporary than thirty-eight days.

Cash cuffed him on the back. "Welcome home. Jace says you had a successful trip."

Sawyer shrugged. "The work half of the trip was productive. The other half was a lot of drinking and catching up with old colleagues. You know the drill." He grinned because Cash, a former FBI agent, had had a one-night stand with a cop at a law-enforcement conference and along came Ellie.

Sawyer suspected there was more sleeping around at law-enforcement conferences than there was at journalism conferences. Either that or Sawyer was an unlucky bastard.

"You met your new neighbor yet?" Sawyer probably should've talked to Cash before foisting her onto his cousin's side of the ranch.

"Not yet. We saw her car parked at the cabin this morning and Aubrey's been hanging out on the porch in hopes of catching a glimpse of her." Cash rolled his eyes. "Have you ever seen this cooking show she's so famous for?"

"A few times." More than Sawyer liked to admit, given that his idea of cooking was nuking a frozen burrito in the microwave or driving over to the coffee shop in Dry Creek.

"I guess I'm the only one on God's green earth who hasn't seen it. Even Ellie knew who Gina DeRose was."

If her reputation continued to take a beating, she'd be filed away in the unemployed has-been pile. She was perilously close now. Then her name would be as obscure as one of those one-hit wonders who no one remembered except for the song.

Sawyer suspected the only reason she'd survived thus far was because Dalton and Associates—i.e. his parents—were master crisis managers.

"No great loss," he told Cash and stifled his own eye roll.

"Who wants burgers and who wants steaks?" Jace called. He was wearing his *Mr. Good Lookin' is Cooking* apron that Aubrey had given him years ago and that he hauled out at every barbecue. The thing had been washed so many dang times the letters were starting to fade.

"Steaks," Aubrey and Charlie shouted from the picnic table, where they'd already made a good dent on a bottle of Pinot Grigio.

The kids all called for hamburgers. Sawyer checked out the offerings that had been laid out on an old wooden trestle table: At least three different salads, a fruit platter, snacks of assorted varieties, and a dozen condiments. He filched one of the bags of chips and joined Jace and Cash at the grill.

"Any of you have time tomorrow to help move the herd to the lower south pasture?" Jace asked. "I took the morning off but could use a hand or two."

"Sure," Cash and Sawyer said in unison.

Sawyer was gone the most and tried to make up for ranch work whenever he was home by doing double duty. They couldn't afford hands and for the most part did everything themselves, including mending the never-ending deterioration of fencing across their 500 acres.

There wasn't anything Sawyer wouldn't do to save the Dalton legacy. Besides a truckload of happy childhood memoires of weekends and holidays on the ranch, it was their grandfather's dying wish that they hold on to the land and make it prosper again.

Jasper Dalton had been larger than life, an almost mythical figure. Cowboy. Rancher. A symbol of honor and integrity and all that was right in the world.

When Sawyer's job took him to the dankest, darkest places on earth, all he had to do was think of his grandfather to keep him centered. To give him hope.

They stood over the fire, eating chips and drinking beer in companionable silence. Cash and Jace had always been more like brothers to Sawyer than first cousins. And with them all living on the ranch together, the three of them had grown even closer. But now that both men had women in their lives, Sawyer sometimes felt like a fifth wheel.

Jace raised his chin and shielded his eyes with his hand to block the sun as he stared out over the fields. "Looks like we've got one more."

Sawyer followed Jace's gaze. Gina was crossing the field, carrying something in one hand and swatting the air with the other. She didn't seem too steady on her feet and Sawyer wondered if she was drunk. "I sort of invited her."

"I thought you didn't like her." Jace jabbed Sawyer in the ribs with his elbow.

"I don't. But she showed up this morning to use my stove and somehow I let our barbecue slip out. What was I supposed to do; say you can't come?"

"Nope. You did the right thing." Jace exchanged a glance with Cash and the two of them grinned.

Sawyer shook his head and stared out over the pasture. Gina had stopped dead in her tracks. Big Bertha stood about a foot away, her bovine nostrils sniffing the air, curious about the interloper crossing the field. The old Angus was well past her production days, but had more than earned her keep on the ranch.

Grandpa Dalton had never been sentimental about his breeding herd. When his cows stopped producing calves, he culled them. But Big Bertha had worked her way into his heart and he'd turned her loose on the ranch to live the rest of her days, grazing under the Sierra foothills sun.

Nice work if you could get it.

"What's she doing?" Cash watched Gina with a quizzical expression on his face.

"I think she's afraid of Big Bertha," Sawyer said.

She continued to stand in the grass with one arm extended as if she was warding off a mugger in downtown LA.

"Hey, Justin," Jace called. "Go shoo Big Bertha away from our guest."

Travis, who'd been practicing his lasso skills on a roping dummy, stopped, and like the rest of them squinted out over the pasture. "Is that her? The movie star?"

"That's her," Jace said. "Go help her out."

Travis trotted across the field while Sawyer laughed his ass off. "I don't know what my mother was thinking sending her here. She's afraid of a goddamn cow."

Jace shook his head but did his best not to join in Sawyer's laughter. Cash being Cash took the high road.

"Leave her alone," he said. "She's clearly not used to ranch life."

They stood, watching as Travis and Sherpa herded Big Bertha away and as Gina continued to totter across the field.

Jace did a double take as she got closer. "Is she wearing high heels and a skirt? You better tell her about the tick problem here."

The woman already had Lyme disease of the brain. "Who the hell wears high heels to hike across a cow pasture?"

Charlie and Aubrey slipped between the fence railings to welcome her. And the three women huddled together, talking.

"You're burning the steaks." Cash nudged his chin at the grill and Jace quickly flipped the fillets.

Sawyer turned his attention to Gina. Despite dressing like she was on her way to happy hour instead of traipsing through cow shit, she looked sexy as hell. Long, shapely legs and today she had her hair down and had actually combed it. It fell in soft waves just above her shoulders. And those blue eyes…they glittered.

Charlie brought her over and introduced her to Jace and Cash. "She brought her famous strawberry shortcake."

Sawyer's cousins greeted her with handshakes. Gina eyed the setup and Sawyer noted the gleam in her eyes. Before his grandmother died, Grandpa Dalton had built the summer kitchen, which rivaled most people's indoor kitchens. Sleek stainless-steel appliances, a pizza oven, wood grill, and smoker. Big log gazebo and a bar. For big events, like Jace's election fundraisers, they set up rows of barbecues to accommodate the crowd. But for anything under a hundred guests, this was more than sufficient.

"I thought you had something else today." A gentleman would've kept his mouth shut and been gracious. But for some reason she pushed his buttons.

"I didn't want to be rude," she said, as if she was doing them a great favor by gracing them with her presence. Bringing the cake, though, had been nice. And unexpected. Gina DeRose struck him as a taker, not a giver.

Maybe he was making a snap judgment based on a paltry two meetings—at least the second one had been more positive than the first—but he was a trained observer, after all. And so far he took her for a narcissist. Weren't most celebrities?

"Gina, you want a steak or a burger?" Jace put a row of burgers on the grill and began to arrange the buns.

"A burger would be great." She slid a glance at the patties resting on the top rack where they could cook slowly without burning.

Jace was merely adequate in the kitchen, but his burgers were legendary. At least in Mill County.

"How do you want yours?"

"Medium rare," she said and gestured at the patties. "How'd you prepare them?"

"Egg, pepper, garlic salt, chili powder, and my secret weapon." When she arched a brow in question, Jace said, "Panko instead of bread crumbs."

Sawyer watched her nod approvingly. The women pulled her over to the picnic table, where they plied her with questions about FoodFlicks. No one mentioned the elephant in the yard and Sawyer couldn't help but wonder whether she was still seeing Danny Clay. Whether they were in love or just having sex.

Cheating sex.

"She seems nice," Cash said.

Sawyer just shrugged and changed the subject. "Any news on Beals Ranch?"

Randy Beals, their neighbor, was upside down on his cattle spread. The Bealses and the Daltons had been friends for generations. But like everyone else who ran cattle in the Sierra foothills, the struggle to keep afloat during drought years was slowly killing them off. Unlike Grandpa Dalton, Randy had borrowed against his land to keep his operation alive instead of culling his herd. Now he couldn't afford to pay the monthly mortgage bills.

"Haven't heard anything," Jace said. "I expect one day we'll drive by and there'll be a *sold* sign on the gate. What happens after that is anybody's guess."

"Anybody's guess?" The vein in Sawyer's neck pulsed. "What'll happen is a big-ass development. You know it, Cash knows it, everyone on Dry Creek Road knows it."

Cash let out a breath. "Not much we can do about it, Sawyer. It is what it is."

"We can buy the damn place ourselves. Randy said he'd give us first dibs when he was talking about selling last winter." But even as he said it, he knew how unrealistic it was. Beals Ranch was twice the size of Dry Creek Ranch and twice the price. They could barely afford the bills on what they already owned.

"Let me know when you win the lottery." Jace sandwiched the burgers between buns and brought the tray to the trestle table, calling, "Food's up."

The kids raced over and Sawyer grabbed the medium rare burger and brought it to Gina. The steaks followed and everyone helped themselves to sides.

"Nice spread." Gina sidled up next to Sawyer. "Does your family do this a lot?"

"Most Sundays, as long as everyone's here. Jace is the county sheriff and Cash is an investigator for the Bureau of Livestock Identification, so they get called out fairly often."

"What does a livestock investigator do?"

"Among other things, solve cattle rustling cases."

"Is that even a thing outside of old Westerns?"

"Like I told you, beef is a billion-dollar business in California. So, yeah, stealing livestock is *a thing.*"

"No need to get huffy about it."

"Huffy?" Sawyer quirked a brow. "There was nothing remotely huffy about that statement."

"Good, then can I borrow your kitchen tomorrow?"

At least this time she was asking. "Why? You planning to go into the catering business now that you're unemployed?"

"Ha-ha, very funny. I'm testing a new recipe and it took me two hours to bake a simple sponge cake in the cabin's poor excuse of an oven."

"Don't show up before one. I've got writing to do." If she was testing, he was tasting. A guy had to eat, right?

Chapter 4

Gina awoke to loud whoops and barks. For a second, she thought she'd died and gone to hell. Then she remembered where she was and realized she hadn't died. But the rest of it was true.

It's temporary, she reminded herself.

She crawled out of bed, padded to the window, and peeked through the blinds. In the distance, past the creek, close to a hundred cows lumbered across a field. Three men on horseback rode in formation, driving the cattle forward, whistling and shouting to keep them in line. Two dogs zigzagged in and out of the herd.

It was a sight to behold, even if it had roused her from a sound sleep. She stood at the window, watching. It was beautiful the way the cowboys seemed to have a sixth sense about which way the cows would move, turning their horses to and fro to keep the animals from straying. She'd never seen anything like it.

Gina grabbed her phone from the nightstand and wandered out onto the porch to snap a few pictures. She zoomed in with the lens and noticed that one of the cowboys was Sawyer. He didn't look so surly on the back of a horse. No, he was actually smiling. And the cowboy hat…it was hot.

She was just about to post the picture to her Instagram account when she remembered that Wendy had warned her to stay off social media. So many haters had come out of the woodwork that she didn't dare even lurk on Twitter or Facebook.

Her mother was probably laughing in her grave. *How did someone like me wind up with someone like you?* Gina forced her mother's favorite refrain from her head and snapped a few more photos.

For the first time since she'd gotten here, she took the time to look around. Really look. The cabin was a squalid POS, but the land was gorgeous. The creek, the gentle rolling hills, the trees, and the mountains in the distance. And so green. Southern California was a sea of brown in July.

She looked for a place to sit to take it all in, started to take a spot on the upside-down wine barrel and thought better of it. All she had on was a nightshirt and the wood looked like it was splintering. Judging by the bottle rings on the oak, someone had been using it as beer rest, not a chair. Later, as soon as she showered and dressed, she'd do a little shopping on the Internet. Maybe buy a rocker.

The sun had made a full appearance, shining like a big orange ball in the sky. Gina went inside to look at the time. It wasn't even eight o'clock. She thought about getting back in bed but was already wide awake.

She put a filter in the Mr. Coffee, scooped in some ground Starbucks, and flicked the switch. Another thing on her to-do list: Get a decent grind and brew and a bag of Italian beans. At least her trip to the Dry Creek Market would sustain her for a few days.

She searched through the cupboard until she found the powdered-sugar doughnuts she'd bought. They were a secret pleasure of hers, rooting back to when she was a kid and used to stash junk food under her bed.

While waiting for the coffee to brew, she jumped in the shower and dressed in a pair of denim shorts, a T-shirt, and tennis shoes. She mentally added jeans and a pair of sturdy hiking shoes or boots to her shopping list.

Last night, she'd felt like a colossal idiot in her Helmut Lang skirt and Fendi sling-backs. Had she lived in her own little bubble so long that she no longer knew how to dress appropriately to a family barbecue?

Well, she wouldn't make that mistake twice.

Yet, everyone had been extraordinarily nice, especially Aubrey and Charlie. The two women had been kind enough not to mention Danny Clay and kept the conversation to cooking and ranch life. It was a relief to talk about something other than her imploding career.

The truth was Gina was so over herself that talking about Charlie and Jace's upcoming wedding, about the women's stepchildren—even about the weather—was a welcome relief. By the end of the evening, she'd so enjoyed herself that she'd forgotten to be miserable. Even Sawyer's insistence that he drive her the short distance home hadn't killed her buzz.

For all his dickness, he could be charming when he wanted to. She supposed a man who looked like Sawyer Dalton didn't have to try too hard. He could scowl and hurl snarky one-liners all day long and still have women fawning over him like he was God's gift to creation.

She hated men like that.

The coffee was done and she pulled out a mug she'd scoured after finding it hiding in the back of a cabinet. That was another thing she needed, dishes. She sat at the table that had been left behind, dunked her doughnut in her coffee, and scrolled through her email.

So far, there weren't any fires to put out. Then again, it wasn't even nine yet.

She eyed the sad little cabin with distaste, wondering how long she'd have to stay here. Her Malibu house wasn't a mansion by any stretch of the imagination, but it had a gourmet kitchen, a pool, a spa, and…running water.

It was weird not having to drive to a set or to her office. She was managing her business—or what was left of it—by email. Thank goodness she had a competent, dependable staff working for her that was picking up the slack in her absence. But she was bored. For her whole adult life, she'd worked hard, building her company.

She would think a break would give her a chance to breathe, a chance to sit back and take stock of her life. Yet, all it did was make her stir-crazy. At least she was cooking again. It had been so long that she'd forgotten how good it made her feel.

She washed and put her mug away, did a little internet shopping, and decided to take a stroll around the ranch. This time, she planned to hike on the road. After what Sawyer told her about ticks, she wasn't taking any chances walking through the brush.

Plus, there were no cows on the road.

The property was vast. Gina didn't know where it started and where it ended. But there were pastures that seemed to go on forever and lots of outbuildings and barns. Some in better shape than others.

She followed the creek in search of Charlie and Aubrey's showroom and studio. At the barbecue, they'd mentioned their fledgling business of selling homemade furniture. Although Gina didn't know a thing about design, she was all for women turning their passions into careers.

The risk was letting the career consume the passion. She knew about that firsthand.

Up ahead, an old weathered barn with a big wooden sign for Refind told her she'd found her destination. An electric tool buzzed as a crew of men framed an adjoining building to the barn. Country music played in the background and no one seemed to notice Gina, who'd had the foresight to wear her hat and sunglasses.

The barn's large sliding doors were open. Gina popped her head inside, but no one appeared to be around. She felt funny about just walking in.

"Anyone here?" she called, doubtful that she'd be heard over the noise. "Round back," someone yelled.

Gina found Charlie sanding a dark wooden secretary that looked straight out of someone's grandmother's house. Next to the hutch was an unopened can of turquoise paint and a box of antique glass knobs.

"Hey." Charlie stopped working and flipped up her goggles. "Welcome to Refind. Come on in. Aubrey's in her office. I'll get her so we can give you the grand tour."

From Gina's earlier peek, the store had been more than she'd expected. For some reason, she'd envisioned something like an antique mall, a mishmash of items laid out in no particular order. Instead, Refind reminded her of a chic showroom that had been built to look like a barn, rather than the other way around. It was like something you'd find in an upscale town in Vermont or wine country.

They entered from a side door. A section in the corner had been cordoned off for clients to sift through fabric and wood samples.

"That's temporary," Charlie said. "Until we get our offices and Aubrey's studio built."

The rest of the barn was set up in vignettes: Living rooms, bedrooms, dining rooms, even outdoor rooms. Light fixtures hung from the rafters, interesting art pieces were affixed to the walls, and there were throw pillows and various other textiles everywhere.

"This is amazing." Gina turned in circles to take it all in. It was even larger than it had looked from the outside.

Charlie led her to the back where heavy canvas curtains partitioned off a makeshift office. "It's a mess right now. The contractors started a few days ago and now it's chaos. We're adding an additional two-thousand square feet. Offices, a workspace for me, and a conference room for Aubrey where she can meet with clients…choose fabric swatches, wood finishes, paint colors, all that kind of stuff."

Aubrey, who sat at an old farm table that had been turned into a desk, motioned that she was on the phone and made the five-minute sign.

They left her to finish her call while Gina wandered the showroom.

"You make all this stuff?" She sat in a club chair done in gorgeous geometric kilim fabric with leather accents and tried not to salivate.

"I find old pieces and either repurpose them or restore them. That came from a garage sale and was originally upholstered in green pleather."

"This? You're kidding." Gina swiveled in the chair. It was as comfortable as it was stunning. "Can I buy it?"

Charlie laughed. "Of course you can. Where are you going to put it?"

It didn't match the beachy theme of her Malibu home. Maybe she'd buy a mountain retreat just for the chair. "For now, the cabin." May as well make the place a little less Bates Motel while she was here.

Aubrey slipped out from behind her fabric wall. "Well, what do you think?"

"I'm buying this." Gina tested the chair's rocking capabilities. Smooth ride. Oh yeah, she was going to spend hours in this chair. But for right now there was more to see. She got to her feet and didn't know where to look first. "Everything is so original…and lovely. How do you both know how to do this?"

"I don't," Aubrey said. "I'm an interior designer. Charlie's the creative one with all the vision."

"Don't let Aubrey kid you. She has an eye like you wouldn't believe. Together we make an awesome team." Charlie's entire face lit up and her passion for her work—for this business—was palpable.

When was the last time Gina lit up like that while doing her show? So long ago, she couldn't even remember.

"So did the two of you know each other before you met Cash and Jace?"

"Nope. Aubrey lived here first with Cash and Ellie. I came later." Charlie let out a nervous laugh. "I was escaping an abusive relationship. Jace and his sons took me in. But that's old news." She brushed it away, clearly not wanting to talk about that part of her life. Gina didn't press. "Anyway, I used to own a successful store in San Francisco, started trolling garage sales here and refurbishing pieces. Word got out, mostly thanks to Aubrey, who had lots of clients looking to furnish second homes. And little by little customers started showing up at the barn, where I'd set up a workshop, to purchase pieces."

"Our aesthetics…well, it's like we were separated at birth, we're so in sync." Aubrey gave Charlie a squeeze. "It only made sense for us to team up. Build on what Charlie had already started at the ranch. The rest is history."

"How does it work?" Gina asked. "People come here to shop or do you and Aubrey go to people's homes?"

"Both," Aubrey said. "At least, that's how we hope it works out. We're still in the infancy stage, but the plan is that I use Charlie's pieces in my design work and that Charlie's clients use me to put together entire rooms or design their remodels."

"Wouldn't you be better off in town?" How would anyone find them in the middle of nowhere?

"Our goal is to lure people to Dry Creek Ranch. The ranch is our inspiration and we think it can be our clients' inspiration too," Aubrey said.

It was actually a brilliant branding strategy, Gina thought. Consumers these days liked the backstory on their products. Charlie and Aubrey had such a sweet and genuine narrative to tell.

She could see the tagline now: *Home is where the heart is and that's Dry Creek Ranch.* Or: *Home on the range.* Gina could think of a dozen catchy slogans off the top of her head. Maybe use the ranch's horseshoe brand on all their labels, she mused. It was really quite innovative.

"And you think people will come this far out?" she asked.

"We do." Charlie nodded. "Especially if we make the ranch part of the Sierra foothills experience. Of course, we'll have to offer more than just a home furnishings store and design studio to make Dry Creek Ranch a destination."

"Like what?" Gina was curious.

"Perhaps a country mercantile, a farm stand, a bakery, even a florist," Aubrey said. "We're still working out the details but we have plans. Big plans."

Gina liked the spirit of it, but Dry Creek Ranch was pretty off the beaten track. Turning it into a destination would need more than a few cutesy country stores. Maybe a theme park, like Knott's Berry Farm, but her gut told her Sawyer and his cousins would never go for that.

Who would?

"Why do you want to turn it into a destination?" Gina had gotten the impression that the Daltons only cared about raising cattle. At least that's how Sawyer had made it sound when he'd snidely pointed out that the ranch wasn't a resort.

Thanks, Captain Obvious.

Charlie exchanged a glance with Aubrey and let out a breath. Clearly, they were deliberating on what or what not to say. For all intents and purposes she was a stranger, after all.

"We'd like the ranch to bring in more money," Aubrey finally said, trying to sound as if it wasn't critical, which only made Gina think it was.

"Money's good." She gave a nonchalant shrug. The Daltons' finances were their business, not hers. And currently she was the last person to give advice.

She ran her hand over a cowhide ottoman to see if it was genuine, which of course it was, and moved on to a sofa that was upholstered in a complementary fabric to the club chair.

"How hard would it be to move all these pieces to the cabin?" She waved her hand at the collection. If she was going to be here for a few weeks she

might as well furnish the place in stuff she loved, instead of the whole homeless encampment theme the former tenant had going on.

"Not hard," Charlie said. "I could borrow Jace's truck and between all of us we could carry everything."

Gina rummaged through her wallet for her gold card. "Let's do it."

A few hours later, she sat in her new living room, admiring the changes. They'd managed to heft the old sofa into Jace's truck for a dump run. The cabin still suffered from neglect and someone's love of dirty beige. But the couch, chair, and ottoman were fabulous.

At two, she loaded her BMW and made the short drive to Sawyer's. As usual, the front door was unlocked and she let herself in, hugging a boneless lamb shoulder and a bag of groceries.

Sawyer sat at the center island with his laptop. He lifted his gaze as she came in and went back to whatever he was doing.

She scanned the kitchen. "Do you have a tagine?"

"I left my last one in Morocco." He rolled his eyes.

"How 'bout a Dutch oven?" She didn't wait for him to answer and searched his cabinets, finding a nine-quart Le Creuset pot. "This'll work."

He shut the laptop and peered at her over his coffee mug. "What's for dinner?"

"Spiced lamb tagine with couscous and a chickpea salad." She found a cutting board in one of the drawers, put it on the counter, and eyed his plaid Carhartt short-sleeved shirt. "I see you have clothes on today."

"Disappointed?"

The truth? Yes. He had lots of faults—crabby personality, for one—but the man had an extremely fine chest. Broad, bronzed, and cut. The rest of him wasn't too shabby, either. Thick dark hair that begged for fingers, blue eyes that reminded her of a trip she'd taken to the Aegean Sea, and a body that was made for sin. Okay, she'd ripped that last line off from *Working Girl*, but it definitely applied to Sawyer.

"Not on your life, bucko."

"Bucko?" He arched a brow, then turned his attention to the groceries she was spreading out on the countertop. "For the tagine, I presume. Didn't know you did Middle Eastern food."

"Just playing around with some new ideas." For her show, everything had to be Italian, so it was nice to try something else for a change. Then there was the fact that there was nothing better to do here than cook. Unless, of course, she counted watching the toppling of her hard-won empire. She might as well test recipes. "I've got to let the lamb come to room temperature. It'll take about an hour."

In the meantime, she got to work on the chickpea salad, sliding a glance every now and again to Sawyer, who'd once again become engrossed in his laptop.

"What's so interesting?" she asked.

"Working on a few things." He flipped the cover down again, got up, and stuck his head in the fridge. "How long until that's done?" He bobbed his head at the lamb.

"At least two hours, I'm afraid." She shoved him out of the way, opened the fridge, and peered inside. There wasn't a whole lot there, not even the leftovers from her soufflé. "I could make you a couple of eggs."

"Nah, I'm not that hungry. The fridge thing is out of force of habit. I had a big breakfast over at Jace and Charlie's after we moved the cattle this morning."

"I saw you," she said. "You woke me up."

He looked at her and shook his head. "In the immortal words of my grandfather, 'This ain't no country club.' Get used to it, princess."

He let his eyes wander over her cutoffs. She couldn't tell whether he was sneering or checking her out. Whatever. She didn't care, she told herself, and finished making her chickpea salad.

"You have any plastic wrap?"

He got off the stool, rummaged through one of the drawers, and pulled out a box. She covered the salad and stowed it in the refrigerator.

"You don't ever have to go into an office?" she asked, wondering how his journalism job worked.

"Nope. I'm freelance, so I mostly work from home when I'm not on assignment."

"What does an assignment entail, exactly?" Most of the journalists she'd had experience with considered camping on her front lawn an assignment. She considered it trespassing.

"I spent much of last year embedded with Special Forces in Afghanistan. The year before, I lived in India for three months while working on a piece about sex trafficking and two months in Brazil, chronicling the start-up of a fair-trade coffee plantation owned by the workers. It just depends on what the story is and how deep my editor wants me to go."

"It sounds dangerous."

"Sometimes. Sometimes it's following a politician around and sleeping in a Marriott every night."

"And you moonlight as a cowboy."

"Not moonlight." He jutted his chin at her. "Cowboying is a way of life. It's what my family has done for more than a hundred years. It's what we'll continue to do long after I'm gone."

Journalist-cowboy. Interesting combination, Gina thought. "Not your dad?" Gina had only met Dan Dalton a few times; she mostly worked with Wendy. But he was about as citified as you could get. Designer suits and shoes that had never touched a cow patty.

"Nope. My grandfather swore that ranching skipped a generation. Unlike his children, his grandkids were infected with the bug."

"And turning the ranch into a business court...you're okay with that?"

Sawyer jerked his head in surprise. "How'd you hear about that?"

"Charlie and Aubrey." She didn't think she was divulging secrets. Aubrey had made it seem that everyone in the Dalton clan was onboard with the idea.

"Let's just say it's a necessary evil to keep the place running."

"I thought beef was a billion-dollar industry." She put her hands on her hips, enjoying turning his own words on him. Just a reminder that she could out-condescend him any day of the week.

"It is. But on our scale—we only run about a hundred head—it's barely enough to keep us afloat. Until we figure out a way for the ranch to make more money...we're in the poorhouse."

She was surprised by the revelation as much as she was by his honesty and felt a twinge of guilt for taking a shot at him. "Are you at risk of losing it?"

"Not yet," he said and left it at that, making Gina wonder if the money situation at the ranch was more dire than he was even letting on.

She didn't press. It wasn't any of her business. Besides, she didn't have any sage advice to dole out. *Don't get accused of screwing someone else's spouse or you'll lose everything.*

Gina slid the lamb in the oven to bake for an hour and got started on steaming the couscous using one of Sawyer's colanders snugly fitted over a pot. In her Malibu kitchen she would've used a traditional *couscoussier* to steam the wheat semolina. But here she had to improvise.

Sawyer rested his elbows on the counter and followed her step-by-step. Even though millions of viewers tuned in every day to see her cook, something about him watching so closely unnerved her. It was as if he knew she was a colossal phony and he wanted to catch her using the wrong ingredient or burning something.

"Anything new from ChefAid?" he asked, handing her the small box of star anise as she reached for it.

"Like what? I told you we were meeting in September."

"Just wondered…you know, after the latest."

"What latest?"

"You didn't hear?"

Gina cut him a look and his face went slightly pale.

Shit.

She lunged for his laptop.

He rested his hand on the top before she could grab it.

"Hear what?" she yelled, her pulse doing a tap dance. It was a pretty good guess that whatever Sawyer was talking about was more bad news. Perhaps staying off the internet to avoid the haters wasn't such a good idea.

She searched through her handbag for her phone. It had only been four or five hours since she'd last scrolled through her messages. But she'd seen lives ruined in the mere click of a keyboard.

She tapped on her phone and sure enough, she had five missed calls, ten texts, and at least six emails marked urgent. She sat on one of the stools, girding herself for whatever new crisis was about to get thrown at her, reading each message.

Sawyer stood over her shoulder. "Sorry, I thought by now you would've heard. But this time you're not sticking me with the dishes."

Chapter 5

Gina DeRose was a walking disaster. Like an eight on the Richter scale of calamities. While some men—like Sawyer's two cousins—ran to women in trouble, he looked for the nearest exit. Unfortunately, in this case that would mean leaving his own house, which he'd actually considered the minute she'd gotten the news and subsequently blew up like a bottle rocket.

She'd hightailed it into his bedroom and for the last twenty minutes had been yelling at someone—maybe his mother—on the phone. From the kitchen, he tried to listen, but was having trouble following the conversation.

He'd give Gina credit, though. She'd rattled off a litany of curse words that he, a lauded wordsmith, would never have thought to string together in quite the way she had.

Impressive.

An entertainment magazine had gotten hold of her and Danny's text messages and had plastered screenshots of them, including a picture of Danny's dick, all over the internet.

Who the hell did that? Sawyer had sexted a time or two, or even three. Especially when he was away on assignment and in the throes of a new relationship. Who hadn't? But why would anyone on God's green earth commemorate his junk in a picture and then hit the *send* button?

Hey, here's a shot of my penis. Wish you were here.

What Sawyer did know was that the dick pic and the texts, which he'd read and were pretty raunchy, weren't going to play well with the ChefAid suits.

Not well at all.

Sawyer's mother had her work cut out for her. And Gina would have to continue hiding here, coming in and out of his house like it was a revolving door. He wasn't too thrilled about that, but at least he'd eat well.

He checked the oven to make sure the lamb wasn't burning. The whole house smelled like Moroccan spices, which for some reason reminded him of Christmas. Maybe it was the cinnamon. The aroma made his mouth water and his stomach growl. He didn't know whether the couscous was overcooking, but decided to leave it alone.

"Can you freaking believe this?" Gina came back into the kitchen, waving her phone in the air.

"I learned a long time ago to never put anything in writing that you didn't want people to see. Privacy is a myth."

She started to say something and seemed to reconsider. Then, because she had to have the last word, said, "You would know, being a professional bloodsucker."

"According to those text messages, I'm not the only one who's sucking, if you know what I mean."

She flipped him off and turned to the stove. "The couscous is going to taste like mush."

"Was that my mom on the phone?" He returned to his seat at the island.

She let out a breath. "My agent, my manager, my assistant. Cynthia Grossman, my publicist, who I'm about to fire."

"What'd she do?"

"Nothing. That's the problem."

Sawyer laughed, though what was she supposed to do? The texts spoke for themselves. "How do you think they leaked out?"

"Obviously not from me."

There was nothing obvious about it. Anyone who had access to her phone, which he assumed her staff did, could be the culprit, but he didn't say anything. Surely someone in her position was smart enough to realize that. "So you think it came from Danny Clay, huh?"

"That would be...I have no idea. All I know is someone is out to get me."

Sawyer had to keep from rolling his eyes. Wasn't that just like a narcissist? She has an affair with another woman's husband, yet someone was out to get her? What a piece of work.

"What?" She squinted her eyes at him.

"I didn't say a word."

"You don't have to. I can hear your judgment from here."

He stood up and leaned his hip against the counter. "Yeah, what am I thinking, then?"

"That I'm a terrible person. But you don't know the first thing about me."

"Nope." Nor did he want to—too much to unpack, he thought, as his eyes did a covert slide down her body. "Hey, I'm staying in my lane. No judgment." Which wasn't altogether true.

"Good, because you don't have a clue of what's going on here."

A lot of bumping and grinding, according to her texts. Hell, she'd sounded like a veritable sex machine.

Really, he didn't know why he was even getting involved. He wrote about peoples' problems for a living, he didn't need to do it in his spare time. But something about her made him want to figure her out. She was like the Saturday *New York Times* crossword puzzle, a challenge. And there was nothing Sawyer loved more than a challenge. Even one who was a full-time pain in the ass.

They wound up eating her lamb tagine between phone calls and temper tantrums. He could only imagine how she must've reacted to the photo, which he'd finally gotten around to searching on the internet. It had been your typical paparazzi wide-lens beach shot. Grainy but clear enough to make out Gina and Danny having a good time. The photo wasn't as salacious as the texts, but it was provocative enough to leave no doubt that the subjects were involved romantically.

Gina cleaned up her dishes and went home, leaving him enough leftovers to last the week. Not such a bad deal. He considered calling his mother and getting her take on Gina's situation, but it would probably be hopeless. Dalton and Associates had a strict confidentiality policy when it came to their clients, as they should.

Instead, he went over the notes he'd taken from interviewing a woman who'd lived on the commune with Angie in New Mexico to see if he'd missed anything.

Five years ago, his sister, Angela, had dropped off the edge of the earth. Angie had always been unreliable, jumping on every cause known to mankind, joining up with fringe groups and traveling to remote areas, living a nomad's life. High-risk? Maybe. But his sister lived by her own rules. It wasn't uncommon for her to disappear for a while, then reemerge a few months later.

But not this time. This time, she'd completely ghosted them, which was so out of character for her that they'd assumed something terrible had happened.

He and his parents had filed missing person reports, hired private investigators, and offered large monetary rewards for any information that would unravel the mystery, without any success.

Then, a few months ago, Sawyer had gotten good information that Angie had been living on a commune in Taos, New Mexico. He continued to plumb the lead but so far had come up dry.

In June, he'd met a woman from the commune who was now living in Santa Fe. But she'd been reticent to talk. It was almost as if she was afraid of something or somebody. She'd been visibly uncomfortable throughout the entire interview, which told Sawyer she knew more than she was saying.

He was considering taking another stab at her, but had a sinking feeling it was hopeless.

He'd lost count of how many times he or his parents had dropped everything to hop on a plane or get in a car and chase down another fruitless tip.

"Hey," came Jace's voice from the bottom of the stairs. "Anyone home?"

"Come up." Sawyer quickly flipped his reporter's notebook closed. His cousins were of the opinion that Sawyer should stop turning his life upside down every time a private investigator found a trail to follow.

But it was his baby sister, for God's sake.

A few seconds later, Jace joined Sawyer at the dining room table. "Damn, it smells good in here."

"Chef Boyardee was over to cook."

"Chef Boyardee is welcome at my house anytime," Jace said while sniffing his way to the inside of Sawyer's refrigerator. "This it?" He held up a covered glass dish with the leftover lamb.

"Yep. You want me to nuke some for you in the microwave?" Sawyer went into the kitchen and made Jace up a plate. "What're you doing home so early?"

"That's what I came to talk to you about. I've got an interview with what may be our first tenants. Two UC Davis grads who want to lease land to grow and start up a flower stand. Charlie's sister hooked them up with us. You remember Allison?"

"The one who owns a nursery in Portland, right?" Jace nodded. "How much land do these Davis grads want?"

Jace stood sentry by the microwave as if hovering would make the food heat quicker. "A few acres."

"A few acres would feed a cow and her calf for a season. That's money in the bank." In the scheme of things, 500 acres wasn't all that much land to run a profitable cattle operation and to lease even a small parcel might not be cost-effective.

"I hear ya. We'll definitely have to make it worth our while financially, otherwise it's a lose-lose."

"How much water will they need?" Water was as precious a commodity as land.

"Don't know yet. These are questions we need to ask them. But I like that it'll at least be agricultural. They're hoping to do flowers for weddings and parties. Also sell to the public. I don't know how that'll work. Something else to ask them. But Charlie and Aubrey like the idea. I'm meeting with them in thirty minutes at the girls' studio. Came by to see if you want to tag along. Cash is in Plumas County today at a cattlemen's meeting."

"Sure, I'll go." Sawyer had put in a solid three hours of work after they'd moved the herd and before Gina had shown up.

The microwave dinged and Sawyer took out the plate of lamb and couscous. He got out the chickpea salad, added a scoop, and slid it down the counter to Jace. "Bon appétit."

Jace didn't waste any time shoveling the food into his mouth. "Wow, this is fantastic," he said around a mouthful.

"When was the last time you ate?"

"Lunch at the coffee shop." Jace ate there at least five times a week. They all did. "I thought you didn't like her."

"Who, Gina?" Sawyer hitched his shoulders. "She feeds me. I don't have to like her."

Jace pointed his fork at Sawyer. "The question is, Why does she feed you?" And then the moron grinned like he was really onto something.

"It's a trade for my kitchen. She doesn't like hers and she doesn't like me, either." Apparently she liked Danny Clay's dick, though. "And after today I'm pretty sure she's going to be here forever."

"Why's that?" Jace got up, found a loaf of bread in the fridge, and sopped up some of the lamb sauce with a slice.

"Someone got ahold of her and that other celebrity chef's sext messages and plastered them all over the internet. Let's just say they're better than anything you get on Pornhub."

Jace's brows winged up. "I suppose sex texts don't jibe with FoodFlicks' family-friendly image."

"Yeah, not even close. I doubt her sponsors are too thrilled."

"She can't hide here forever." Jace scraped his plate clean and stuck it in the dishwasher.

"Let's hope not." Though if Sawyer was being truly honest, he hadn't altogether minded her company. She had a quick wit and was fun to spar with.

"You ready to go?"

They hiked across the field to Charlie and Aubrey's old barn. Whether on foot or horseback, Sawyer never grew tired of the place. The sights and

smells changed with the hours. He loved every inch of the land, its rugged hills and rolling pastures and the way they stretched out forever, making everything else seem small in comparison. Most of all, though, he loved the way his family's history was steeped in these foothills.

He and Jace caught up with the creek, which wound its way through the property like a snake. Maybe tomorrow he'd sit by the water's edge with his laptop and do a little writing outdoors, then take a dip. The most popular spot was a swimming hole next to Cash's old cabin where the water was deep and the current calm.

But now with Gina living there he planned to avoid the place like the Ebola virus. As much as he appreciated dueling with her, he didn't want to get sucked into her drama. Not like he had this afternoon. Sure, he'd brought some of it on himself by asking a lot of questions. He tried to chalk it up to the fact that he was a journalist, naturally inquisitive—but that wasn't completely true.

For whatever reason he was drawn to her, which was an anomaly. While his parents were fixers, he'd never had a knight-in-shining-armor complex. In general, he steered clear of women with a lot of baggage.

"What are you so quiet about?" Jace asked as they got closer.

"Just working out a story in my head and trying to figure out the hook."

There was a 1950 candy-apple red Chevrolet pickup parked next to the barn. Sawyer wasn't an expert on classic cars, but someone had taken real good care of that baby.

Jace let out a long, low whistle "I like these girls already."

They took a few minutes to admire the truck. Yep, the women had good taste in pickups, Sawyer would give them that. But he was still on the fence about leasing them land.

He and his cousins had to do something to support the ranch, but he wasn't sure this was the answer. The idea of people traipsing in and out like it was a shopping mall didn't sit well with him.

Then again, neither did losing their legacy.

Voices came from inside the barn. He and Jace climbed over a stack of lumber and circled a sawhorse to get through the entrance. The construction crew must've punched out for the day. Either that or the crew had taken a break so they could hold their meeting without the cacophony of buzz saws in the background.

Charlie and Aubrey were sitting with two young women on a pair of Charlie's custom sofas in the showroom. Pretty girls, Sawyer thought, though they looked like teenagers. One was blonde, the other a brunette. Both dressed in jeans and graphic T-shirts. The brunette's had a picture of a

John Deere tractor and the words *I'd rather be f-ing.* Cute, Sawyer supposed, but not the most professional to wear on an interview.

Damn, I'm getting old.

"This is Ava and Winter." Charlie made the introductions while Sawyer and Jace pulled over two chairs.

"Tell me what you have in mind," Jace said. He'd never been one for small talk.

"We need about three acres to grow our flowers," Ava said and went on to list the genus and species of about a dozen plants in Latin. For all Sawyer knew, they were roses and snapdragons. Both girls vibrated with so much enthusiasm about it that it made Sawyer dizzy. It was if they were talking about the Giants clinching the 2010 World Series after a fifty-six-year losing streak.

"And we'd need a building we could use as a shop," Ava continued. "Nothing as big as this, of course." She looked around the Refind showroom, which used to stable Grandpa Dalton's horses.

Before the drought, when the cattle business was booming, he'd built a state-of-the-art barn where the horses currently lived and over time this one had gotten a little long in the tooth. The new construction and addition would return the old barn to its earlier splendor, even if it no longer housed Grandpa Dalton's prized cutting horses.

But the rehab cost money, a fact Sawyer couldn't lose sight of. Hence the meeting with the Powerpuff girls.

"Just big enough for a couple of refrigerator units, a workspace, and a small showroom," Ava continued in a way that sounded more like an apology than a business transaction.

Sawyer supposed he and his cousins were expected to pay for the build-out. Between lumber, labor, electrical, and plumbing, it wouldn't be cheap.

"What kind of rent are we talking about?" Sawyer asked.

Winter cleared her throat. "Uh, what were you thinking?"

Sawyer exchanged a glance with Jace and tried not to laugh. Fresh out of college and raring to go without a clue. But so damned earnest that Sawyer had to force himself to stay firm. Otherwise he'd give away the whole damn store.

"Let's come back to that," Jace said. "Right now, I'm more interested in your model and whether it fits in with our vision."

"We want to basically be a farmers' market for flowers," Winter said. "Straight from the field to the consumer. We're also planning to do floral arrangements, wreaths, that sort of thing, for weddings and special events and to sell from the shop."

Charlie grinned proudly and Aubrey nodded her head as if the graduates had re-created the wheel.

"You have a business plan with your profit-and-loss projections?" Sawyer asked.

Both women looked at each other blankly.

"I could help them with that," Charlie rushed in. "They're farmers," she said, trying to smooth over the girls' lack of business acumen. But to be a successful farmer you had to have a strategy, not just a dream.

Jace flicked up the brim of his Stetson and flashed a gooey smile at Charlie while Sawyer threw up a little in his mouth. If Ava and Winter failed they wouldn't be able to make their rent, which wasn't going to help Dry Creek Ranch.

"We could have the plan to you by tomorrow," Ava quickly volunteered, clearly unaware of how long it took to put together a comprehensive executive summary, market analysis, marketing plan, and sales strategy. Weeks, even months.

They were so gung ho it was hard to fault them for being in way over their heads.

He looked over at Jace, who looked back at him. Ah, jeez, they were going to do this. They were going to let these two novices run a flower shop from their ranch because Jace was so in love with his fiancée that he couldn't think straight and would do whatever she wanted. And she clearly wanted the girls.

Sawyer was just a sucker, plain and simple.

Too bad Cash wasn't here. He was a pragmatist, unlike the rest of them. He would've put the brakes on this so fast there would've been skid marks all the way to Dry Creek Road.

"Get us that plan and we'll take it from there," Jace said.

The girls took off in their vintage red truck and Sawyer turned to Jace, Charlie, and Aubrey. "You know this is crazy, right?"

Jace shrugged. "Farming's good."

Sawyer shook his head and hiked back to his loft apartment where a phone message from his mother awaited. He hit *return* on her number and she picked up on the third ring, a sign that whatever she had to say was important. Usually, they played phone tag for a day or so before they connected. His father was a little easier to get, but was often too distracted to carry on a coherent conversation.

"Have you seen Gina?" Sawyer's mother asked by way of a greeting. "I'm worried about her."

"She was here a few hours ago. I assume you know about the texts? She was making phone calls while she was here. I presumed you were one of the people with whom she was talking."

There was a silent pause. "I haven't been able to reach her in the last hour. Would you be a doll and make sure she's okay?"

No. He threw his head back and let out a sigh because his mother had the magic touch where he was concerned. She could wheedle him into doing anything. "I'll do it this time. But Mom, I'm not her keeper. I've got a story to write and a ranch to manage."

"Thank you, sweetheart. Tell her to call me, please."

He tapped his head against the wall in frustration and grabbed his keys off the hook. This time he was driving. It was too damn hot to walk.

Her BMW was parked in front of the cabin, so why the hell wasn't she answering her phone?

He jumped down from his cab, climbed the stairs, and tapped on her door. When she didn't answer he banged harder. "Anyone home?"

Still no answer.

He went around the side of the cabin and found her sitting on the creek bank with her feet dangling in the water. She had on a ridiculous floppy hat and a pair of big red plastic sunglasses, reminding him of vintage photographs he'd seen of Hollywood starlets. He stopped to surreptitiously watch her and despite himself enjoyed the scenery. She looked like a cover shot for *Life* magazine.

Sensing his presence, she flicked her head and caught him staring. She pushed the sunglasses down her nose and stared back without saying a word.

"My mom's looking for you." He hiked over to her spot and sank down beside her.

"Why? Because if there's more bad news, I don't want to know about it."

"She didn't say. Publicist-client privilege. But she's worried about you."

She turned her head and looked at him. "I think she's the only one in the world who is."

He couldn't tell if she was telling the truth or just feeling sorry for herself. He didn't have time for either but continued to sit there, anyway.

"You should call her." He pried off his cowboy boots, slid off his socks, rolled his pant legs up, and dropped his feet into the creek. The water was colder than he expected, but it felt good in the heat.

She nodded but didn't make a move to get her phone. "Who were the women in the red truck? I saw them drive toward the gate a little while ago."

"Farmers. They want to lease some land from us to grow flowers and sell them from the ranch."

"As part of the business plan Aubrey and Charlie have?" she asked.

"Yeah."

"Flowers are nice, but they're not going to turn this place into a destination."

"Who said anything about turning Dry Creek Ranch into a destination?"

"I thought that was part of the plan." She lifted one foot out of the water and Sawyer watched her wiggle her toes.

Her nails were painted bubblegum pink. A little cutesy for a woman who ran a multimillion-dollar enterprise, but for some reason he found them hot—and he wasn't usually into feet.

"Not my plan," he said. "I just want something that will bring in a steady income in addition to the cattle."

"And you think flowers will do that?"

No, he didn't. "Maybe. They just graduated from ag school and they need land. We've got it. It's a win-win."

Gina didn't say anything, just continued to nod her head. But she was skeptical. Sawyer could see that.

"What would you do?" he asked her.

"It depends what your objective is. If you're just looking for pocket change, a flower shop might do the trick. But according to what you told me, it sounds as if you need a steady flow of income. Significant income, right?"

He didn't want to go into any more financial details about Dry Creek Ranch with her. Truthfully, he was tired of talking about money. Lord knows he and his cousins had been going around and around about it since the day the lawyers had read their grandfather's will and trust.

"Why's my mother the only one who's worried about you?" He was violating his don't-ask, don't-care policy with her. But surely she had family and friends who realized how precarious her situation was and cared about her. Even though she'd made her own bed—so to speak—it did leave her business on shaky ground.

Take Paula Deen. The celebrity chef had never fully recovered after her fall from grace. There was no reason to believe Gina would, either.

"My mother's dead and even if she were still alive, she'd say I was ultimately destined to be a failure."

Sawyer drew back. "Mommy issues, huh?"

Gina let out a mirthless laugh. "Big-time. I was adopted at birth and a great disappointment to Sadie DeRose. I wasn't beautiful enough, popular enough, smart enough, social enough to meet her expectations. She thought she and my father had found the perfect mother to birth the perfect child. And it turned out that I was merely average."

Sawyer thought she was far from average. By anyone's standards she was a huge success. And beautiful. He might not like her, but any objective person could see she was someone special.

"What about your father?"

"Gino?" Her face lit up. "He adored me. Unfortunately, he died when I was nine."

"*The* Gino DeRose?" Sawyer didn't know why he hadn't put the connection together sooner. DeRose. The man was a legend in the film industry. A director whose body of work had changed the face of foreign cinema. "Wasn't your mother an actress?"

She bobbed her head in a combination that was part-nod and part-shake. "Besides a few roles in my father's films, she never really broke out. By the time I came along, she'd all but given up. I was her great hope."

"Did she at least get to see your cooking show?"

"In its very early iteration. I don't think she understood the cultural phenomena of FoodFlicks. I may as well have been a car show model to her."

Sawyer suspected as many people watched FoodFlicks as they had Gino DeRose's films. Perhaps even more. "What about your various business ventures? She must've been proud of those."

"Most of it came later…after she'd passed. It doesn't matter. It wasn't her dream for me. She wanted me to be what she couldn't be. A movie star with a shelf full of Oscars and a face like Angelina Jolie."

He turned to her, tilting his head to one side to take a long look. A thorough look. "You have a good face, Gina. I'd take your face over Angelina Jolie's any day."

She leaned back, rested on both elbows, and studied him as if she was waiting for the punch line to a joke. When none came, she said, "That's the nicest compliment anyone has ever given me. You know what, Sawyer Dalton? You're okay."

"Right back atcha."

They held each other's gaze and moved close enough so that their legs were touching. The heat between them was palpable.

For a long while they didn't talk, letting the sounds of the creek fill the silence. In those quiet moments he wondered about Danny Clay. Hadn't Clay ever told her she was irresistible?

Sawyer wanted to ask, but resisted. They were having a moment. A weird moment, but he didn't want to disrupt their tentative cease-fire. *Why* was a whole other story. One that he was going to put on the back burner while he enjoyed the sun, the creek, and the pretty woman sitting beside him. Even if she was a natural-born disaster.

Chapter 6

In the middle of the week, Gina got so stir-crazy she decided to take a field trip. If she wore a thin disguise—the shades and floppy hat—and stayed in her car no one would recognize her. And it was such a pretty day. Too hot to stay inside when she could enjoy the comfort of her BMW's top-of-the-line automatic climate control.

She set out with no particular place in mind other than State Highway 49. Once there, she'd planned to go north and let the highway take her wherever it led. But like the first time she'd tried this nearly a week ago, she got lost on a back road where verdant pastures dotted with cattle and sheep stretched out like a never-ending roll of outdoor carpet. Instead of pulling over and setting her GPS, she decided to follow the road to the end of the line. It had to lead somewhere. And who knows, maybe if she kept going she'd find civilization?

In the meantime, her surroundings didn't suck. Gina, born and raised in Los Angeles, had never considered herself a country girl. But the landscape appealed to her. In fact, she could look at it all day as long as she was within walking distance of a Peet's Coffee and a Whole Foods. So that pretty much ruled out Mill County.

Take lots of pictures, she told herself. When she got home, she'd blow them up to poster size and hang them in her office. While she was at it, she'd take a couple of shots of Sawyer too. Just for the view.

She wasn't ready to forgive him for forcing her to live in a cabin that was better suited as a meth house than a real home. But he was nice to look at and had been a good ear when she'd needed one.

Nothing she'd told him by the creek side had been classified. Most of it had been spilled across the pages of her bestselling memoir. Still, it had

been nice to confide to someone real, not a faceless fan. And his reaction had been perfect. Not pitying or patronizing...but sweet.

You have a good face, Gina...I'd take your face over Angelina Jolie's any day.

The words gave her goose bumps. She replayed them in her head a few times and her chest gave a little kick. The weight that had been clamped to her chest these last weeks began to lift.

Then the phone rang and that tightness clutched her again. She glanced down at the caller ID. Robin, her agent.

Gina answered on Bluetooth. "What now?"

"Candace filed for divorce two hours ago. She just put out a statement."

"Oh God. What does it say?"

"The usual. 'After much thought and careful consideration, we remain business partners and friends. Please respect our privacy at this difficult time.' So on and so on."

"Nothing about me in the statement, then?" Gina held her breath.

"No, but I suggest you stay off social media and the internet for a while. It's gotten pretty ugly."

Gotten? By Gina's estimation it had been ugly the day that stupid picture surfaced.

"Candace's fans are upset about the breakup and are understandably lashing out at you," Robin continued.

Gina exhaled and tried to steady her hands on the steering wheel. "What's going on with FoodFlicks? Do I still have a show?"

"I wish I knew. No one at the network is returning my calls. I could bluster, say that we'll take the show to a lifestyle or DIY channel, but it would be an empty threat. My messages at both networks have also gone unanswered. Let's be honest here: You're toxic right now, Gina. I don't even think I could get you on *Celebrity Big Brother* at this point."

Celebrity Big Brother? Is that what her life had been reduced to? She felt like vomiting. "What do we do now, Robin?"

"We wait it out, let Wendy Dalton work her magic, and hope for the best." There was a long pause and Gina knew more was coming.

"Just say what you have to say," she told Robin.

Robin cleared her throat. "I would be derelict in my duties as your agent...as your friend...to sugarcoat this. Your television career as we know it may be over. Timing is everything in this industry and this thing with the Clays has really disrupted the clock. I've got another call. Let's talk next week."

Gina pulled over to the side of the road and rested her head against the windshield. Suddenly the day didn't seem quite so sunny. Without her show…well, she didn't know who she was without it. And it propelled everything else. The Gina DeRose brand, the merchandise, the endorsement work, her entire company.

At least she wouldn't go broke. Her father had made sure she'd inherited well and she'd always been good with money, making sound investments. But her whole identity was wrapped up in the celebrity of Gina DeRose. Maybe it was superficial, but it was who she was. It's how she'd reinvented herself into someone who mattered.

She took a couple of deep breaths and got back on the road. No sense wallowing in something she couldn't fix. And being a control freak, that's what really galled her. Her hands were tied.

Fifteen minutes later, she found herself in town. Not Dry Creek. But the buildings looked similar. Nineteenth century, if she had to guess. Probably built sometime around the Gold Rush. A sign on one of the businesses told her she was in Grass Valley. She'd never heard of it, but Sawyer had mentioned something about a kitchen store here.

Drivers inched their way up the main drag, searching for parking. Pedestrians jammed the sidewalks, window-shopping at a collection of boutiques and galleries. And what did you know? Restaurants and cafés lined the streets.

The town was definitely larger than Dry Creek and from the looks of the crowd—mostly families, carrying shopping bags—a major tourist draw.

She drove in search of the kitchen store and found it on her second pass down Mill Street. It was a large shop, judging by the two plate glass windows decorated with clever kitchen displays. Finally, she found a parking lot off Mill and squeezed into one of the spaces and questioned the wisdom of going inside.

Laney from the coffee shop had recognized her instantly in her sunglasses and hat. Who's to say anyone else wouldn't? At the same time, she really wanted to shop. Sawyer had a well-stocked kitchen when it came to pots and pans, but he didn't have much in the way of baking supplies and she only had two warped cake pans she'd found in the cabin. She'd love to get a few pie dishes, a tart pan, and parchment paper.

It was impulsive, but she decided to risk it. Before leaving her car, she adjusted her hat in the visor mirror and hiked up the street to the store. It was surprisingly well stocked and even carried ChefAid mixers, food processors, and coffee makers. It was also packed with shoppers, which

made her nervous about being discovered. As it turned out, the throngs of people made it easier to hide in plain view.

The store was three stories high. The basement featured a demo kitchen for cooking classes. The ground floor focused on gadgets, cookbooks, wine, olive oils, and cheeses. And the third level had small appliances and dishware, including the Gina DeRose brand.

Before she knew it, an hour had passed and her hand basket was full. On her way to the checkout counter, she realized her only method of payment was plastic. Her name was on every credit card she owned.

Shit.

She rifled through her wallet and managed to scrape thirty-eight dollars together. It wasn't enough to pay for everything in her basket. She did some quick calculations and could only afford the pie dish and a tart pan.

She considered finding a teller machine, but every minute she was out in public she risked being recognized. Living like this was getting old. Fast. But it was better than the alternative of having the paparazzi up her ass.

She paid for her supplies and got back in her car, deciding that her adventure for the day was over. Maybe she'd try to bake a pie in the oven from hell or visit Aubrey and Charlie at their shop. It was strange not having meetings to attend or a show to tape, or a public appearance to make. She should be out-of-her-mind bored, but oddly she wasn't. Last night, she'd spent time on her laptop, looking up recipes for inspiration. She'd even read a book from beginning to end, lying on her new sofa.

It was a new experience having enough hours in the day for leisure time. And it was depressing as hell. It would be one thing if she didn't have the weight of her entire portfolio resting on her shoulders. Then maybe she could actually enjoy relaxing. But she was constantly on edge, waiting for the next surprise attack.

As she pulled up to her cabin, she saw Sawyer's Range Rover across the creek, parked at Cash and Aubrey's house. She felt a tickle in her stomach and blamed it on indigestion. Inside the cabin, she unpacked her two purchases and sorted through her pantry to see if she had the required ingredients to make a pie. On one of her walks to Charlie and Aubrey's barn, she'd noticed a wild blackberry bush near the creek, brimming with fruit.

She changed into a pair of jeans and tennis shoes. The tick warning had scared the bejesus out of her. All she needed was Lyme disease to cap off the shit storm that had become her life.

It had cooled considerably since the first time she'd left the house. According to her phone, the temperature was a balmy ninety degrees.

But if she walked in the shade it wasn't too bad. The day was so clear she could see the mountain peaks of the Sierra. Maybe all the way to Nevada.

She'd done a cookbook signing in Tahoe a few years back. Other than that, though, she'd never spent much time in this part of California. Except for promotional junkets and the obligatory trip to New York for the annual James Beard Awards, she rarely left LA. And even then, it was a series of airports and hotels.

She found the berry bush, which was thick as a forest, covered in plump, ripe fruit. Gina plucked one off an overgrown vine and popped it in her mouth. It was a tasty blend of sweet and tart. Perfect for pies.

While her culinary focus had always been on savory dishes, she was a fine baker. She was also a fine eater of her baked goods. When the pie was done, she'd bring it to Sawyer. It would look better on him than on her. But not before she had a taste of her labor.

She filled her pie dish with berries, wishing she'd brought a bigger container. There was enough fruit to bake dozens of desserts. If things got any more dire, she might just open a bakery and give Laney a run for her money.

Sawyer's Range Rover pulled up alongside her and his passenger window slid down. "What are you doing?"

"Picking berries. I assumed it was okay." They were just going to waste, feeding the birds and rotting on the bush.

He shrugged. "Knock yourself out."

She wanted to ask him where he'd been yesterday when she'd borrowed his kitchen to make a cassoulet, but bit her tongue. Perhaps he'd been trying to avoid her. She didn't fool herself that their creek-side truce had suddenly made them BFFs.

"Did you eat any of that cassoulet I left in your refrigerator?" she asked instead.

"I had three helpings. Hope you didn't have other plans for it," he said, but didn't seem terribly concerned that she might've.

"Nope, just testing recipes."

He shut off his engine and leaned across the seat. "How come you never take anything home?"

"The mice and rats." As far as she could tell the cabin was rodent-free, but she liked reminding him that he was a cad for dumping her there.

"They don't eat much." Both sides of his mouth hitched up. "Just be careful of the bears and mountain lions. You go out today?"

Aha, he was keeping tabs on her comings and goings? Don't be delusional, she told herself. He just happened to notice that her car was gone while he was at Cash's. "To that kitchen store you told me about."

He rubbed his hands over his scruff. Apparently, he no longer shaved. "That wise?"

"Probably not, but I needed a few things and it was a nice store."

He didn't say anything, just seemed to study her for a few minutes. "Well, I better get home."

"You mind if I use your oven to bake a pie?" She knew she was becoming an imposition but asked anyway. Why? She didn't know. She'd been perfectly prepared to bake in the cabin. The walls were closing in her, that's why.

"Uh...I guess." He didn't sound thrilled about it, so she decided to do it just to antagonize him.

"Great. I just have to go home and grab my ingredients and the new pie dish I bought. See you in a little while."

She rushed to the cabin and gathered up her supplies, including her freshly picked berries. Despite the danger of facing more negativity on the World Wide Web, she opened her laptop to research crusts. The best ones were made with lard and she didn't have any, or even Crisco. She could do all-butter, but it tended to make the crust puffier than she liked. Cream cheese, though, made a fantastic substitute for Crisco. And she had a package she'd bought to smear on the crappy frozen bagels she'd gotten at the Dry Creek Market.

She did a Google search for Rose Levy Beranbaum's cream cheese–to–butter ratio. As far as Gina was concerned, Beranbaum's *Pie and Pastry Bible* was the definitive manual on crust or anything having to do with pie.

When she was a girl, cooking in her parents' Beverly Hills kitchen, she had attempted to make every recipe in the book. Sadie had complained that it was making her fat and demanded that Gina stop. Until her mother had issued the no-more-baking edict, Gina had gotten two-thirds through the tome, which was thicker than the Old and New Testament combined.

She searched for the recipe, trying to stay focused and not peek at the day's news or YouTube videos of the late-night shows, or TMZ. How she loathed TMZ. It took all her willpower not to take a quick look at her fan email, which would just be masochistic. Unfortunately, though, she was one of those people who slowed down to look at car accidents. The pull to search her name was like a magnetic force.

Nope, not going to do it.

Yet, she deliberated when it came time to power down. Then her phone rang and she was saved by the bell.

Bye-bye internet.

She slammed down the top of her laptop, rushed across the room, and searched her purse. Her phone had sunk to the bottom and she had to swim through the flotsam to pluck it out.

"Hello," she answered, afraid she had already missed the call. "Hello?"

"Gina, it's Danny."

Chapter 7

Sawyer reached into the overhead storage bin and pulled out his carry-on. It had only been a four-hour flight from Albuquerque to Sacramento, but his legs were happy to be standing again. The seats in economy were too damn cramped for someone six-two.

He handed down a second bag to a middle-aged woman who'd sat in the seat next to him. She had not been subtle in her attempts to set him up with her daughter. Sawyer had pretended to be interested but his mind was on other things.

It had been his second trip to New Mexico in search of answers about Angie. He'd gone Friday on a whim, convinced that if he dug deeper, talked to more people, he'd get somewhere this time.

Yet, he had more questions now than when he'd started.

His source, the cagey woman he'd originally spoken with, was even more tight-lipped than she'd been the first time. Though she had let it slip that Angie had left the commune—*commune* being a fancy way of saying *cult*—to do humanitarian work overseas. When he tried to pinpoint her on where overseas, she said she didn't know.

He wasn't buying it. But that's all he had. So it pretty much left him with the entire world to search.

The heat hit him as soon as he stepped outside to catch a shuttle to the overnight lot. It had been cooler in Santa Fe, or maybe just drier. He'd only been gone two days, but was anxious to get home. Sleep in his own bed.

He turned on his phone and scrolled through his emails and messages. Nothing that couldn't wait until he got to the ranch. Traffic was manageable this late in the evening and he hoped to make good time.

Wishful thinking. What should've been an hour drive turned into two. A big rig jackknifed on the freeway, leaving a backup miles long. By the time he pulled through the ranch gate, he was in a foul mood.

And it only got worse when he found a little BMW parked in front of his garage doors.

"At least have the freaking decency not to block me from getting in," he muttered under his breath and left his Range Rover in the driveway.

Sawyer slung the strap of his go bag over his shoulder and went inside. Something smelled good, like fresh-baked bread.

"You're here." He unceremoniously dumped his bag on the floor.

"Hungry?" She looked up from something she was reading on his kitchen counter. It appeared to be his mail.

He swiped the pile of bills and assorted other paperwork off the counter, shoved them in a drawer, and grunted under his breath.

"I'll take that as a *yes*. Sit down and I'll make you something."

It was the least she could do after constantly invading his space. Ever since they'd had their moment on the creek bank, he'd been avoiding her, even leaving his house when he knew she was coming over to use his kitchen.

But in all honesty, seeing her again...shit. He liked it. He liked having her in his kitchen again.

"Let me change first," he said. Between the stuffy plane and the heat, he'd have to scrape his shirt off like wallpaper. On his way to the bedroom, he adjusted the air-conditioner to sixty-five.

He emptied his pockets and dropped his loose change, phone, and wallet on his dresser. In the bathroom, he stripped, washed up, and put on a fresh pair of jeans and a T-shirt. On his way back to the kitchen, he glanced at the clock on his nightstand.

"You're here late." He took a seat at the island. "Are you baking bread?"

She blew out a breath. "Yeah and it sucks. It's tough and flavorless. Nothing is coming out right. Maybe it's the altitude."

"We're only at a little more than twenty-four-hundred feet, hardly Mount Whitney." He got himself a beer out of the refrigerator, popped the cap, and took a long drag. "You want one?" He figured if she did, she would've helped herself, since she'd helped herself to everything else in his house. That is, everything but him. Not that he was interested.

"I'm good."

He tipped the neck of the bottle back to take another swig and held her gaze, letting his eyes slide down her torso. "Are you?"

What the hell was he doing? After the creek-bank moment he thought he'd gotten clarity.

Gina DeRose was off-limits.

First, because she was his mother's client. Second, because she was involved with another man. A married man. And third, because he didn't particularly like her kind.

"Not really." She sank into one of the barstools. "In fact, I'm pretty shitty. Last I looked, I lost two thousand Twitter followers. My Facebook wall is covered in hate posts. And don't even get me started about the memes."

He could only imagine. "Not good for your bottom line, huh?"

"Nope." She looked so defeated that he almost felt sorry for her. Almost.

She went to the refrigerator, took out a casserole dish, and set it on the counter while she preheated the oven. When he pulled back the foil she said, "It's baked ziti. I made it yesterday, but it's usually better the second day. Where have you been, anyway?"

"Work trip," he lied because he didn't want to discuss Angela right now.

"What kind of work trip?" she pressed.

"It's a long story." He took another pull on his beer and reclaimed his stool at the kitchen island. "And I'm done with work for the day." He gave her a pointed look.

She dropped it, launching into a litany of complaints about being exiled to Timbuktu. "There's no place to buy decent cheese around here. And good almond paste? Forget about it."

"I don't know about almond paste, but there's a goat and sheep farm on Cattle Drive Way where they make their own cheese. Technically, they're not allowed to sell it to the public. I think it has something to do with it not being pasteurized. But I'm guessing a crafty woman like yourself could get your hands on some. You won't be disappointed."

She perked up and just as quickly lost her enthusiasm. "I can't be seen in public, remember?"

"You went to the kitchen store."

"In a hat and glasses with the rest of the badly dressed tourists. But at someone's farm? I'd look like a freak."

He'd seen her in her getup. Not a freak. More like a Hollywood type, trying to hide her identity, only to call more attention to it. He knew the drill; he'd grown up in Beverly Hills, after all. Probably not far from where she'd grown up. They definitely hadn't gone to the same schools—his was private—because he would've remembered meeting Gino DeRose's daughter.

"What? You want me to go there and buy the damn cheese for you?"

She flashed her TV smile. "Yes, please."

"And what will you do for me?" He hitched his brows.

The oven bell dinged and she slid the baked ziti in. "Feed you."

"You do that in exchange for my kitchen. Time is money, honey. You want me to buy you cheese, you've gotta do something for me in return."

"Like what?" She lifted her chin in challenge as if to say, bring it on.

About a thousand things, all of them sexual, came to mind. "I don't know yet. Give me time to think about it."

"Take all the time you need," she threw back.

He got another beer out of the fridge and his stomach growled. "Can I have a slice of that bread?" He nudged his head at a loaf wrapped in a towel, resting on the countertop.

She cut a few pieces, arranged them on a bread plate, and slid it over to him. "Eat at your own risk."

He grabbed the butter out of the fridge, slathered a pat on one of the slices, and took a bite. She hovered over him, watching.

"Nice and soft, just like Wonder Bread," he said as he chewed off another bite.

She snatched the plate away and elbowed him in the arm. He chuckled because he liked getting a rise out of her.

"It's too tough, isn't it?"

Was she kidding? The bread was freaking fantastic. Crusty on the outside, soft in the middle, and still warm from the oven. "Nope. Now give it back to me." He reached out and tugged the plate back.

"What about the flavor?"

"It tastes like bread."

She put her hands on her hips and glared at him.

"Okay, fine. I taste malt and maybe a little honey. Not too yeasty. I actually think it's bold in the flavor department. Yet, it doesn't overwhelm the palate." Oh, for Christ's sake, he sounded like one of those douchey foodies who were always talking about mouthfeel and throwing around words like *artisanal* and *curated*.

"Wow, you got the malt. Is it too much?"

Jeez, how was it that one of America's most famous chefs was so damned insecure? "Nah, I thought it was pretty balanced."

"I used less yeast and I retarded the fermentation by refrigerating the dough to help the flavor stand out more. But I still think it sucks. You don't, huh?"

"Nope. Then again, I wouldn't turn down a Little Debbie variety pack. So what the hell do I know?"

He saw her face fall and kicked himself for being an asshole.

"It's as good as anything I've ever had at La Brea, Röckenwagner, Tartine, Acme," he quickly amended, ticking off every great California bread bakery he could think of. "You planning to bake bread full-time?" When she shook her head, he said, "So what's the big deal?"

She deliberated, then said, "I've got a thing about being perfect." She took a long pause as if she'd just come to that revelation, then added, "It's sort of exhausting, if you want to know the truth."

"Yeah, I would imagine so. I'm guessing this has to do with your mommy issues." He wasn't much for armchair analysis, but it didn't take Carl Jung to figure out that Gina's mom had turned her daughter into a head case.

"Probably" was all she said about it. "What about you? What's your kryptonite? Or are you perfect?"

"Pretty much." He winked and then for no reason at all said, "My sister went missing five years ago. The thought of her out there, alone and in trouble, keeps me up at night. The alternative, that she's dead, is even worse."

Gina jerked back in surprise. "My God, Wendy never said anything. How…what happened?"

That was the question he'd been asking himself for years. "One day she just stopped calling. It was as if she vaporized. No money trail, no social media presence, no contact with her friends, no nothing."

"Do you think…could it be that someone hurt her?"

"Maybe. But there's information to indicate that two years ago she was involved in this group, some kind of communal farm that was off the grid in New Mexico. As far as I can tell it doesn't exist anymore. And that's where the trail ends."

"Was she close to your family? I mean, why wouldn't she call?"

"We were close. That's why none of it makes sense."

She pulled the baked ziti out of the oven and served them both before joining him at the counter. "What about that communal farm? I mean, not to judge, but it sounds kind of sketchy. Especially because it's the last place she wound up."

You think? "Yup. Angie has always been attracted to weird shit. Normally, I wouldn't find a communal farm all that weird, or sketchy, just a bad remnant of the seventies. But I'm with you on this one. I just spent the last two days digging around Taos and there's nothing on these people. Not so much as a footprint. They were either ghosts or shady as hell."

"That's where you were, huh? Maybe you and your family should hire a private investigator."

"We have. At least a dozen of them. The last one came up with the Taos lead. I confirmed it with a former resident of the commune, who had a picture of Angie. But she's not saying much."

"What about the police? Can't they get this woman to talk?"

He shook his head. "There's no law that says she has to speak with us."

He took a bite of his ziti and another one after that. Maybe somewhere an Italian grandmother made it better, but it was the best ziti he'd ever had. For all her nutty insecurities, Gina DeRose could cook.

"This"—he stabbed his fork at his plate while he chewed the rest of his mouthful—"is incredible."

"It's in my frozen food line." She ladled a second helping onto his plate. "Back to your sister. I think we should make another trip to New Mexico."

He swiveled to the side to look at her. "We?" He was unaware that they'd suddenly become a team.

"Yes. In case you haven't noticed, I'm on sabbatical from life. I've got time for this."

"Gina, this isn't a cozy mystery novel where the celebrity chef moonlights as a detective. The best investigators in the business, including me, have failed to find Angie. This is my baby sister, not some game to keep you amused while you deal with the fallout of your affair."

"There was no affair," she blurted.

He stopped eating and put his fork down. "What are you talking about?" In his line of work, people liked to manipulate the facts by twisting words. Maybe a blow job or tantric sex wasn't an affair in her book.

It damned well was in his.

"I'm saying I never slept with Danny Clay."

"Well, your texts say differently."

"I know what they say. The problem is, I never wrote them. In fact, I've never texted Danny in my life. We're barely acquaintances, let alone sex-starved love bunnies. I've maybe met him three times at most—once on set of the FoodFlicks' *Junior Chef Competition* and twice at Tyler Florence's annual Feed the First Responders event. That's it."

"What about the picture of you two on the beach?"

She squeezed the bridge of her nose. "I don't know. But I've never been on a beach with Danny Clay. Not ever."

Sawyer didn't know what to think. The evidence spoke for itself. "Did you tell my mother this?"

"Of course I did. She believes me."

His mother believed whatever the client paid her to believe. "Yet, she hasn't launched this as a defense, has she?"

Gina pinned him with a look. "It's pretty hard to prove a negative."

Or an out-and-out lie, especially when there was proof to the contrary. Photos. Texts. "Why would someone set you up like this? Or him?" It seemed like a lot of trouble to go to. And what was the motive?

"I don't know." She began rewrapping the baked ziti. Sawyer got the impression it was an excuse to keep busy and not to have to look him in the eye. "I certainly know people who don't like me. Television is a cutthroat business. But this is extreme."

"Yep. And methodically planned. What about Clay? Does he have enemies?"

"Like I said, I barely know him. All I know is that he and Candace used to own a catering company, shopped a pilot about entertaining to FoodFlicks in the early days, when the network was just starting. And it's been a runaway hit ever since."

Sawyer took another bite of his ziti, weighing the credibility of Gina's story. The texts could easily have been manufactured. But the photo of her and Danny Clay together? He supposed it could've been photoshopped. But it seemed pretty far-fetched.

Then again, her defense was so implausible that it just might be true.

At the start of his journalism career, when he covered the night crime beat at the *New York Times*, he'd quickly learned that liars typically went with believable stories. It was the crazy stories, the ones that were stranger than fiction, which almost always turned out to be true. And Gina's bordered on nuts.

"So someone randomly decided to blow up your life?"

"That's what it looks like." She put the casserole dish in the refrigerator. "You don't have to believe me, but it's true."

"What's the strategy, then?" He got up and tossed his empty beer bottles in the recycling bin.

"Your mom says we should wait it out. That going on the defensive will only call more attention to the situation." When he pulled a face, she said, "What? You think we're doing the wrong thing?"

"No, not without proof that you've been set up." It bothered him, however, that if this really was a frame job the person responsible would get away with it.

"You're the investigative reporter; how do I get proof?" She stood with her back pressed against the counter, looking determined.

"I would start by making a list of people who would stand to gain from your fall or from hurting the Clays." There was the possibility that

Danny and Candace had been the intended targets and Gina was merely collateral damage.

"That would be a very short list," she said. "I don't have partners and even if I did, the business's success rides on the Gina DeRose brand. If I go down, the business goes down. It's that simple."

Sawyer agreed. That's why her story didn't make a whole lot of sense. Unless, of course, someone was exacting a personal vendetta. "Then who has an ax to grind?"

She threw her hands up in the air. "No one off the top of my head. But who knows? I run a multimillion-dollar enterprise; there's bound to be people I've pissed off along the way."

"There you go. Those are the names that should go on your list."

She nodded, but her expression told Sawyer she thought a list was a waste of time. "When are we going to New Mexico?"

Her intentions were genuine. She was high-maintenance, but at her core she was a good person. If nothing else, he'd learned that about her over the last couple of weeks. But this was his cross to bear, no one else's.

"You and me?" He shook his head. "Try never."

Chapter 8

The next morning, Sawyer met with his cousins at the coffee shop. The topic of where he'd been the last couple of days hadn't come up and Sawyer steered clear of the subject. Cash and Jace would only accuse him of being compulsive.

Laney sat them at their usual table in the back of the restaurant, near a bull horn hat rack where they could hang their Stetsons. Not five minutes passed when she returned with coffee. A chorus of chicken and waffles went around the table as she took their order.

With Gina using his house as her personal test kitchen, it had been days since he'd eaten at the coffee shop. It was usually his home away from home.

"How's our friend?" Laney asked in a whisper.

Cash passed a glance at Sawyer and Jace. "What friend?"

Laney poked him in the arm. "Don't be coy with me, boy. I know who you're harboring over at the ranch. I've got her recipe for strawberry shortcake to prove it. Now don't tell me you think I'd run to the tabloids?"

Not to the tabloids. Laney had more class than that. But Sawyer wouldn't put it past her to blab all over town that Gina was holing up with the Daltons. Dry Creek didn't know from discretion. The entire town ran on gossip.

When none of them responded, Laney put her hands on her ample hips. "Fine, be that way. I have half a mind to drive out there and pay her a visit. As for you boys, no chess pie. I've got three pieces left and none of you are getting any of it." She walked off in a huff.

"How long are we supposed to keep Gina a secret?" Cash asked. He and Jace turned to Sawyer.

"How the hell should I know?" Then, apropos of nothing, he huffed out a breath and blurted, "She says she didn't do it." Cash and Jace looked at Sawyer like they had no idea what he was talking about.

"Did what?" Cash asked.

"She didn't sleep with Danny Clay." Sawyer didn't know why he was telling his cousins. It wasn't like they could give two shits. But for some unfathomable reason it seemed important to him that they know Gina was innocent. "The whole thing was fabricated by someone who is either out to ruin her or the Clays."

"That's what she told you?" Jace arched a brow. "And you actually believed her? Man, you've got it bad for the woman."

He didn't have anything for Gina DeRose. Well, maybe he wanted to get inside her pants. He chalked that up to being a guy. And hormones. Nothing more. Gina might be attractive, even amusing, but she was a head trip. Spoiled, self-centered, and a headache. He liked no-drama women.

"She told my mom the same story."

"And does she believe Gina?" Cash asked, demonstrating the same open skepticism as Jace had.

That's what Sawyer got for having two damn cops for cousins. If someone said the sun was up, the two of them went outside to check.

Sawyer started to hedge, then realized: What was the point of obfuscating? "I didn't talk to my mother about it. Crisis manager-client privilege and all that shit. But I believe Gina." He locked eyes with Jace, who was shaking his head. "Give me a little credit, asshole. I'm an investigative journalist, for God's sake."

Jace threw up his arms. "Seems like there's a lot of evidence to the contrary. Just saying."

"*Just saying*. What are you? A fifteen-year-old girl?"

Cash chuckled at Sawyer's quip, but made it clear he agreed with Jace. "Aren't there pictures? Texts? The dude's dick?"

Yep, there was all that. Still, Sawyer believed her. Her story was too ludicrous not to.

"You and I both know with good photo software anything is possible. Hell, William Randolph Hearst knew how to do it more than a hundred years ago. Remember: 'You furnish the pictures and I'll furnish the war.'"

From Cash's expression he still seemed dubious. "How does she plan to prove it?"

Sawyer shrugged. "We're working on it."

"*We're*?" Jace's brows shot up again. "Now you're her champion. Just the other day you couldn't stand her."

Cash, the grown-up in the room, ignored Jace and asked Sawyer, "What would be the motive to spread rumors about her? Who has that big of a grudge against her? Or something to gain?"

These were all questions Sawyer had asked himself. Gina sure didn't think there was anyone who would go to this end to ruin her. "It might be someone out to get the Clays and Gina was just an unintended casualty."

"Sounds a little out there to me. But if your instincts say she's telling the truth, I'll go with it because you're usually right. Not always, but usually."

Jace glanced at his watch. As Mill County sheriff, he usually had meetings and briefings in the morning. "You have a thing for this woman?"

"Hell no," Sawyer said and even to his own ears sounded too defensive.

"For a guy who isn't into her, she sure spends a lot of time at your place." Jace topped off his cup from the carafe on the table.

"She likes my kitchen."

"Are you sure that's all she likes?"

Sawyer was preparing a pithy comeback when Mitch Reynolds walked in. Jace bristled. The two of them used to be best friends until Mitch started screwing Jace's other best friend's wife. At the time, Mitch had been engaged to Aubrey. The whole ordeal had ended in a complicated mess that had almost lost Jace the sheriff's race.

On top of that, Mitch, a developer, had been caught up in a scam to swindle Randy Beals out of his ranch so he could build a golf-course community. Jace had arrested him, but Randy wouldn't press charges because his kids had also been involved in the conspiracy.

Mitch bobbed his head at them. Sawyer wasn't sure if Mitch was being cordial for appearance's sake or if the gesture was his equivalent of waving his middle finger. Whatever. The guy could go screw himself for all Sawyer cared.

A few minutes later, Randy came in the coffee shop and joined Mitch at his table.

"What the hell's that about?" Sawyer said.

Jace watched the two men across the restaurant. "What do you think it's about? Randy's so desperate to sell, he's willing to make a deal with the devil."

"I don't want that asshole as a neighbor." Sawyer drained the last of his coffee and poured himself another cup.

"Are you kidding?" Cash said. "You said it best, Sawyer. When he's done with Beals Ranch, it'll be half-acre lots with mini-mansions and an eighteen-hole golf course. Our neighbor won't be Mitch, it'll be two thousand new families."

"Who'll complain about the smell of our cattle," Jace added and rubbed his hand down his face. "Shit."

Maria, who'd been working at the coffee shop as long as Sawyer could remember, brought their food while Laney took orders at another table.

Jace doused his chicken with hot sauce. "Our only hope is that the city won't allow Mitch to develop the land, that it'll have to stay agricultural."

Jace was delusional. The tax revenue alone would be difficult for any municipality to turn down. And then there was the fact that it was happening all around them. The land was just too damn valuable for ranching or farming.

"Any way we can appeal to Randy?" Sawyer asked and looked to Jace because he'd known Randy his whole life and had grown up with the Beals kids.

"It's not like I can tell him who or who not to sell to. He's got to do what's best for him and Marge. And last time I talked to him they were drowning in debt."

Basically, there wasn't a whole lot they could do to prevent the inevitable.

They ate and moved on, talking about Sawyer's article, a cattle-rustling arrest in Texas that Cash was keeping tabs on, and eventually came around to the topic that was supposedly the reason they'd met for breakfast in the first place.

The flower farmers.

"Well, are we going ahead with letting them lease the property or not?" Sawyer looked to Cash, who'd been briefed.

There was no question Jace's vote was *yes*. Whatever Charlie wanted, he wanted. And Charlie was in favor of a flower shop. Aubrey, too.

"I don't see how it could hurt." Cash pushed his empty plate aside. "If they don't pay their lease, we own their crop."

"Flowers?" Sawyer pulled a face.

"I did a little research and cut flowers are damned profitable," Cash said. "On average, about thirty thousand in sales per acre."

Jace perked up. "No shit?"

"Maybe we should eliminate the UC Davis girls and plant them ourselves." Sawyer was joking, but he had no idea flowers grossed so well. A cow-calf pair needed roughly two to five acres of land. Without doing a lot of fancy math, Sawyer was thinking the flowers had a bigger return. At least in the short term.

"You want to be a farmer?" Cash didn't have to ask because the answer was a resounding *no*.

They were ranchers, born and raised, even if Sawyer and Cash grew up in the city. As Grandpa Dalton used to say, it was in their DNA and nothing could change that, not even Beverly Hills. Or in Cash's case, San Francisco.

"What about the shop they want?" Sawyer supposed the three of them could build it themselves to save on labor costs.

"If we're planning to lease out business space, we'll have to supply the infrastructure," Jace said. "No way around that, right?"

Cash nodded. "It doesn't mean we have to supply them with a refrigeration system or any of the other bells and whistles they need for a floral shop. Just bare bones is the way I see it. The rest is up to them."

Sawyer agreed. "What about fencing for their fields? Anything deer-proof will cost a hell of a lot of money."

"I think that's on them, too," Cash said.

"The big question is water." Jace looked from Cash to Sawyer.

"I say we give them two price options," Sawyer said. "One with water, one without. They could always truck in their own tank."

"Yeah, I'm good with that." Jace glanced at his watch again. "We'll have to come up with some numbers."

"We might also offer profit sharing." Cash hitched his shoulders. "Farming's always a gamble, but as far as the flowers, I like the returns. Something to think about, anyway."

Sawyer glanced over at Mitch and Randy's table. The men were in deep conversation, which couldn't be good.

"I've gotta motor." Jace reached for his wallet and Sawyer swatted his hand away.

"I'll take care of the bill. You can get it next time."

Jace and Cash left at the same time. Sawyer squared up with Laney at the register and went into the kitchen to say hello to Jimmy Ray, who was up to his ass in alligators. The dining room was hopping.

Every Wednesday the local cattlemen met for breakfast. As always, five big tables had been pushed together to accommodate them.

"Sawyer," one of the cowboys called him over. "How you boys doin'?"

It didn't matter that he and his cousins were all in their mid-thirties or that Jace was the county's sheriff. To this group of ranchers, his grandfather's best friends, Sawyer, Jace, and Cash would always be "boys."

Sawyer took an empty chair at the table. "Fair to middling. How 'bout you, Joe?"

"Real fine as long as the price of beef holds." He grinned. "Your grandfather would've been real proud of you boys." Joe turned to look at

Mitch's table and in a low voice said, "Randy's kids are already counting the money. Damned shame."

Sawyer didn't say anything even though Joe was right. He had no love for Jill Beals Tucker or her brother, Pete. "I got to get home and do some writing. It was good seeing you, Joe."

"When's that war book coming out?"

"Late next year."

"I'm looking forward to reading it. Say hi to Jace and Cash for me."

"You just missed them," Sawyer said.

"Both of them are doing a good job. I heard Cash caught those rustlers out of Plumas County. Heard he traced the thieves to a Nevada ring trafficking in stolen livestock, farm equipment, and methamphetamine."

It was the first Sawyer had gotten wind of it, but wasn't surprised. Cash was a great cop and unfortunately livestock theft was often tied to the drug trade. Sawyer rose before Joe jawed his ear off. He still had to finish the piece for *Forbes*.

By the time he got outside, the temperature had climbed into the nineties. In a few hours, it would soar to triple digits.

He passed Gina's cabin on the way to his barn apartment. Her BMW was parked in front. He considered stopping in but decided against it. The undeniable zing between them had ratcheted up a few dozen notches since he'd learned she wasn't involved with a married man. Now, it was the kind of zing that resulted in two people getting naked and falling into bed together. And in their situation that wasn't advisable for all the reasons he'd already determined—namely, that she was his mother's client, a wreck, and he didn't need the drama.

But that didn't mean she didn't tempt him beyond reason. So it was best to avoid her as much as possible. It was difficult because she'd made herself at home in his house. Then again, he hadn't exactly dissuaded her from using his kitchen. He'd like to say it was because he enjoyed eating her food. But on the days she didn't show up it wasn't her mouthwatering meals he missed. It was her company, her smart mouth, and her impressive capacity to give as good as she got.

And of course, there was the fact that she was nice to look at. All legs and sweet curves.

He passed her place and went directly home. Inside, he switched on the air-conditioning and booted up his laptop. He planned to make a sizable dent in the article that was due at the end of the month. But instead of working on the piece, he found himself noodling around on the internet.

First, he pulled up Gina's website, read her bio, and flipped through her photo gallery. There were lots of pictures of her on the set of her show, making various dishes in the test kitchen. There were also shots of her posing with a number of celebrities, including the cast of the *Today* show.

The woman was damned photogenic. But the bright lights, makeup, and overly coiffed hair made her look a bit like a Barbie doll. Plastic. He preferred her without all the shine and gloss.

After spending a good thirty minutes trolling around her site, he went in search of the infamous photo. It only took two minutes to find it again. The beach shot of her and Danny was plastered on every celebrity site and tabloid on the internet. He searched for the photo with the best resolution and blew it up on the screen. For a while he just studied it, examining the different angles of the picture. To the naked eye—at least his—he couldn't tell whether the photograph had been doctored. It looked like the real deal to him. There was no question the woman in the photo was Gina.

Was it a cut-and-paste job? The answer to that was above his pay grade. But surely there were experts who could tell.

Sawyer suspected his mother had already consulted with a few forensic photographers. He picked up the phone to call her, then, just as quickly put it down. His mother was too professional to discuss Gina's case with him, even if Gina had.

Unable to leave it alone, he searched through his contacts, found who he was looking for, and punched in his number.

"Hey Shooter, it's your buddy, Sawyer Dalton." The two had worked together at the *Times,* been roommates in Tel Aviv when he was the bureau chief there, and had kept in touch over the years. Carlos Gonzales, aka Shooter, was one of the best photographers in the business. "How good are you at determining whether a photo has been doctored?"

"You mean like photoshopped?"

"Yeah, like sticking somebody's head on somebody else's body. Or splicing two people together. That sort of thing."

Shooter laughed. "Dude, what are you working on?"

"You'll keep this on the Q.T., right?" Shooter was good people. Not the kind to spread confidential information. "It's for a friend. She's a celebrity chef who the tabloids are having a ball with. Love triangle, racy photos, that kind of bullshit. But she says the picture that's getting all the attention is fabricated. I was hoping you could take a look at it, see what you think."

"Is this that Gina DeRose thing?"

"Yeah," Sawyer said, surprised. He wouldn't have expected Shooter to pay attention to tabloid fodder. The guy had been in Turkey for the last six months, covering the plight of Syrian refugees. "How'd you know about it?"

"Dude, you'd have to live under a rock not to. Send over the original and I'll take a look."

"I don't have the original, just a copy from the internet. Will that work?"

There was a long pause. "It'll be tough but I'll see what I can do. Email it to me."

"Thanks, buddy. I owe you one."

He saved the photo and sent it as an attachment to Shooter. Instead of pulling up the article he was supposed to be working on, he searched a few sites on flower farming. Damn, Cash was right. There was good money in growing cut flowers.

He continued procrastinating when notification of an incoming email flashed in the right-hand corner of his computer screen. On the small chance it was Shooter responding with a verdict, he went to his inbox. Nope, not Shooter. A note with a Gmail address he didn't recognize. Probably a press release. He got lots of those.

Nope, not a press release. Just a concise message. Only six words.

Stop searching for me. I'm safe.

He stared at the note for a while, reading the two sentences over and over again. Was it some sort of a very unfunny joke? Or was it Angie reaching out to him? But why after five years? It didn't make sense. No, it was probably someone trying to mess with him. But who in God's name would do something like that?

For a second, his mind flitted to his conversation with Gina. She'd offered to go with him to New Mexico and search for Angie.

Nah, he told himself. She had no reason to toy with him that way. She might be self-centered, but from his observations she wasn't sadistic. Only someone really warped would do something like this.

He replied to the message, *Who are you?* but a few minutes later his email ricocheted back to his inbox with the heading that it was undeliverable.

A person with mad computer skills might be able to trace it. But cyber forensics wasn't in Sawyer's wheelhouse. It might be in Cash's, though. And if not, his cousin would surely know someone from his FBI days who could track where the email had come from.

He wondered if the sender could possibly be the woman in Santa Fe. The one who'd been reticent to talk to him. Perhaps she was trying to throw him off. Whoever it was clearly wanted him to stop searching for answers.

But why? He suspected the reason would lead him to Angie. Dead or alive.

Chapter 9

Gina decided to risk another trip to the kitchen store in Grass Valley. This time, she was loaded with cash so she could purchase anything she wanted without having to use a credit card. It was still chancy, but she was climbing the walls of the cabin.

On her way out, she stopped by Refind to see if there was anything Charlie and Aubrey needed. A couple of times, they'd grabbed her groceries or sundries in town and she wanted to return the favor. That's how it was here at the ranch. Everyone looked out for one another.

The construction crew had moved from framing to walls and windows and were making enough racket to turn a person brain-dead. Gina went in search of her friends, only to find them in bright yellow hard hats in the middle of the crazy. They were picking out the locations for outlets and switches before the drywall went up.

"It looks as if they're making progress," Gina said over the noise.

The two women led her away from the mayhem to a small Airstream trailer that Aubrey had temporarily set up as an office. At least here they could hear themselves talk.

"They say two more weeks max." Charlie hitched her shoulders. "But you know how that is. Two weeks could very quickly turn into six months. In the meantime, we're going deaf."

"Where'd you get the trailer?" The interior was sad. Lots of Formica finishes and worn vinyl upholstery.

"Craigslist. Charlie's planning to rehab it and make bank when we resell it. These things are supposedly collector's items. But first we have to get through this." Aubrey waved at the barn.

"So far, it looks great." Gina was impressed with the expansion's design. The new build was definitely in keeping with the rustic vibe of the barn. They'd gone with wood siding made from reclaimed lumber. Even the windows had been recycled from a hundred-year-old farmhouse.

"I'm headed into Grass Valley. You need anything? Earplugs, maybe?"

"An industrial-size bottle of aspirin," Charlie joked, then eyed Gina's disguise. This time, she'd gone with a straw cowboy hat and a pair of mirrored aviators she'd picked up online.

"What? It's not working?"

Charlie laughed. "I know who you are so it's hard to tell. Maybe tuck your hair up."

Gina pulled her hair back and twisted it up underneath the hat. "Better?" She didn't wait for an answer because it was as good as it was going to get, short of her becoming a brunette. "How 'bout you, Aubrey. Anything?"

"I'm good. But I was just about to take Sawyer to pick up his Range Rover at the mechanic. You could save me the trip."

"Sure." Sawyer had spent much of the past week working on his article. Every time she'd gone over to use his kitchen, he'd either locked himself in his room or worked outside on his porch. She'd sort of gotten used to his company and their little banter routine. It wasn't like she missed him—*Liar!*—but having him around made the days pass faster. "What's wrong with his Range Rover?"

Aubrey shrugged. "All I know is that Jace followed him to the shop this morning and took him home and I was supposed to drive him to pick it up. But now I have you to save me the trouble." She did a little hip-shake happy dance.

"I'll go over and get him."

"Don't forget dinner at Charlie's tonight. Just us girls."

Gina had been looking forward to it ever since they'd invited her a couple of days ago. The last time she'd had a girls' night was in the dorms at San Diego State. Sadie had had her sights set on USC for Gina. But Gina's GPA hadn't been high enough to get in. Another epic fail on Gina's part.

"The pie is cooling and ready to go," she told Aubrey. "And of course, strawberry shortcake." The cake had been a special request of Travis and Grady, who'd be away but wanted slices when they got home.

Charlie had gotten the strawberries at a nearby farm stand. The blackberries for the pie came from the bush that kept giving. She had so many berries that she'd made a buckle, a pandowdy, and a *crostata*. Gina had delivered them to Laney and Jimmy Ray for review. Jimmy Ray said

they were the best desserts he'd ever eaten and Laney had thrown a soup ladle at him. The woman had a temper.

Maybe while she was at the kitchen store she'd buy an ice cream maker and if the shop carried it, some good vanilla beans, too.

She drove to Sawyer's and tooted her horn. He came out onto the balcony, looked down at her car, and glowered.

She stuck her head out the window and shouted up, "I'm taking you to get your Range Rover." She added "asshole" under her breath.

He went back inside and came down a few minutes later in a pair of worn jeans and T-shirt that stretched across his broad chest. His hair was damp, like maybe he'd just showered, and a few dark tendrils curled against his neck. He looked like a walking Super Bowl ad for Ram trucks or something equally testosterone-driven.

He got inside the passenger side of her car and pulled the seat back as far as it would go. "Where's Aubrey?"

"She asked if I'd give you a ride because I was going to town anyway." She backed out of his driveway and headed to Dry Creek Road. "Unless you want to come with me to the kitchen store first?"

"Tess'? What for?"

So we can hang out, stupid. "So you can carry my stuff to the car."

He snorted, then glanced at his watch. "Buck said my car wouldn't be ready until two, so I've got a little time to kill. But first let's stop off at Beals Ranch. I want to talk to Randy about buying his stock trailer."

"Will he recognize me?"

"I doubt it, but even if he did he isn't the type to spread it around. Ranchers have a tendency to keep to themselves...shun the press."

"Okay." She had nothing else to do. "Tell me where to go."

He gave her directions. About twenty minutes later, they passed a Century 21 *for sale* sign, boasting "cattle property" and drove through an elaborate gate. From the top of the gateposts swung a large iron cattle-brand emblem and the words Beals Ranch.

"Do they raise cows, too?"

"Yup, but the ranch is on the market."

He guided her to a home that had been oversold by the impressiveness of the gate. It was a faded yellow farmhouse with a wraparound porch that had seen better days. And the cement walkway up to the front door could use a power washing. There were three pickup trucks and a Subaru Forester parked in front of a four-car garage, which seemed excessive given the size of the house.

A couple of kids played on a tire swing that hung from a big oak tree in the side yard. Sawyer waved as he got out of the car. A dog barked from the porch and someone yelled for it to be quiet. An attractive woman about Gina's age came down the steps and gave Sawyer a hug.

"What a nice surprise."

"I wanted to talk to your dad about his stock trailer."

Sawyer introduced the woman—Jill—to Gina. There was something off between them; Gina could feel it right away. She wondered if maybe Jill and Sawyer had dated and the relationship had ended badly. Whatever it was, she sensed a gnawing discomfort between the two.

"Daddy's on his way home. He should be here any minute." Jill turned to the kids on the swing. "You guys go wash up. Your father's coming to get you for lunch at the coffee shop."

The kids ran up the steps and into the house.

"You want to come in…have something to drink while you wait?"

"Nah," Sawyer said. "I don't want to impose."

"No imposition and it's hot out here." She ushered them through the front door.

The inside of the house was as worn as the outside but surprisingly cozy. Lots of family pictures and braided rugs. Someone had a penchant for cutesy inspirational signs because they were everywhere. Bless this house, life is better on the ranch, kiss a cowboy, and chasing cows will be your fate if you don't shut the gate.

Jill led them to the kitchen, which hadn't been updated since the eighties: Cream-tile countertops, oak cabinets, and white appliances. Still, the room exuded warmth. Gina could tell a lot of happy family meals had been prepared in here.

"You want a soda, juice, or lemonade?" Jill asked.

"Ice water is fine." Sawyer was being polite but not friendly.

Gina planned to ask him about it when they left.

"Do you live around here, Gina?" Jill asked and Gina wanted to kick Sawyer for using her real name. The good news was Jill didn't seem to recognize her, not in Gina's hat and glasses.

"Just visiting for the day." Gina waited for the inevitable follow-up questions—Oh yeah, what brings you to Dry Creek? Where you from? Aren't you that bimbo celebrity chef who slept with Danny Clay?—but Jill just nodded. It struck Gina that maybe Jill thought she was Sawyer's girlfriend.

Gina would've disabused Jill of that notion, but it was actually a good cover.

Jill brought them each a glass of water and motioned for them to take a seat at the round oak table in the breakfast nook. There was a sliding glass door half-covered in dog and little-hand smudge marks that looked out onto a garden.

"Is your dad selling to Mitch?" Sawyer asked.

The question had been delivered bluntly and Gina heard an undertone of…something. Anger, maybe. There was a strange undercurrent going on here that she couldn't read. Another thing to ask him about later.

"They're in negotiations," Jill said and let her eyes drop to her feet. "Brett's on his way over to spend some time with the kids. I think he's planning to hang out with Jace later, but I know he'd love to see you."

Gina got the sense Jill was trying to change the subject with her abrupt non sequitur about Brett. She assumed Brett must be Jill's ex and that Jill didn't want to discuss the sale of her family's ranch, which was probably emotional.

Gina watched Sawyer, trying to figure out what was going on here. He definitely didn't like Jill, who seemed perfectly nice to Gina.

Sawyer glanced at his watch and feigned surprise at the time. "We've got an appointment in town that we'll be late for if we don't giddyup. I'll catch up with Brett this evening." He stood abruptly. "Tell your dad I dropped by and I'll call him later."

Sawyer gently took Gina's arm and guided her out of her chair. Jill walked them to the door and Sawyer made a beeline for Gina's BMW.

"What just happened there?" Gina started her car and nosed down the driveway.

"A couple of more minutes in Jill's presence and I was going to let her have it. She's getting everything she ever wanted."

"What is it that she wants? And who's Brett?"

"It's a long, ugly story and Brett is Jill's husband."

She slid Sawyer a sideways glance. "I've got nothing but time."

"You're going the wrong way. You were supposed to make a left on Dry Creek Road, not a right."

Gina sighed. These blasted country roads had her all turned around. She hung a U-turn and headed toward the highway.

"Are they broken up?" Gina assumed if Brett was coming over to spend time with his kids he lived elsewhere.

"Yep."

"Why?" For a man in the communications business, he was awfully tight-lipped.

"Among other reasons, she cheated on him with Brett's best friend," he finally said.

She turned in her seat to face Sawyer. "Seriously?"

"Watch where you're going." He nudged his head at the road. "Yeah, seriously. She cheated with Mitch, the guy who's about to buy her family's property and turn it into fucking leisure land."

"How does that get Jill exactly what she wants? And what do you mean by leisure land?"

Sawyer huffed out a breath. "Here's the *Reader's Digest* version because the full version is complicated. Last summer, Jill and her brother stole their parents' cattle in a ploy to force them into selling the ranch. That way Mitch could come in and swoop up the land for a good price and develop it. In return, Mitch was going to give Jill and her brother, Pete, a cut. But Jace and Cash got wise to their little conspiracy and busted them before the deal could go through. If it wasn't for Randy refusing to press charges against his kids they'd all be in prison now."

"Are you saying that without the money from their cattle they would have defaulted on their loan?" Gina had no idea what cattle were worth, but it seemed like there had to be livestock insurance against theft, market fluctuations, disease, or any of the myriad things that could go wrong in the livestock business.

"Yep. Most ranchers don't have a lot of reserves and can't afford insurance. We're living paycheck to paycheck, so to speak."

"Okay, but if they got their cattle back, why are they being forced to sell now?" It didn't make sense.

"They didn't get their cattle back. By the time Jace and Cash figured out what was going on, the Bealses' cattle were already hamburger meat. As part of the resolution, Mitch agreed to pay Randy and Marge restitution for the stolen cattle. But they were already so far in debt that the only way to crawl out is to sell. Which means Mitch is going to wind up with the property anyway. And when he's done developing it, we'll be living next to a retirement golf-course community with rows of mini-mansions and fake lakes. It's not anything my cousins and I want for a neighbor."

"Why don't you guys just buy it?"

He let out a rusty laugh. "You mean with all the millions we'll make from leasing land to two college grads who want to go into the flower business? We're having enough trouble holding on to Dry Creek Ranch, let alone buying more land."

They'd been talking so intently that Gina had lost track of directions. Again. "Did I miss the turnoff for the highway?"

"It's coming up in about a mile. Did you just get your license or something?"

"Did anyone ever tell you that you're a moron?"

He laughed. "A time or two, yes. Why don't you pull over and let me drive?"

"Not in this lifetime, pretty boy."

"Pretty boy?" He slanted her a glance and quirked a brow. "How is it that you're able to find your way around Los Angeles but can't manage a small country lane that only runs in two directions?"

"I manage to get around here just fine without you in the car."

"You still find me distracting, huh?"

She blew out a loud raspberry. "Still high on yourself, I see."

"Turn right up here to get on forty-nine."

"I know where I'm going." Frankly, she would've missed the turn had he not said something. To compensate, she hung the right a little too sharply and her tires squealed.

He exaggerated a grab for the roof handle. "Slow down there, Mario."

She looked over at the passenger seat where his long, denim-encased legs were splayed wide. The tip of his boots reached the front of the floorboard, even with the chair extended all the way back.

"What do you want at Tess'?" he asked.

"Maybe an ice cream maker, not sure yet."

"Then why are we going?"

"To get out of the house, mainly. And to spend quality time with you." She flashed a saccharine smile. "So are Jill and Brett getting a divorce?"

"You sure are interested in people you don't even know."

"It's better than thinking about myself."

"I thought that was your favorite pastime."

She reached up, took off the silly straw cowboy hat, and flung it in the back seat. No one would recognize her in the car. And it was hot as Hades today and the hat added ten degrees.

"Well, are they divorcing or not?"

"I think they're trying to work it out, at least according to Jace. I don't know Brett all that well, only that he's a vet, who came back from war in a wheelchair."

"Oh my God. He can't walk?"

"He's a paraplegic."

She gasped. "That is so sad. And then his wife sleeps with the best friend. Holy crap."

"Yep. The whole thing was a shit show. After the separation, he moved to Sacramento and enrolled in a vocational training program for disabled vets. Carpentry, I think."

He cocked his head. "Speaking of cheating spouses, I'm having a friend look at that picture of you and Danny Clay on the beach to see if it was doctored."

"To see? The picture's completely one-hundred-percent bogus," she said, heated, then reminded herself that he was trying to help her. "But thank you." Gina was surprised he'd gone to the trouble. The fact that Sawyer even believed her was a minor miracle. She suspected no one else would. "Your mom is also having it looked at by an expert she knows."

"I wouldn't have expected anything less from her. But I figure it doesn't hurt to get a second opinion."

"We were never together on the beach or anywhere else. But there's no question it's me in the photo, though there are a few inconsistencies."

"Like what?"

"Let's just say some of my anatomy was either augmented or mixed and matched with Dolly Parton's."

He boldly gazed at her chest and grinned. "I wasn't going to mention it. But, yeah, I noticed the disparity. Like a lot."

"Thanks." She elbowed him in the shoulder.

He bobbed his head at the road. "You're about to miss our exit."

She jammed in front of a pickup towing a horse trailer just in the nick of time to make the turn. It had only been a few days since she'd last been here, but she'd already forgotten where the store was.

Recognizing that she was once again lost, Sawyer guided her to a public parking lot. They were just about to get out of the car when he remembered her hat and reached into the back seat to get it. He tucked her hair behind her ears and put the hat on her head, sweeping a few more locks under the rim. The sensation of his hands brushing against her skin did something odd to her insides. For a while they both sat there, holding each other's gaze.

He bent forward, his eyes darkening as he stared at her lips. She moved closer until their mouths were just a whisper away from each other.

And then, just like that, he opened his passenger-side door and the moment was lost.

Neither one said anything as they hiked up the hill to Mill Street. But she thought about what it would've been like to feel the pull of Sawyer's mouth on hers the whole way to the kitchen shop.

Right before they went inside the store, she adjusted her sunglasses and whispered, "Can you tell it's me?"

"If anyone looks close enough, yeah, probably." His eyes took a slow stroll over her breasts. "Then again—" She kicked him in the shin before he could say more.

She left him at the door and went in search of the ice cream makers, once again marveling at what a great store it was. Every bit as good as Williams Sonoma or Sur La Table.

On the second floor she found the appliance section and perused the ice cream machines. The store had everything, from the old-fashioned kinds that you cranked by hand to frozen custard machines. There was even a ChefAid one that made gelato, frozen yogurt, and ice cream.

Under different circumstances she would have simply called ChefAid and asked them to send her the machine. It was common practice in her profession. Nothing like a little product placement to move merchandise.

But for now, her show had been canceled. And at the rate things were going she would no longer be affiliated with ChefAid.

She read the features on the various boxes, trying to decide which one to choose. The Cuisinart appeared to have more bells and whistles then the ChefAid. Yet, she still felt loyal to the brand. Misguided, since they obviously had no loyalty to her.

Sawyer came up behind her, his lips grazing her ear, nearly knocking her hat off. "What did you find?" His breath felt warm against her cheek and his front pressed against her back, sending tremors down her spine.

"Uh...which one do you think?" she stammered. It had been a long time since a man had reduced her to a nervous schoolgirl. Even her voice had risen to a high pitch.

I am so not doing this with him.

She'd avoided dating and relationships at all costs. Too much disappointment involved. Men were either intimidated by her success or competitive with her because of it. She told herself her reaction to Sawyer was merely a symptom of loneliness. And...hot cowboy. Which was a whole new species of man in her world of chefs, television producers, and corporate tycoons.

"They all look the same to me. I'd say whichever one makes the most ice cream at one time." His lips ticked up in the corners. It was obvious to Gina that he knew just how charming he was.

There was no question he had a healthy ego. And why shouldn't he have one? Good looks, impressive job, a killer smile, and a drool-worthy set of abs. On top of that, he was part owner of a nice chunk of real estate. He was a fabulous catch by anyone's standards.

The thing was Gina didn't think Sawyer wanted to be caught; otherwise he wouldn't still be single. In her experience, the emotionally available ones were always the first to get taken. All the rest had dated her at one time or another.

She'd grown so tired of putting herself out there that she'd focused on work instead of finding her one and only. Because he didn't exist, she reminded herself and turned her attention back to ice cream makers.

She narrowed the offerings down to two, including the ChefAid, which delivered the most features. In the end, the ChefAid won out. Sawyer carried it to the cashier's counter while she continued to browse. She'd never been much of a shopper—a passive-aggressive swipe at her mother, whose second home was Saks Fifth Avenue. But she could get lost in a kitchen or restaurant supply store for hours.

About twenty minutes later, with a basket full of crockery and gadgets she didn't need, she found Sawyer in the barware section, talking with a middle-aged blonde who smiled up at him with obvious familiarity. Though she was dressed like one of Gina's late mom's friends—lots of gold jewelry, white designer capri pants, and a pair of Jimmy Choo sandals—she wasn't a tourist up from the city. She appeared to know everyone working in the store.

Sawyer caught sight of her out of the corner of his eye and silently signaled that she should stay away. Gina crossed the floor and took the stairs down to the lower level to hide out. It wasn't a hardship because there was a clearance rack to explore.

She was immersed in the *Moosewood Cookbook* when Sawyer found her.

"The coast is clear." He tilted his head to see what she was reading. "You ready to giddyup? The store is mostly empty now."

"I'm ready." She handed her basket to him and he rolled his eyes but didn't balk at carrying it up the stairs.

"Who's your girlfriend?" When Sawyer appeared confused, she said, "The blonde wearing Fort Knox around her neck and on her wrists. You too looked quite cozy, chatting next to the Riedel stemware."

"Jealous?" He winked and flashed another one of his I'm-sexy-and-I-know-it smiles. "That was Tiffany, Jace's former campaign manager."

"Campaign manager?" This didn't seem like a place where one needed a campaign manager. But what Gina knew about small towns and politics she could fit in a quarter-teaspoon. "For what election?"

"Sheriff. It was a pretty contentious race."

When it was their turn at the counter, the cashier graced Sawyer with a blinding smile that hurt Gina's eyes, even with her sunglasses on. The

woman mostly ignored Gina while she paid for her items. It appeared that as long as Sawyer was around, Gina didn't need a disguise.

"What do you mean by contentious?" Gina asked as they were leaving the store. The idea of small-town life intrigued her for some odd reason.

"Jace had a fierce opponent." Sawyer rolled his eyes and laughed. "A local hardware store owner with zero law enforcement experience ran against him and almost kicked his ass."

"Holy crap, I'm living in freaking Mayberry." God, she missed LA: the smog, the crime, the corruption, the bullshit. At least she understood those things. Everything here was so…quaint.

"Not Mayberry." He tweaked the brim of her hat. "It's just folksy. Nothing wrong with that."

She didn't understand how someone as erudite as Sawyer loved living in the sticks. She did, however, like the hot cowboy shtick he had going on.

Her purse rang. Sawyer stopped on the sidewalk until she rescued her phone from the bottom of her bag. She checked the caller ID and grimaced.

"Who is it?" Sawyer glanced over her shoulder at her display screen.

No sense keeping it a secret, since she'd already confided in him. "Danny Clay," she said.

Sawyer's expression darkened. He pierced her with a long, hard look and took off toward the car at a swift pace.

"Hold up," she shouted, then remembered she was in public and in a quieter voice called, "Sawyer!"

He didn't stop and she had to jog to keep up.

By the time she got to the car she'd worked up a sweat in the blazing heat. "What? Now you don't believe me?"

"You told me you barely know the guy and yet he's calling you on your private cell phone number. What do you want me to believe? I'm not that fucking gullible, Gina. I was trying to help you but I don't like getting used. Or played."

"Can't you let me explain? He's a victim in this too. His reputation is shot and his wife won't talk to him anymore. All because someone did this to us."

"How do you know his wife isn't talking to him? You told me you've never said more than a few words to the dude. Now, suddenly, you know his whole goddamn story."

Gina let out a long breath and unlocked the car. Sawyer put her shopping bag in the trunk and folded himself into the passenger seat. Granted, she hadn't known him long, but she'd never seen him this angry, not even when he'd found her squatting in his apartment.

She got in the driver's seat and turned on the ignition just to get the air-conditioner going and rested her forehead against the steering wheel. "He's been calling me. I don't know how he got my private number, but it wouldn't have been terribly difficult. We all run in the same circle. He's just as confused about what's going on as I am. Neither of us has a clue about who would want to ruin us or hurt Candace. Because—let's face it—she's probably been the most wrecked by this. According to Danny, she believes he's been unfaithful and is absolutely crushed."

Sawyer didn't respond. Gina got the impression he was deliberating on whether she was telling the truth. She couldn't blame him for being skeptical. The whole story was like something out of *The Twilight Zone.*

After a long stretch of silence, he turned in his seat and looked at her. "Have you told my mother that the two of you have been in contact?"

She squirmed. "No, not exactly."

"What does *not exactly* mean?"

Not exactly meant Gina hadn't broached the subject at all with Wendy, who would have a complete shit fit if she knew Gina and Danny Clay were exchanging regular phone calls. "I was afraid she would have the same reaction as you. The first time he called, I didn't pick up. But he left a long message, begging me to return his call because he was just as baffled as I was about the pictures, the texts, the entire crazy story that we'd been having a love affair for the ages."

"And you did, of course." Sawyer banged the back of his head against the seat. "Let me drive."

"Why?" They were having an important conversation and he suddenly wanted to take the wheel of her car? The man was confounding.

"Because I want you to start at the beginning and you have enough trouble finding your way around even when you're not talking. I've never met anyone with a worse sense of direction."

She started to argue, but he was right. Mill County was a maze as far as she was concerned. And she had no idea where his mechanic was located. So why not let him drive? She got out of the driver's seat and switched sides with him. Sawyer pulled onto Main Street and headed in the direction of the highway.

"Start with his first call," he demanded. The man was bossy.

"There really isn't much more to tell. We've talked a few times since his initial message. The first time was when I came to Dry Creek Ranch. He wasn't going to give up, so I figured what was the harm in taking his call. In any event, neither of us can figure out who's behind this or why. He told me that at first he thought I had staged the entire scandal as a publicity

stunt. But he quickly realized that the rumors were hurting me as much as they were hurting him. Together, we've been taking your advice and brainstorming who our possible enemies are."

Sawyer hopped on the on-ramp, one hand on the wheel, totally at home driving her car. "It's a supremely bad idea for you two to be talking on the phone. If it ever leaked the press would have a freaking field day. And inevitably it will leak. Everything does. Take it from me, leaks are my bread and butter."

Of course, he was right. He was a reporter and knew how these things worked. But in this situation it seemed like her only hope was to team up with Danny to prove their innocence.

"Given that we're both affected, what's the harm in us working together to find out who's trying to screw us? What else do we have to lose? Candace has already filed for divorce. The future of both our shows is in jeopardy. And our brands...Ha." She laughed. "We can both kiss future endorsements good-bye."

Sawyer turned to the side and pinned her with a look. "You're kidding me, right? The entire world thinks the two of you are having an affair. Your phone calls...Come on, you've got to realize how incriminating it looks."

Not if you're innocent, she wanted to scream. But he was right. The court of public opinion had already deemed her a liar and a cheat, regardless of the truth.

"There's got to be a way that we can communicate with each other. He might discover information that could help clear this mess up and vice versa. Shouldn't we be in this together?"

There was a long pause. Gina could tell Sawyer was mulling the conundrum over in his head.

"Let me think about a safe way you two can talk without the tabloids catching wind of it. It's your scandal, not mine. But until you have a truly private way to communicate, I'd suggest no more phone calls."

He took the exit to Dry Creek. She recognized Mother Lode Road, where the coffee shop was. But when he turned off on a side street and drove for a few miles, she was in unfamiliar territory.

"Where are we?" The homes were close together with dirt driveways. In almost every yard there were a few goats, sheep, dogs, chickens, or a combination of all four.

A double-wide trailer in the style of a ranch house sat at the end of the cul-de-sac. Two tow trucks were parked on what passed for a lawn and a metal garage with four bays took up most of the property. In one of the inlets, she spied Sawyer's Range Rover.

"This is Mama's." Sawyer parked under a shady tree in the dirt. "She owns the only tow service in town. Her son, Buck, is the local mechanic. You mind waiting while I check to see if my truck's ready?"

"Sure." It wasn't as if she had anything better to do.

She pulled her hat down to cover her face. Today, she'd taken too many chances of being recognized. But what was she supposed to do—never leave her cabin? Even on the ranch there was Aubrey and Charlie's construction crew. Wendy and Linda had told her to keep a low profile, not to lock herself away from all human contact.

She cracked the window for air, and watched Sawyer walk to the garage to the strains of "Save a Horse (Ride a Cowboy)" blaring from one of the car bays.

Ride a cowboy.

The thought had crossed her mind a time or two. Or three or four.

He returned a few minutes later and slid back into the driver's seat. "Buck is waiting on parts, so no truck today."

"It's a good thing I waited." It was a long walk home, she assumed, even though she didn't have the foggiest notion where they were.

"Yup." He reached inside his pocket and handed her his phone. "Put Danny's number in there and I'll call him to fill him in on the new protocol not to reach out to you anymore."

So they were back to that again. He slid her a glance as if it was a test to see if she'd go along with him contacting Danny.

"You still think I'm lying, don't you?"

"I believe you." But his voice held a slight waver. Sawyer Dalton was nobody's fool.

She respected him for that. It was the reason he was such a successful journalist. Despite her self-imposed banishment from the internet, she'd run a Google search on him. Sawyer had cred, writing for just about every respected publication out there. He hadn't lied when he said he didn't stoop to covering celebrity gossip. His stories were about wars, coups, corruption, and world leaders. And when he wasn't traveling the globe, he was helping to run his family's ranch.

Nope, Sawyer Dalton was no dupe.

"Good," she said. "Because I'm telling the truth. What should we tell your mom?"

"We? We shouldn't tell her anything. You, however, should tell her the truth. She works for you, I don't."

"Which raises a good question. Why? Why are you helping me?" Though she welcomed his advice—she could use all the support she could get—

she wondered about his motivations. He'd made it more than clear that he thought of her as a self-indulgent pest, who had commandeered his kitchen and got away with it because she was Wendy Dalton's high-paying client.

There was a long silence; only the hum of the air-conditioner and the sound of tires swooshing against the pavement.

He finally said, "The sooner your name is cleared, the sooner you can go home. Besides, I'm getting fat with you around."

"Don't you worry, I'll be out of here faster than you can count to ten." She threw her head back. "Oh, how I long for civilization." But honestly, Dry Creek Ranch was beginning to grow on her.

Unfortunately, so was its owner.

"Civilization?" He raised a brow. "I'd hardly call Hell-A civilized."

He pulled through the open ranch gate, which as long as Gina had lived here had never been closed. She didn't know why they had a gate in the first place. Maybe it was to keep the animals in. But she'd never seen a cow on this side of the property and the dogs hung out at Jace's house.

"Right, living in the Clampetts' old place down by the river is the height of civilization," she fired back.

"I'd say it's a sight more civilized than running the paparazzi gauntlet in La-La Land."

She'd used up all her pithy responses for the day.

"What are you cooking tonight?" His stomach rumbled as he continued up the blacktop road, past Jace and Charlie's ranch house, to his loft apartment.

"I thought you were watching your girlish figure." Nothing about Sawyer Dalton's physique was girlish. Nope, he was all man, right down to his big 'ole cowboy boots. "Anyway, you're out of luck, bucko. Tonight, I'm hanging out with Aubrey and Charlie."

"What about that new ice cream maker? I thought we should test it out."

"I bet you did. Unfortunately for you, I'll be testing it all by my lonesome at the cabin and bringing it for dessert for our girls' night."

He parked her car in his driveway and let the engine idle. "So you're not coming up?" He said it as if he was disappointed.

"Not today," she said. "Why, you afraid you'll miss me?"

He cut the motor and rubbed the bristle on his chin. "Maybe," he said. "One thing I'll say about you is that you're entertaining."

She turned in her seat to face him. "And my food. Don't forget you'll miss my cooking when I go, even if it is making you fat." She took a slow turn down his T-shirt–covered torso, pausing on his abs. Nope, not an inch of fat on him.

"I guess I could always buy your frozen entrées. Try to choke 'em down." The light in his blue eyes sparkled. He was enjoying teasing her.

"Then you'll have your kitchen back."

"Yep. Can't wait." He reached across the console and took off her sunglasses. Next came her hat.

She suddenly felt naked without them. Especially as he sat there, gazing at her face. She started to finger-comb her hair, but he pushed her hand away and held it in his much larger one. Then, he did something completely unexpected.

He leaned in, covered her mouth with his, and kissed her.

For a hard man, his lips were soft. And exquisitely pliant as they moved over hers, roaming until his tongue was licking into her mouth. She opened for him, letting him take the kiss deeper. He tasted good, like heat and desire, and she practically climbed over the center divider for more of him.

But he made it clear he was the one still in the driver's seat, tilting her head so that he moved over her and controlled the kiss exactly the way he wanted it. And, boy, did Sawyer Dalton know what he was doing. That one hand was still holding hers and the other he'd cradled behind her head. It was his mouth doing all the work. The hot pull of it was enough to make her panties melt.

He took his time exploring and tangling his tongue with hers. She felt his bristle against her face. It tickled. And the musky scent of his aftershave was like a special kind of aphrodisiac. Her nipples tightened and her body tingled. And her hands wanted to fill themselves with him. But when she tried to touch him, he caught her hand and held it still, along with her other one.

It was slow, erotic torture. Just his lips and his tongue, making her temperature rise.

He hummed something low in his throat and lifted his head to look at her, heat simmering in his blue eyes. Once again, he dipped down and caught her mouth for another kiss. Just a short one this time, but sensual just the same.

Then he straightened up, opened the door and got out, tossing her the keys, before he went inside.

Gina sat there, her entire equilibrium off-balance. What just happened? She traced her finger over her swollen bottom lip, trying to pull herself together. Trying to quell the ache between her legs.

The bastard had kissed and run and had left her...well, she wouldn't say unsatisfied. That had been about the most satisfying kiss she'd ever had. But to just walk away like that...to just leave her in the car all hot

and bothered…She had half a mind to go after him and demand that he finish the job.

She didn't, of course. She had more pride than that. Instead, she went home and made ice cream, hoping it would cool her off.

Chapter 10

"You think it's legit?" Sawyer stood at Cash's table, staring at his laptop as his cousin studied the email.

"I think it's a legitimate email. The question is whether the sender is legitimate." Like Sawyer, Cash tried to reply to the message, only to have it bounce back.

"Is there a way to trace it?" No matter how many times Sawyer reminded himself to be skeptical, even to dismiss the email, something about it told him it was a trail to Angie.

"Maybe," Cash said. "I'll talk to a friend of mine from the Bureau, see what he can do.

"More than likely it was sent from a disposable email address or a burner. Lots of people are using them now when they sign up for things online to keep from getting spammed. If it's a burner, it can probably be traced to the owner of the email address." Jace leaned back on a dining room chair.

Cash poked Jace in the ribs. "You break that chair and Aubrey will break your legs." They were supposed to be watching a baseball game while the women had their girls' night at Jace's place. Ellie was away at horse camp and the boys had gone on an overnight fishing trip with the family of one of Travis's best friends.

"How is it that you're so up on disposable email addresses and burners, anyway?" Cash asked Jace.

Sawyer wondered the same thing. There weren't a lot of cybercrimes for a sheriff in Mill County.

"When Charlie filed her restraining order against that douchebag, Ainsley, I researched it."

Last winter, Charlie had fled her abusive ex and had hidden out on Dry Creek Ranch, where Jace had fallen madly in love with her.

Sawyer was thrilled that both his cousins had found their soul mates, even if he felt like he was living inside a freaking romance novel. Then again, he had two gorgeous women in his life, who fussed over him.

Nothing wrong with that.

He subconsciously touched his lips with his finger, thinking about his and Gina's kiss. On a scale of ten, the kiss had been a solid fifteen. It had taken all he had not to throw her over his shoulder, caveman style, and carry her up to his loft apartment. Not happening, he reminded himself. His mother would have a meltdown. The kiss was bad enough. And Gina… was a walking aneurism.

But despite it, he was attracted to her. A lot. Which was weird because she wasn't even his type. Too high-maintenance, too much of a prima donna. How many times had she made disparaging remarks about Cash's old cabin and the ranch?

The Clampetts.

The Daltons were no *Beverly Hillbillies*. The Clampetts had at least struck oil on their land.

"What if it's a disposable?" Cash asked, bringing Sawyer back to the conversation at hand.

"Dunno," Jace said. "That's as far as I got. Don't have to worry about it anymore." His lips curled up into a self-satisfied grin. "Not now that Ainsley is doing life."

They were all quiet for a few seconds, remembering one of the worst days in Jace and Charlie's lives. Everyone had recovered, thanks to Jace. And against all odds, the lovebirds were getting married in October. The best time of year on the ranch. Warm days filled with light.

"Let me see what Ken can do in the computer forensic lab," Cash said, breaking the silence. "He owes me a few favors. But Sawyer, my gut tells me this isn't Angie. Why would she wait five years to contact you? Or any of us, for that matter. Yes, we all questioned her lifestyle choices. But no one, including her, questioned our love for her. She knew there wasn't anything we wouldn't do for her."

Sawyer had thought the same thing himself when he'd first opened the email. Why now? Why after five years? But on further reflection, he was convinced that the note had something to do with him going to New Mexico and nosing around. He was getting closer to the truth about why his sister disappeared. And someone didn't want him to. Those six boldfaced words—*Stop searching for me. I'm safe*—had to be Angie-related.

In all these years, he'd never lost hope. And that had to mean something. "Then who?" Jace asked. "Who would've sent it and why?"

"Could it have something to do with a story you're working on?" Cash got them all another round of beers from the fridge while the forgotten ball game played in the living room. Sawyer caught glimpses of it from the dining table.

Though the cabin's layout was a carbon copy of Gina's—same open floor plan—the similarities ended there. Aubrey's magic decorator touch was stamped on every surface: From the refinished floors and brightly colored walls to the painted kitchen cabinets and sophisticated window treatments.

"Not that I can think of." And Sawyer had racked his brain trying to find a possibility there. "But half of being a reporter is a fishing expedition. I get a tip, make a lot of calls, and when nothing pans out, I usually stop working on the story. But who knows? I might've spoken to someone about something that seemed like a big story at the time and have completely forgotten about it. Still, the message doesn't make sense for something like that, unless someone's trying to yank my chain. And I just don't see it."

Jace nodded. "Me neither. It's either someone pretending to be Angie or it's Angie."

Cash let out a long breath. "I don't think any of us should get our hopes up. The chance that it's Angie after all this time...well, it's a long shot." That was Cash, always the voice of reason.

For once, though, Sawyer felt like this could be something solid, something that might at least end the mystery to what had happened to his sister. "How long do you think it will take this buddy of yours to trace the email?"

Cash popped the cap off his beer. "I'll ask Ken to make it a priority. But if I know anything about the lab, he's backed up fifty ways from Sunday. The Northern District has more cybercrime than they can handle."

Cash didn't like to call in favors, especially because he'd left the Bureau on a bad note. The FBI's fault, not Cash's. "Thanks for doing this—it means a lot," Sawyer said.

Cash scowled. "I'd do anything for Angie. You of all people should know that, Sawyer. We're family."

Sawyer nodded. Cash and Jace were more like brothers than cousins. But they'd been down the Angie bogus-tip road so many times that he wouldn't blame anyone for giving up. At least this time, Jace didn't think Sawyer was going off half-cocked. Even Cash, for all his caution, appeared to think there might be something to the email.

"I'll wait before I say anything about this to my folks," Sawyer said. His parents, more than anyone, had been devastated by his sister's disappearance.

"That's probably a good idea," Cash said. "It would be good to have something concrete first, something that won't end in disappointment."

They sat around the table for a while, absorbed in their own thoughts. The ball game continued to play in the background, but no one seemed interested in watching it.

Sawyer's mind shifted to his meeting that morning. It still rankled. "I went by Beals Ranch today and Jill all but confirmed that Randy is selling to Mitch," Sawyer told his cousins.

Jace flicked his bottle cap across the table and sighed. "Jill would know. What did Randy say?"

"I didn't see Randy. I went over there to inquire about buying Randy's stock trailer, but he wasn't home. Just Jill. She said Brett was in town."

"Yeah, we had a couple of beers earlier. But he never said anything about Mitch buying Beals Ranch."

"He might not know about it," Sawyer said. "Jill was vague. She's probably counting her inheritance." It wasn't quite fair. She had moved to the ranch to help her parents to make amends for what she'd done. But Sawyer wasn't feeling all that forgiving.

"Sounds like we'll be living next door to the seventh circle of hell." Jace shook his head and pointed the tip of his beer bottle at Sawyer. "And I'll fight it with everything I've got."

"We'll fight it," Cash said, his second reminder of the day that family sticks. As Grandpa Dalton used to say, "Together, we're cowboy strong."

"How is Brett?" Cash asked. "How's his program going?"

"It's going so well that he's planning to move back next month and start work for his uncle's cabinet company. He says he's hoping to work things out with Jill." Jace scowled. There was no love lost between him and Jill. Understandably, Jace blamed her for delivering the final blow to Brett, who was already on shaky ground to begin with. He'd been deeply depressed even before he'd found out that his wife had been stepping out on him.

"That's great," Cash said. "Carpentry is a good trade."

Jace, stoic like their grandfather, gave a faint nod. Sawyer suspected his cousin was still grieving what had happened to Brett in Afghanistan and didn't want to talk about it. Brett had come back from the war a hero, but a different man than the one Jace had grown up with.

"Yup." Jace nodded, then sidetracked. "Saw you driving Gina's BMW earlier. What's up with that?"

"She took me to pick up my Range Rover, which still needs new brake pads. Buck can't get the parts until tomorrow."

"She still peddling that story about being set up?" Jace took a long drag on his beer. "Why don't you have an expert look at the picture?"

"Already working on it."

"If you need a second opinion I might have a forensic guy who can help," Cash offered.

"Thanks." Sawyer and his cousins didn't always agree, but they always backed one another up. It had always been that way, even when they were little kids. When Jace's family had been killed in the auto wreck, they'd spent an entire summer on the ranch, comforting him. When Jace's wife, Mary Ann, deserted him and their kids, Sawyer and Cash were back at the ranch to support him. When the FBI fired Cash for a case his bosses screwed up, they'd rallied. When Angie went missing, his cousins pooled their law enforcement experience to help find her.

They were Daltons. Cowboy strong.

They moved to the living room, but it was the eighth inning and the Giants were so far behind that the game was too painful to watch.

"They suck this season," Jace said, grabbing the remote off the coffee table and flicking off the TV. "By the way, I gave the flower girls their options with the numbers we agreed on. They went for the pricier number one—we supply the water. I'm just waiting for the signed contract, but it looks like a thumbs-up on the land lease and shop."

"Is that what we're calling them? The flower girls?" Sawyer suppressed a laugh.

"Yep. I guess we're farmers now."

Cash feigned a shudder because no self-respecting rancher called himself a farmer. "What do you think Grandpa would've thought of what we're doing?"

"He would've liked it a hell of a lot better than a golf-course community, I can tell you that," Jace said.

They were saving the legacy and that's what mattered. And to Sawyer's mind, Grandpa Dalton would've appreciated the creative way they were going about it. Aubrey and Charlie's design studio and furniture shop. Even the flowers.

"I met a saddlemaker who might be interested in studio space and a small storefront." Cash swung his arm over the back of the sofa. "He's a hand at one of the ranches I inspect. Does beautiful work and is ready to make a go of it full-time. Good guy; you'll like him."

"I can get behind a saddlemaker." Jace walked back to the kitchen and stuck his head in the fridge. "You have anything to eat around here that isn't kale?" Cash was a bit of health nut.

Cash returned to the kitchen, pulled a bag of chips down from the pantry, and tossed them at Jace. "Here, go ahead and give yourself a heart attack."

Sawyer eyed the chips. He hadn't eaten anything since lunch and was starved. He remembered Gina's leftovers in the fridge and got to his feet. "I'm heading out. See you guys tomorrow."

As he started for the trail that cut across the field to his place, he stole a glance at Gina's cabin. The lights were out and her car wasn't in the driveway. It appeared that she was still with Charlie and Aubrey at Jace's house. All for the better, he told himself as he crossed the moonlit pasture.

But the whole way home he thought about their kiss.

* * * *

Gina had had three glasses of wine and a margarita and was feeling more than a little tipsy. Her pie, strawberry shortcake, and homemade ice cream had been the hit of the evening. But Charlie's cheesy beef quesadillas were nothing to sneeze at. In fact, Gina planned to borrow the recipe and put her own spin on it. It would be a nice venture outside the box to cook something other than Italian food, even if it was just for a dinner, alone.

Danny had called her two more times. But on Sawyer's advice, she'd let his messages go to voicemail. She agreed with Sawyer. Until she and Danny had a safer way to communicate, she wasn't taking any chances.

Sawyer.

Her thoughts had drifted to him throughout the evening. She suspected he'd met up with his two cousins to watch the ball game at Cash's place. That's where Jace had gone, according to Charlie, so the women could have the ranch house to themselves.

Or maybe Sawyer had a date. He probably had a whole private life she knew nothing about. Right at this very minute, he could be hooking up with one of the locals.

But there had been the kiss.

"Maybe FoodFlicks did it to drum up publicity," Aubrey said, interrupting Gina's visit down memory lane. Because that kiss was something to remember.

She'd given them the 411 on her and Danny Clay. Why not? She had done nothing wrong and wanted to shout her innocence from the rooftop. Shockingly, her new friends believed her. If only the rest of America would.

But how did you prove something didn't happen when all the evidence said that it did?

"Nah, that's not the kind of publicity a family-friendly network wants." Charlie uncorked a second bottle of white and refilled their glasses. "Maybe it was one of those tabloids. Don't they do stuff like that just to get readers?"

Tabloids certainly played fast and loose with the truth, at least in Gina's experience. But make things up wholesale? That seemed like a multimillion-dollar lawsuit waiting to happen.

"I've gone through every person I've ever met or done business with and no one stands out. In fact, everyone—my investors, my staff, my producers, and the companies I represent—stand to lose. That's why I can't figure this out."

"Maybe whoever did this is out to get Danny. Or maybe Candace. This has got to be worse than awful for her…Not that it's not awful for you too." Charlie began clearing their dinner dishes from the table. "But you know what I mean."

"Charlie has a good point. This whole thing could be designed to hurt Candace and you're just a means to the end. Her husband, her show, her public humiliation all in one fell swoop." Aubrey shook her head in commiseration with Candace.

"It would help if I could talk to her and compare notes," Gina said. "But according to Danny, she's holed up somewhere and refusing to talk to anyone. I assume when she does, I'll be the last person on her list."

"Uh-uh," Aubrey said. "I'm with Sawyer on this. You can't talk to any of the Clays until the three of you are a united front. Otherwise the press will find out and it'll look like you and Danny really are an item."

"I'm one-hundred percent with Aubrey on this." Charlie sliced herself a sliver of strawberry shortcake and gave both of them a sheepish grin. "It's so good I want seconds."

"Hey, no judgment here." Gina was about to go in for thirds. She no longer had to worry about the camera adding ten pounds.

"I know you're right," she continued. "But I'm dying to talk to Candace. First, to plead my innocence. Second, to see if the three of us can figure this out together."

Aubrey licked a drop of whipped cream frosting off her finger. "Having once been falsely accused of cheating on my ex-fiancé, I speak from experience. Don't do anything to fuel the flames. People will believe what they want to believe until you have solid proof."

"You were engaged to someone before you married Cash?" It was the first Gina had heard of an ex.

"It's a long story." Aubrey waved her hand in the air dismissively. "What I'm saying is that without proof that the pictures and texts are fake, you're—"

"Screwed," Gina finished. Aubrey was right and it was beyond frustrating. "But how do I get solid proof when I can't even talk to the other victims?"

Both women murmured their understanding. It was a challenge, to be sure. But having two women friends to share her angst with was a bonus she'd never expected from hiding away in the boonies. Besides Sawyer, who'd become the object of her late-night fantasies, Charlie and Aubrey had become one of the best perks of temporarily making her home at Dry Creek Ranch. She now had pals, which in her former life hadn't been the case. No time for girls' nights out or gossiping on the telephone.

Or maybe she hadn't let herself make the time.

That protective shell she wore like armor wasn't exactly a friend magnet. But it sure the hell kept her from getting hurt. It took ten years of therapy to learn that she wrapped herself in her accomplishments, instead of human connections. Dr. Peggy Regis, her two-hundred-dollar-an-hour shrink, attributed most of Gina's fear of relationships to her father's death and her mother's disapproval.

The bottom line was Gina had—among other neuroses—abandonment issues, according to Peggy.

In high school, Sadie had never approved of her friends. Not that she ran with a bad crowd, just mid-listers in Sadie's eyes. The children of Hollywood and Beverly Hills parents who weren't household names. Some of Gina's inner circle didn't even live in Beverly Hills, but had used the address of employers or relatives to get into the 90210 school district. Sadie considered those kids leeches, too beneath a DeRose.

So when Gina went to SDSU her mother directed her to rush the most prestigious sorority on campus, a consolation for not getting into USC and for making shitty friend choices in high school.

Gina's heart wasn't in it. Not really. Not when she had next to nothing in common with most of the girls other than wealth and privilege. She'd even overheard two girls in the sorority house whisper behind her back that she wasn't Alpha Chi material, which everyone knew meant she was either not pretty enough, not popular enough, or not rich enough. Lord knew the last one didn't apply, leaving Gina to assume it was the first two.

It came as no shock when she didn't make the cut. Still, it ruined her freshman year. Her peers' rejection and Sadie's stinging displeasure had been overwhelming.

The experience set Gina's social course for the rest of her college years. *Keep my head down, my mouth shut, and get out as fast as I can.*

She'd graduated in four years, a major feat given that it took most students that long to find parking in the overcrowded lots.

But Sadie was no longer alive to approve or disapprove of Gina's friends. And when it came to Charlie and Aubrey, Gina wouldn't have cared, anyway. They were smart, accomplished women, who unlike the rest of the world, didn't think she was a home-wrecking slut.

"Enough about me." The entire point of a girls' night out was to laugh and eat and drink too much. "Let's talk about something cheerful."

Aubrey and Charlie exchanged conspiratorial glances.

"You and Sawyer seem to be spending a lot of time together." Charlie covered the cake with a glass lid, one of her charming, vintage tableware pieces. "I'm saving the rest for the boys. Back to Sawyer. What's going on with you two?"

"Uh, nothing," Gina said too quickly, conveniently leaving out the kiss. "Nothing at all." Jeez, even to her own ears, she sounded like she was protesting too much.

"Really? Because it looks like there's something going on to me," Aubrey said. Between her and Charlie, she was the more outspoken one.

"Nope. Just friends. Well, not even friends. More like chef and professional taster. I cook, Sawyer eats. That's about the extent of our relationship."

Charlie's eyes were laughing at Gina. "He appears to be doing more than just sampling your recipes." She made it sound sexual. "Hasn't he been advising you, giving tips on how to avoid negative press? He has to like you, or he wouldn't get involved."

Gina shrugged. "His parents represent me. He's just taking part in the family business. So what's the deal with his sister?"

Again, Aubrey and Charlie exchanged looks. This time, not conspiratorial but surprised.

"He told you about Angie?" Aubrey lifted the cake lid and took another swipe at the whipped cream.

"A little. I offered to go with him to New Mexico to check out this commune where she supposedly lived. I mean, it's the least I can do since he's helping me out. But he wasn't interested."

"He didn't tell you the latest? About the email?" Charlie asked.

Gina shook her head. "No. What email?"

Charlie turned to Aubrey. "I guess it's okay if we tell her, right?" Aubrey nodded. "It was an anonymous email, someone saying they were safe and that Sawyer should stop his search."

Gina's mouth fell wide. "Angie sent it?"

Aubrey hitched her shoulders. "We don't know for certain. But, yeah, that's the consensus. Cash is having a friend in the FBI cyber lab see if he can trace it."

"Who else could it be?" As far as Gina knew, Sawyer was only searching for one person. His sister.

"We just don't want to jump to conclusions," Charlie said. "Sawyer deals with a lot of weirdos in his line of work. A lot of reporters do. Everyone wants their fifteen minutes of fame."

"What if it is her, though?" None of it made any sense to Gina, unless Sawyer's sister wanted a permanent separation from her family. Then why not just say she didn't want them to contact her? Period. But from everything Sawyer had said that wasn't the case. They were close—the whole family was—according to him.

Charlie blew out a breath. "That's the big question. It was nice of you to offer to help, though."

"Why? He's helping me."

Both Charlie and Aubrey smiled. It was a knowing smile, but they had it all wrong. There was nothing going on between her and Sawyer.

Except for the kiss.

"How long until Cash's friend knows something?"

"I guess when he can fit it in." Aubrey gave a half shrug. "Until then, we wait."

Sawyer didn't strike Gina as the type to wait. He'd continue his own investigation until Cash's FBI buddy came through. That much she knew. She'd offer whatever help she could give, though tracing anonymous emails wasn't exactly her forte.

They spent the rest of the evening gossiping about people Gina didn't know. But she enjoyed the conversation just the same. It was a close-knit town and it sounded like everyone was up in everyone else's grill. Same as FoodFlicks without the nastiness.

"Have you signed up the flower growers, yet?" she asked, curious about how this little village of shops and agricultural pursuits would work. The concept very much appealed to her business side and on the nights she didn't fantasize about Sawyer naked, she played around with ideas of ways this plan of the Daltons could be more profitable.

"We did." Charlie pumped her fist in the air.

"Cash talked to a saddlemaker who's interested too." Aubrey cleared the rest of the table and started loading their dinner plates into the dishwasher.

"Is that very lucrative, saddlemaking?" Gina's only exposure to horses and saddles had been her sixth birthday party. Sadie had gone with a petting

zoo theme, including pony rides. And there had been a lot of protests and tears when her father had tried to hoist her onto the back of a shaggy little Shetland named Mike. Petting had been fine. But riding, a no-go.

Sadie had pouted and whined that they were missing a golden photo opportunity. Just one of a long list of her mother's complaints about Gina.

"Are you kidding?" Aubrey straightened from the dishwasher and stretched. "The price people will pay for a good show saddle is through the roof. Some of those saddles have more sterling silver than a jewelry store. According to Cash, this saddle guy does a lot of custom work."

"No question saddles fit in with the ranch motif. As long as the guy can pay his rent. You ever consider talking to Laney and Jimmy Ray? That sarsaparilla they make is a license to print money. Just a stand here, nothing that would cut into their coffee shop business. Can you picture it? Folks browsing in Refined, strolling through the flower shop, popping in to watch the saddlemaker, all the while working up a powerful thirst."

"It's brilliant." Aubrey clapped her hands. "They could serve it in cute Mason jars, maybe sell slices of Laney's chess pie or ramekins of her berry crumble."

"Do something seasonal for the holidays," Gina continued. But it was the sarsaparilla that would draw people in. She hated to think of Laney and Jimmy Ray's winning concoction confined to a life of obscurity.

"What a wonderful idea." Charlie turned on the dishwasher and grabbed a pad of paper from one of the drawers. "I want to take notes, share it with the guys, and then we should approach Laney and Jimmy Ray. They're spread thin at the coffee shop, so they'd probably have to bring someone else in. We'd have to do the build-out ourselves. Laney wouldn't have the patience for it and Jimmy Ray has got his hands full. Plus, the money. I'm not sure they'd want to make the investment until they knew it would pay off."

"Just a kiosk would do it," Gina said. "There's got to be prefab ones you can buy."

Aubrey started searching on her phone. "It would have to fit in aesthetically with the ranch. Nothing janky, like the ones you see at the mall."

"I'm sure we could get someone to build something. Even Dennis and his crew," Charlie said.

Aubrey looked at Charlie and narrowed her eyes. "If we want it done by the twelfth of never. Because that's how long he's taking to finish our job."

Gina heard the construction whenever she walked to Sawyer's house. The contractor and his people appeared to be zipping along. But she

supposed it was easy to become impatient when you were living in it, trying to run a business.

"I'm sure one of the guys knows someone." Charlie dismissed Aubrey with her hand. "The bigger challenge is getting them to go along with it. Not so much Laney, but Jimmy Ray."

"I could talk to them," Gina volunteered, though she was an outsider. The Daltons would probably have better luck. But her mind spun with so many ideas she couldn't help getting caught up in the planning. And food was her bailiwick. "Or the three of us could, with me explaining the concept. You've got to have a concept in the hospitality industry."

"If that doesn't work we can sic Jace on them," Charlie said. "There isn't a thing they wouldn't do for him."

"Hey, they stand to make bank on this," Aubrey added. "It's a win-win for both of us."

Gina didn't see how Laney and Jimmy Ray's sarsaparilla could lose as long as Aubrey and Charlie got the kind of traffic they were hoping for. Getting people here was the key, which meant they'd need something significant. Something people would travel for.

"I'm calling it a night, ladies." Aubrey wrapped up the last of the quesadillas, stashed them in the fridge, and grabbed her purse.

Gina supposed it was her cue to leave too, though she was enjoying herself and didn't relish going back to her hot, empty cabin. The evenings in Dry Creek were cooler than the days. But the temperatures still hovered in the low eighties. Living by the ocean, she'd grown accustomed to cool sea breezes. Here, she had the creek, which didn't temper the heat but was sure nice to listen to.

"You want a ride?" she asked Aubrey, who unlike her had walked over.

"Nah, the exercise will do me some good." Aubrey patted her belly.

They walked out together and even though it was closing in on ten o'clock, there was enough moonlight to illuminate the path everyone used for going back and forth between the cabins and the ranch house.

Gina considered leaving her car and joining Aubrey for the short stroll. But suddenly she had somewhere else she wanted to go.

Chapter 11

Sawyer was tweaking his nut graph on the *Forbes* piece when someone rang the doorbell. He glanced at the clock. The girls were probably still doing their thing and Jace needed a place to hang out until he could go home.

"Door's open," he yelled down.

The sound of footsteps came up the stairs.

Sawyer didn't bother to look up from his computer. "Cash kick you out?" His cousin had adopted the hours of a cow cop. Early to bed, early to rise.

"How come you didn't tell me about the email? The one from Angie?"

He swiveled his barstool around to find Gina in his entryway, not Jace. She had on the same short skirt she'd worn to the barbecue that first week she was here and a stretchy sleeveless top that gave her a boost in the chest department. Not the legendary Gina DeRose rack of cooking show lore, but enough to fill his hands. Instead of the high heels, cowboy boots. That visual alone made his blood rush south of his belt.

"We don't know that it's Angie," he said, trying hard not to ogle her and failing miserably.

"Who else could it be?"

Who else indeed? But it was better to keep his expectations low, that way he wasn't disappointed. "Don't know. But the timing seems odd. Why now, after all these years?"

"Because for the first time you have a solid lead. New Mexico. She likely knows you've been talking to people from the commune, asking questions."

Beautiful and smart. But Gina DeRose had enough troubles of her own. He didn't plan to make his her part-time hobby while she waited for the dust to settle on her own situation.

"Maybe," was all he said. "Your hen party over?"

"I hate that saying. It's condescending. What if I called your night out with the guys a cock party?"

He eyed her up and down, not even bothering to be discreet about it. Cock party?

His cock wanted to party right now.

"Did you come over to use my kitchen or to berate me for being a chauvinist?"

"I came over to find out why you hadn't told me about the email. We spent all day together and not one word." She plopped down on the stool next to him. "I tell you all my stuff."

"That's so I can help you go home. Back to the bright lights and glitter." He winked.

"You're being a dick."

"Dick is my default."

"What're you going to do if Cash's friend traces the email to Angie?" She wouldn't let it go.

He let out a breath. "It won't be that cut-and-dried. But if the signs point to it being sent from her, I'll find her."

"Even if she doesn't want you to?"

"I don't believe that," he said. "There's more to it, more to the story."

"Like she's in trouble?"

He nodded and turned away, staring out the window. "Why are you really here?"

Rarely did women show up at his house after ten p.m. without sex in mind. If that's why she'd come, he'd send her home. As much a temptation as she was, he'd proven he could restrain himself. The kiss had been a slip, a momentary lapse in judgment. He wouldn't let it happen again.

Maybe when she fixed her life and was no longer his mother's client they could meet up for a drink in Malibu. Tear up the sheets for a night and make a plan to do it again sometime. But not under these circumstances. And definitely not while she was living less than a mile away.

Sawyer liked his space and freedom too much to hook up with the girl next door.

"You have air-conditioning and I don't." She got up, moved to the living room, and made herself at home on his sofa.

"If you're going to suck up the free air-conditioning you could've at least brought ice cream."

"We ate it all. Now that I've got the machine, I'll make you some tomorrow."

He saved his work, shut down his laptop, and joined Gina on the sofa. She kicked off her boots and tucked her legs under her ass, showing more of those glorious legs of hers. He considered moving to the chair but stayed put, either to punish himself or to prove his mettle.

"What were you working on?" She nudged her head at his computer on the kitchen island.

"An article for *Forbes* that's due next week."

"What's it about?"

"The fall of globalization." Normally, he could've spent hours talking about his current work. The research, the interviews, the thesis of the story, things that bored his cousins to death. But not tonight.

Tonight, he was having trouble focusing on anything other than Gina stretched out on his couch in that tiny skirt, wondering what she had on for underwear.

"It sounds dull as dirt."

"It's my life's work, so thanks."

"It is not. I liked your story about that Malawi kid who studied library books so he could build an electrical windmill to bring water to his home."

"You read that?" He'd written it years ago. Since then, the kid— now a man—had been the focus of a documentary and had penned an autobiography.

"Mm-hmm. You're a good writer."

He laughed because she sounded surprised. "Yeah, I get by."

"If you could only be one, which would you pick: cowboy or writer?"

"Cowboy writer." He grinned. "How 'bout you? Chef or celebrity?"

She took a long time to answer. "Celebrity."

He'd expected her to imitate his cop-out answer with celebrity chef. But she'd surprised him. "Yeah?" He tilted his head sideways. Why was he not surprised?

"The thing is I'm a better celebrity than I am a chef."

He didn't know about that. She was quickly on her way to being a washed-up celebrity. But on that, he held his tongue. "Your show is good, Gina. I don't even cook and I watch it." He left out that he especially enjoyed the T&A part of the program. "But your cooking"—he held his hand over his heart—"incomparable."

"Don't get carried away. Whatever skills I had I've lost. And even when I was good, I wasn't Thomas Keller or Nancy Silverton good."

"I disagree. And I've eaten at the French Laundry, Per Se, Bouchon, and Ad Hoc. I freaking lived at La Brea Bakery and spent my childhood

eating at Campanile before Nancy and Mark split up. You're every bit as good as them."

"Nancy and Mark?" She rolled her eyes at his familiar use of Chef Silverton and Chef Peel's first names.

"Hey, my parents are Wendy and Dan Dalton." His lips curved up. "They handled the press on the divorce."

"I'm not doing anything innovative or extraordinary," she said, getting back on point. "Everything I do is basic. My signature is strawberry shortcake. Enough said, right?"

"Isn't Nancy famous for grilled cheese sandwiches? And Keller, a version of an Oreo cookie. It's all in the execution."

She shook her head. "You know what? For a cowboy you're an awful big know-it-all."

"Nah, I'm just smart as hell. And hungry." He got to his feet before he did something stupid like kiss her again. Because the mood in the room was definitely veering in that direction.

He stuck his head in the fridge, wishing he could stick the lower half of his body in there too. All of Gina's leftovers were gone. He'd powered through her baked ziti in less than two days. "You want something?"

"I gorged on Charlie's cheesy beef quesadillas. I couldn't eat another thing."

"Quesadillas, huh?" He searched his dairy drawer for cheese, found a package of stale tortillas on the top shelf, and piled his ingredients on the counter.

"You want me to make them for you?" she asked as he fumbled with a cheese grater.

"I can do it." Although hers would be edible. His, not so much.

She came over and grabbed the butter before he closed the fridge door. "Go sit down. Watching you is painful."

Not half as painful as watching her bending over to preheat his oven in that short skirt.

"You have any steak?"

He looked at her pointedly. "I own a cattle ranch." Then he got up and opened his freezer.

"Holy cow." She laughed at her own pun, which really wasn't that funny. "You've been holding out on me, Dalton."

"It's fresh, *DeRose*. Help yourself. But it's a little late for beef." Nighttime had never stopped him from grabbing a burger when he was out on the road on assignment. But when he was home, he tried to adhere to somewhat of a normal schedule, which included not eating heavy meals before bedtime.

"I wanted to test out Charlie's recipe. With a twist, of course." She eyed the freezer shelves filled with various cuts wrapped in white butcher paper, each package efficiently labeled. "I'll take you up on your offer, though. Not tonight. But I can't wait to play with your meat." It took her a second, then her face flushed. "Yeah, that sounded...weird."

He thought of a dozen double entendres he could fire back, but was afraid it would hurt to talk. Instead, he concealed the lower half of his body underneath the granite ledge of the kitchen island while she finished grating the hunk of cheddar cheese he'd butchered.

"Not what I would normally use, but it's all you have." She gazed around his kitchen. "You have a red onion?"

"Maybe in the pantry." He started to get up and thought better of it. She didn't seem to notice and found what she was looking for.

"I don't know how old that is." Hell, he couldn't even remember buying it.

"Not old. I brought it for the *panzanella* salad." She filled a bowl with apple cider vinegar—another staple he didn't know he had—sugar and salt, then began slicing the onion. "Nice knife. Mine's better, though."

"What's that for?" He bobbed his chin at the vinegar mixture.

"It's to pickle the onion. Technically, it takes an hour. But I won't make you wait." Her lips ticked up in a teasing smile.

Did the woman know what she was doing to him?

"Seems like a lot of trouble for a quesadilla." Something he'd always thought of as kid food. Ellie, Travis, and Grady lived on them.

"Even simple dishes should be elevated to be the best they can be, according to you, Mr. Cowboy Know-It-All."

"Well, this cowboy know-it-all is starved." Starved for something entirely different than food.

He continued to watch her work, gliding through his kitchen in that stretchy top that left little to his imagination. Damn, he needed to date more. Have sex more. He wanted to tell himself that his infatuation with Gina was due to his dry spell. But he had a strict policy of never lying to himself.

Their chemistry was off the charts. Apparently, he had a thing for self-indulged smart-mouthed women whose lives were falling apart. Or maybe he just had a thing for Gina. And that wasn't going to work.

Just a taste.

"Pass me the spatula."

He leaned across the counter and swiped the cooking tool from a crock Aubrey had artfully arranged on his island. Instead of tossing it across

the kitchen to her, he came up behind her while she heated a skillet over his six-burner range.

"Here you go," he said so close to her ear that he could smell her shampoo. Something botanical.

She turned. "Thank you."

Their eyes met and held. And that's when he knew he was screwed.

He slid her away from the cooktop, boxed her in against the counter, and covered her mouth with his. She tasted like whipped cream, strawberries, and wine. Starved for more, the kiss became frenzied. She fisted her hands in his shirt, going up on her toes for more.

He pressed into her, his erection straining against his button fly. She moaned. It was the single best sound he'd ever heard.

"More?" he asked, making sure he wasn't reading things wrong.

She tilted her head back. "God, yes."

His hands roamed, first cupping her ass to pull her tighter against him. Then to her stomach, where he inched his way under her shirt. Her skin was warm and soft and he wanted more of it. He dragged her top over her head and tossed it away, leaving her in a black lace push-up bra that reminded him of the pinup girl calendars in Buck's garage.

Sucking in a hard breath, he explored, working his hands up her rib cage. She hooked her thumbs into the waistband of his jeans and tugged.

"What?" he whispered. "You want them off?"

Her head fell back. "I—uh—please."

He lifted her onto the countertop and undid the front clasp of her bra. She let the straps slip down her shoulders while he took his fill of looking at her. Beautiful. Not the sex kitten chef she played on TV. Real flesh-and-blood woman.

Ravishing woman.

He slowly pulled her straps the rest of the way down and tossed the bra in the same vicinity as her shirt. His hands reached for her breasts, weighing each one in his hand. He ran his thumbs over her nipples, watching them pebble to hardened buds.

"Sawyer," she said in a breathy voice.

He kissed her again, letting his lips trail down her throat to the valley between her breasts. Then took each perfect globe into his mouth, sucking and laving until she nearly came off the counter.

He moved over her stomach, kissing and swirling his tongue around her belly button. Her skin tasted like a mixture of salt and perfume.

"You're killing me." Her voice was barely a whisper.

He cocked his head to the side and looked up at her. "Don't die." His hands slipped under her skirt, filling his palms with two bare ass cheeks.

Ah, mystery solved. A thong.

He dragged the scrap of lace down her legs and kissed the inside of her thighs. "Mmm, you taste good."

Her hands were in his hair, her head tilted back, her eyes at half-mast, and her pretty breasts on display.

Man, she turned him on.

He went back to kissing her, letting his lips skim higher and higher. She whimpered when he reached the promised land, dipping his tongue in for a taste. Gina pressed against his mouth, begging for more.

He pulled her closer to the counter's edge and spread her legs wide.

"Oh, yes, yes," she cried as he sucked and simultaneously rubbed her with his finger.

"Good?" He could feel her muscles tensing.

"So, so good. Sawyer...please." Her hands gripped his head tighter.

He slipped a finger inside of her while he licked her with the tip of his tongue. She bowed up.

"Let yourself go, baby."

"Oh." It came out as a moan as she clenched and climaxed.

But he wasn't through yet. He lifted her into his arms and carried her to his bedroom, where he kicked the door closed and laid her in the middle of his king bed.

It was time to get Gina DeRose out of his system for once and for all.

* * * *

Gina lifted her butt off the bed and shimmied out of her skirt, growing impatient. "Hey, why am I the only one naked?"

"Working on it." With one fluid motion Sawyer yanked his shirt over his head.

She watched his muscles bunch with the efficient movement. Still recuperating from his thorough ministrations and an orgasm that was now her gold standard, she stared at his chest. A chest she never tired of looking at. He was even more bronzed than the last time she'd seen him shirtless. Probably from working around the ranch in the hot sun.

Her eyes moved lower where he flicked open the buttons on his fly and shucked his boots and jeans. Both landed on the floor with a hard thud. He stood over the bed in a pair of black boxer briefs that struggled to contain the hard bulge inside.

His ass was a true work of beauty, she noted as he walked to the side of the bed. Round and firm. All that time with his legs clamped to a horse's barrel were apparently better than squats. Perhaps she should learn how to ride.

He scraped open the drawer on his nightstand, retrieved a box of condoms, and placed them on the table. For a second, she let her thoughts wander to how many women had shared his bed, then shooed petty jealousies away. Neither of them was a virgin, though it had been at least two years for her.

"What are you thinking about?" He crawled next to her and planted another one of his heart-stopping kisses on her mouth.

"That you're a man who knows what he's doing."

He chuckled and kissed his way down to her breasts. "Let's see how I do."

"So far I'd give you a solid B-plus," she lied, not wanting to feed his already inflated ego.

"You and I both know that's bullshit." He flicked his tongue over her nipple and she nearly screamed with the pleasure of it. "In the kitchen...that was an A-plus performance. I have the scratches on my scalp to prove it."

She ran her hands through his dark hair. "You do not. What you have is a head the size of this ranch."

"Wait until you see the rest of me." He lifted up and rolled his shorts down his legs, giving her a nice view of his impressive erection, then winked.

She climbed on top of him and held his hands over his head while she kissed her way down his chest.

He broke free with ease and palmed her butt. "You're welcome to stay on top, but I get to touch."

"Touch all you like." She wrapped her hand around his thickness and squeezed. "Because I plan to touch too."

"As you wish." He rolled her onto her back and nestled himself between her legs.

She arched up and rubbed against him, trying desperately to soothe the ache in her center. He kissed the side of her neck and nibbled on her earlobe.

"Sawyer?"

"Hmm?"

"I want you." She tried to roll him under her but he wouldn't budge.

Finally, he relented, but not before swiping one of the condoms off the bedside table and suiting up.

She straddled him, guiding him inside of her. When he was seated all the way in she flinched.

"You okay?" He gripped her hips.

"Uh-huh." But the truth was it hurt a little. "Slow at first, okay?"

He stroked her back, giving her plenty of time to grow accustomed to him. She loved the way his blue eyes were filled with heat and how he leaned up to spread kisses across her chest.

As she got more comfortable, she began to move. Slowly at first, trying to find her rhythm. He let her set the pace, his big hands rocking her hips.

"Good?"

"Mmm." She closed her eyes as she increased the tempo, feeling him fill her with his upward thrusts.

His hands reached for her breasts and she opened her eyes to find him watching her, his arousal so heightened it was written all over his face. No man had ever looked at her like that. With fire and passion dancing deep in his eyes. It made her feel sexy and empowered and…it stirred her.

She rode him harder, resting her hands on his chest for leverage. He matched her stroke for stroke. He seemed to sense when she was close, because he reached between them and worked her with his fingers. The friction, the fullness—all of it—was enough to send her over the edge.

She threw her head back and closed her eyes as shards of light exploded behind her lids. Her body convulsed and the orgasm rolled through her, seeming to last forever. She cried out as it shook her to the core.

He rolled her under him and took the lead, slamming into her over and over again. She wrapped her legs around his waist so he could go deeper. Every muscle in his body strained to hold back. The fact that he'd been able to go this long spoke to his stamina.

His breathing quickened, his muscles tensed, and with one final thrust he called out her name before collapsing on top of her, slick with sweat. They just laid that way for a few minutes, trying to recover.

"Holy shit," she said.

He lifted up on one elbow and peeked down at her. "Kind of intense."

"You're not kidding."

He rolled off her and swung his legs off the bed. "Be right back."

She watched him cross the room to the master bathroom in all his naked glory, then wondered whether she should get dressed. She didn't want to. If he didn't act weird about it, she'd like to stay. Cuddle. Maybe spend the night. But she had no idea where they stood. Whether what they'd just done was the start of something or a one-off.

He came out of the bathroom a few minutes later and got back in bed. She needed to go too, but was more self-conscious than him. His T-shirt was on the floor, so she hung over the side of the mattress, picked it up, dragged it over her head and got up.

The house was hot, or it might've just been her. In the bathroom, she stripped, got in Sawyer's giant walk-in shower and used the handheld head to rinse off. The cool water felt good and she tried hard not to overthink what had just happened.

Live in the moment, she told herself. *Don't start analyzing everything to death.* They'd been dancing around their attraction to each other since she'd gotten to the ranch. Until now, they'd dealt with it by throwing barbs and pretending not to like each other. Perhaps they didn't. Lord knew they didn't have anything in common.

But the chemistry? It was off the charts. So, they'd wound up in bed? It didn't mean anything.

By the time she found a towel, she'd convinced herself that it was just a hookup. A summer fling between two consenting adults with time on their hands. And if she kept telling herself that, she wouldn't be devastated when he lost interest. Because he would. They always did.

At least before everything had gone to hell, she'd had her career. Stardom. Now, she was back to where she started: Sadie DeRose's disappointment of a daughter.

She wrapped the soft bath sheet tighter around her and padded into the bedroom to find him sitting on the edge of his bed in a pair of boxer shorts. Well, that hadn't taken long. He was already done with her.

"I guess we got that out of our systems," she said, going for a preemptive strike.

He crooked his finger at her. "C'mere."

"Why?" She searched for her clothes on the floor.

"Because I said so."

"Who died and left you boss?"

He rolled his eyes, sprang to his feet, and grabbed her around the waist. "Thank you."

"For what?" She snatched up her thong, which had landed on the arm of his leather club chair.

"For rocking my world." He dipped down and kissed her.

When she gazed up at him the heat was gone, but his blue eyes were smiling.

"You're welcome."

"Do you have something you want to say to me?" He looked smug.

"Not particularly."

"Bullshit. I blew your mind."

She ran her fingers through his lightly furred chest. "If you say so."

He shook his head and slipped into his jeans, leaving the top button undone. "We both know I did, but whatever." Sawyer strolled out of the bedroom.

She followed him into the kitchen, thinking she should probably leave. It had to be after eleven. "What are doing?"

He held up the package of tortillas and grinned. "Quesadilla time."

Chapter 12

Gina woke to pounding on her door. In her sleep-induced haze, she glanced at her cell phone on the nightstand. It was seven in the flipping morning. She'd fallen into her own bed about three, after she'd left Sawyer's.

Who the hell came calling this early in the morning?

She pulled the blanket over her head, hoping that if she ignored the knocking whoever it was would go away. But the banging just got closer. It sounded as if someone was tapping on her bedroom window.

She yanked the covers off, padded across the floor, and pulled the blinds up. A man—a stranger—stood there with a camera lens pointed at her face.

"Gina DeRose, did you get what you want? How do you feel about Candace Clay filing for divorce?" he shouted, snapping a succession of pictures.

She flinched, then jerked the blinds closed. Scooping up her phone, she ran to the bathroom and hid in the tub.

"Please answer, please answer," she prayed aloud as she hit Sawyer's number. It made more sense to call Aubrey and Cash. They were just across the creek. And Cash was law enforcement. But Sawyer was press. He'd know how to deal with the bloodsucking leech.

"Morning," he answered on the second ring, sounding more chipper than anyone had a right to this early. And after what they'd done all night. "Didn't you get enough last night?"

"A tabloid photographer is outside my window," she whispered.

"What? I can't hear you."

She repeated herself, raising her voice just a fraction, afraid the person outside would hear her. Which was ridiculous. He'd seen her. He knew she was here.

"On my way," he said. "Until then, don't go outside."

She considered crawling out of the tub back to her bedroom. Still in sleep shorts and a tank top, she'd like to at least put on a bra. Run a comb through her tangles. But she didn't budge, fearful that the man would capture her on camera, streaking down the hallway like a lunatic. She could already see the headlines: Insane Celebrity Chef Lives in Old Unabomber Cabin.

How the hell had he found her?

She shot Wendy a text, giving her a heads-up. At some point today, there'd be pictures of her with crazy hair all over the internet. Outside, she heard a commotion and climbed out of the clawfoot to see what was going on.

She stood on the toilet seat to peer outside the window. Cash had the photographer pinned against a tree. Sawyer must've called him.

A short time later, Sawyer joined Cash. She hadn't heard his Range Rover and suddenly remembered that it was still at the mechanic's. He must've run the whole way.

She dashed to her bedroom, changed into a bra and T-shirt, slipped on her new cowboy boots, and flew out the back door.

"Who the hell do you think you are—?"

Sawyer cut her off at the pass. "We've got it under control." He held up the memory card from the digital camera, which was currently in Cash's hand. "Jace is on his way."

"You hurt my camera and I'll sue you," the man bellowed. "You don't have a right to take people's equipment."

Sawyer looked up at the sky as if he was praying for patience. Then he turned to the man and in a voice that was surprisingly calm said, "Come on, you were trespassing and staring into a woman's window like a freaking Peeping Tom."

"I'm just trying to make a living." The photographer stared at Gina and started to say something, but Sawyer held up his hand.

"Don't even think about it. The sheriff is on his way to deal with you." He looked at Cash and said, "Give him his camera."

"I need my goddamn memory card back, that's what I need," the photographer yelled. "It's my property. You have no right to keep it. If you don't give it back you'll hear from my lawyers."

"By all means, tell them to give us a call." Sawyer grasped Gina's shoulders, turned her around, and told her to go back inside the cabin.

"Not until he tells me how he found me." She put her hands on her hips. "Who told you where I was?"

"I'm not divulging my sources." He jutted his chin at her.

Gina hoped that Laney or Jimmy Ray hadn't sold her out. But someone had. How else had he found her?

"You want a story? An exclusive? Then tell me who your source is," she demanded.

Sawyer took her by the arm and dragged her to the front of the cabin. "The guy's a bottom-feeder. Don't bargain with him. When you have an exclusive to tell, you'll give it to a reputable news organization. This guy is a stringer. He'll sell whatever you give him to the highest bidder."

She let out a breath and pinched the bridge of her nose. "If he found me, others will too." She'd have to leave and find a new place to hide. She didn't want to go. Not now. Not when she…she just didn't want to have to leave.

"We'll lock the gate," Sawyer said.

A locked gate was the last thing they needed while they were trying to get Charlie and Aubrey's business off the ground. A business that relied on visitors.

They looked up as Jace's sheriff's SUV bounced along the rutted road, stopping short of the front porch.

He stuck his head out the window and let his Oakleys slip down his nose. "Where is he?"

"Around back," Sawyer said.

Jace hopped out of the cab in full sheriff's gear: badge, holster, gun, the whole nine yards. Gina had never seen him in uniform before. He was hot in jeans and a flannel shirt. In the uniform, he was smoking. Not as good-looking as Sawyer, but Charlie was a lucky woman. Aubrey too.

"Is he mad at me?" Gina whispered as Jace crossed the yard to the rear of the house. She'd brought this upon them. Besides having someone invade his private ranch, Jace had better things to do with his time than chasing some jackass with a camera off his property.

"Nah, that's his cop scowl. He reserves it for trespassers." Sawyer maneuvered her onto the porch. "What did the photographer say to you?"

"Nothing really. He pounded on the door first, then came to the window. I opened the blinds to see who it was and he started snapping pictures." She scanned the area, suddenly realizing that she hadn't seen a car. "How did he get here?"

"Probably parked on Dry Creek Road and hiked in."

"Oh God, you don't think he was here all night?" The idea of a stranger creeping around in the trees while she was in the cabin alone gave her the willies.

"I doubt it. Why wait until morning to knock? Better to hit-and-run before he got caught and thrown off the property."

Sawyer made a good point. "Is that how you do it?" she asked just to be snarky. It was kind of a rotten thing to say, especially after he'd flown to her rescue.

"I call ahead, make an appointment." His lips ticked up. "And if that doesn't work I go in for an ambush."

She didn't know whether he was joking. But somehow she didn't see Sawyer skulking around someone's house, hiding in their azalea bushes. He was more Robert Redford in *All the President's Men*, following the money. Not some skeevy guy with a paunch and suspenders, stalking celebrities with a big-ass camera lens while they slept.

Jace brought the skeevo around front and started to load him into the back seat of his vehicle.

"Last chance to give your side of the story," the photographer told Gina, then nudged his cuffed hands at Jace. "Here, give her my business card."

"No can do," Jace said and pushed the camera guy's head down so he wouldn't hit it on the door.

After Jace drove away, Cash went home.

"You want coffee?" she asked Sawyer, who looked like he'd been up for hours: clean-shaven and dressed in his usual jeans, T-shirt, Stetson, cowboy boots.

"Yep." He led the way into the cabin and hung his hat on a wall hook that had been there before she'd moved in.

"I guess Candace is going through with it…She's really divorcing Danny."

"You already knew that. Why? Did the photographer say something? Because you know divorce filings are public record, right?"

"I know. Candace also put out a statement." Just the same, hearing the prowler yell it at her with such vitriol… well, she felt guilty, like it was her fault. "I'd hoped to talk to her, convince her that this whole thing is ridiculous. I'm really tempted to call Danny. Maybe there's still time to fix this."

Sawyer put his hand on her shoulder. "If her own husband can't convince her of his innocence, how do you expect to? I don't know anything about the state of their marriage, but let's put it this way: I believed you and we've only known each other a few weeks. What does that say about the Clays? As far as talking to them: Like I said yesterday, nothing good can come of it."

Gina let out a frustrated sigh. "I want my life back, Sawyer. I want the Clays to have their lives back. And him"—she nudged her head outside to where the intruder had been driven off by Jace—"he won't be the last

member of the paparazzi to show up at Dry Creek Ranch. Mark my words. They're like roaches. There's never just one."

He rubbed his chin and sat at the kitchen peninsula. It was really too narrow for stools but Gina had stuck two she'd picked up on Amazon there anyway. She flicked the switch on her fancy new coffee grinder.

When the noise from the grinder stopped, Sawyer said, "You need to call my mom today. Fill her in on your morning visitor."

She'd already planned to, though it left a sour feeling in her stomach. Wendy would undoubtedly find Gina new accommodations. For everyone involved, including Gina, it was the right thing to do. But leaving Dry Creek Ranch…she had friends here.

And there was Sawyer, also a friend. But something more complicated than that.

"I texted her as soon as I found the bloodsucker in my yard. But you're right, I should tell her everything that happened."

"You can call her while we go to pick up my Range Rover," he said.

"Okay." She scooped the ground coffee into the machine, filled the reservoir with water, and turned on the switch. "You want breakfast?"

She didn't wait for him to answer, just grabbed the basket of fresh eggs from the fridge that Aubrey had brought over the other day and started making an omelet. There was a bell pepper in what passed for her pantry and she began dicing it. The familiar task, along with the sound of the knife clicking on the wooden board, instantly helped to calm her nerves.

Sawyer watched as a companionable silence fell over them. It was as if sitting in her kitchen, the simple domesticity of it, was the most natural thing in the world between them.

"Maybe you should stay at my place for the next few days," Sawyer blurted.

She suspected he was as surprised by his offer as she was. On the heels of sleeping together, a woman less realistic than Gina might misconstrue the invitation. But she knew it for what it was. He was offering safety from the paparazzi, nothing more.

"I'll be fine," she said, though the offer was tempting on many levels, least of all escaping the press.

"If you change your mind, you're welcome to stay."

Gina noted that he hadn't insisted and wondered if he was relieved that she had declined his invitation.

She found the omelet pan in one of the cupboards and popped a couple of slices of bread in the toaster. Throughout breakfast, both of them steered clear of mentioning their night together. What was there to say about it,

anyway, besides the fact that it was probably the best sex Gina had ever had? Which really wasn't saying much. She'd never been that into it. Now that she'd had a taste of Sawyer, she was probably ruined for all time.

"What are you thinking about?" He reached for the butter and spread his toast with it.

"Nothing."

He looked at her for a few seconds. Really looked, but didn't say anything. She suspected he'd also returned to their night together. Whether it had been as transcendental for him as it had been for her was another story. Doubtful. She was pretty sure he'd been with a lot of women, more than she wanted to think about. She'd merely been another notch in his belt, so to speak.

"Thanks for coming to my rescue," she said when the quiet grew awkward, unable to remember whether she'd properly expressed her gratitude.

"Not a problem." He took his plate to the sink, poured himself a second cup of coffee, leaned against the counter, and sipped.

She rose from her stool. "I'll just clean up real fast and we can go."

He let his gaze drift down her body until it rested on her cowboy boots.

She looked down at herself, still in her pajamas. "Yeah, I guess I better shower and change first."

"I'll do the dishes. You go get ready."

But as she started to leave, he followed her into the bedroom. She sat on the edge of the bed and pried off her right boot.

"Remind me to get you a bootjack." He lifted her left foot and finished the job, leaving her barefoot.

She'd put the boots on so fast when she'd spotted the photographer outside her window that she'd forgotten socks. He played with her foot, running his fingers over her red toenail polish. Then he reached for her arms and tugged her up from the bed. In a flash, his mouth covered hers.

"We're not doing this again," he said against her lips.

"Okay." But it seemed to her that they were.

"Last night was a mistake."

If he hadn't snaked his tongue into her mouth right after he'd said it, she would've been offended.

"We can't let it happen again," he said as he reached under her T-shirt and unhooked her bra.

"Why not?" she whispered, though she could think of a dozen reasons off the top of her head, starting with the fact that sleeping with her crisis

manager's son, while breaking up the marriage of her former colleagues, was probably in poor taste.

"Colossally bad idea." He slipped her bra off, leaving her in nothing but her sleep shorts.

"Agreed," she said, and began undoing his belt.

She was taking too long because he shooed her hand away and undid the buckle and the buttons on his fly by himself. He didn't even wait to get his pants all the way down, just tugged her shorts off, pushed her against the dresser, spread her legs wide, and entered her from behind.

She let out a sort of scream-moan and he froze.

"Ah, jeez, did I hurt you?" He started to pull out.

"No, no." She pushed her bottom against him in a wanton plea for more.

He moved inside her. Slow at first, which drove Gina crazy. It was good—wonderful—but not enough. The need inside her had grown to fever pitch. She ground her butt against him in a not-so-subtle message to pick up the pace.

Sawyer moved her to the bed, bent her over the footboard, and took her harder. Deeper. Faster. It was the most adventurous she'd ever been with a man, but Sawyer made her feel safe. And uninhibited. Sexy.

Despite the way she'd been branded on television—the chef with the *abbondanza* cleavage who made tasting her own dishes look like oral sex—she'd never felt particularly sensual.

Not until Sawyer.

He reached around and worked her with his fingers. With the other hand, he fondled her breasts while continuing to thrust inside her. He did it over and over again until a multitude of sensations washed through her like a tidal wave, making her body shudder and clench with exquisite pleasure.

A few more strokes and she felt a subtle change in Sawyer's body. He jerked, threw his head back, and shouted out her name.

Afterward, he wrapped his arm around her waist to keep her from collapsing. She could hear him breathing hard behind her. He kissed her softly on her neck and led her to the clawfoot tub.

Only under the hot spray of the showerhead did it occur to her that they hadn't used a condom.

Chapter 13

"Go ahead and call her," Sawyer said. It was the first words he'd spoken since they'd left the cabin.

He'd taken her keys and deemed himself the designated driver, mostly because he liked driving her car. But partly because she had a lousy sense of direction and he wasn't in the mood for getting lost on the way to Mama's.

He only half-listened to Gina tell his mother the details of their morning trespasser. He was too busy revisiting his and Gina's bedroom scene. Clearly, there was something seriously wrong with him. It was bad enough that he was having sex with his mother's client and a woman with enough issues to fill the *Diagnostic and Statistical Manual of Mental Disorders*. Sawyer didn't do issues. He didn't do anything that required even a modicum of complications. He got enough of that from his work.

And then to add to his stupidity, he forgot to wear a damn condom. It wasn't like he never fucked up. He did, more than he'd like to admit. But forgetting protection…That had never happened. Ever. Then again, he'd never been this sexually caught up. It wasn't to say he didn't like sex. He liked it. A lot. Had it as often as he could. But this was…different.

Ever since that morning he'd come home to find her hunkered over her computer in his bed, there'd been this charged electricity between them. She pushed his buttons, even though he wasn't the kind of guy to rouse easily. It was sort of a love/hate thing, though that was a little strong. More like an admire/you-bug-the-shit-out-of-me thing. What it had proven to definitely be, though, was a I-have-to-have-you thing.

Which had disaster written all over it. And now he had to worry about… babies. He had nothing against them per se as long as they were someone else's.

"We didn't use a condom, you know," he said the second she hung up with his mother.

"I know."

He waited, hoping she'd say she was on another form of birth control. But she said nothing.

"We'll have to monitor the situation," he said and realized he'd made it sound like he was talking about North Korea and its nuclear weapons cache.

"Yep," was all she said.

At the last minute, he decided to ditch the highway and take a circuitous route of back roads to Mama's. Traffic, he told himself. But it was eleven o'clock and it was freaking Dry Creek, not the 405 at rush hour.

"What did my mom say?" He'd circle back to the condom dilemma in a few minutes. Give her time to absorb how irresponsible he'd been.

"That she heard through the grapevine that Candace is pitching a new show to FoodFlicks."

"Yeah, so?" It hardly seemed newsworthy. "Stands to reason that without her husband in the picture, she'd want a new gig."

"It just seems kind of soon, don't you think?"

"Not if it's her livelihood."

Gina let out a breath. "I guess."

"What? It seems opportunistic to you?"

"No, you're right. What is she supposed to do? Sit home and collect unemployment?"

"Did my mother think it was odd?"

"No, just interesting. She's meeting with my manager next week to strategize how to deal with ChefAid."

Hopefully by then he'd hear back from Shooter about the photo. "She say anything else or have any ideas how our lowlife friend found you?"

Gina shook her head. "I'm wondering if someone recognized me at the kitchen store. Maybe the cashier wasn't as oblivious as she seemed."

"Could be." He took a right on Gold Trail, an old mining road. When they were kids, he, Jace, and Cash used to ride their horses out here and shoot beer cans with their BB guns. "Someone had to have recognized you when you were out with me and put two and two together. Otherwise, how would they have found you on the ranch?"

"You don't think it was Laney or Jimmy Ray, do you?"

"No way. They and my grandfather go back to when dinosaurs roamed the earth. They can keep a secret. You think Tiffany might've recognized you?" Jace's former campaign manager wasn't a malicious person, but she did have a big mouth. Pretty much everyone in Dry Creek did.

"I don't know. She seemed too wrapped up in you to even notice me."

"I wouldn't bet on it. Tiffany may seem oblivious, even like one of those vapid ladies who lunch. But she's sharp as a steak knife. I learned that during Jace's campaign."

"If it is her, do you think someone—maybe even Jace—could ask her to zip it? I'd like to not have to move again."

He glanced over at her. "Thought you hated it here and were dying to get back to *civilization*." He mimicked the way she'd said it when she was trying to provoke him.

"I do and I am," she said. "But who's to say that the next place your mother finds for me to hide isn't Siberia. At least Dry Creek Ranch has Wi-Fi."

Hell yeah, it did. He'd emptied his bank account to get high-speed internet on the ranch. If Jace and Cash had had their druthers they would still have dial-up.

"Besides," she added, "I'd miss Charlie and Aubrey."

He slid her another glance, this time hitching his brows above the rim of his sunglasses. "Charlie and Aubrey, huh?" He was flirting when what he should've been doing was putting the skids on whatever this was that they were doing. Yet, he couldn't help himself. Just like he couldn't help himself from tearing off her PJs this morning after watching her bounce around the kitchen, making him crazy with those long legs of hers.

"I might miss the sex." She flashed him a cheeky grin.

He started to say that she was going to miss it all right because they weren't having any more. But he knew the words for what they were: Lies. As long as she lived here, they were having sex. Lots of it. The sooner he came to terms with that the better off he'd be.

"I'll ask Jace to feel out Tiffany," he said. "If he thinks she knows something, he'll tell her to keep it on the down low."

"Thank you."

"You're welcome. Now put on your disguise, we're almost there."

* * * *

That evening he took the situation up with Jace and Cash. Both agreed that it could've easily been Tiffany. Sawyer thought Jill was also a possibility and kicked himself for exposing Gina that way.

"Nah," Jace shook his head. "Even if Jill had recognized Gina, it wouldn't have occurred to her to call the *National Enquirer* or any of those other

rags. I've known her all my life. What she did to Brett…but this thing with Gina doesn't have her mark. Take my word for it.

"Tiffany is the more likely culprit. If it was her she didn't do it to be spiteful." Jace had a soft spot for his old campaign manager. "There's not a mean bone in her body. She just likes to talk, like everyone else in this town. She also likes to one-up everybody with the quality of her gossip. I suspect finding out that Gina DeRose is hiding at Dry Creek Ranch was quite a nugget. More than likely she told a friend, who told another friend, who knew someone who works for one of the tabloids. She wouldn't have intentionally sent a stranger with a camera to our back door."

Sawyer hung his arms over the top rail of the fence as they watched the horses graze in the pasture. It was a pastime they'd adopted when he and Cash had moved to the ranch. The women did their wine and cheese; he and his cousins watched the livestock and pretended to be masters of their domain.

"Could you talk to her, express how important it is that she not tell anybody else?"

"Yup."

"What did you do with the camera guy?"

"Cited him for trespassing, gave him a stern lecture about how lucky he was that he didn't get his ass shot off, and sent him on his way. He whined about getting his memory card back. I ignored him."

"What do we do about the gate?" Cash held out a slice of apple to Ellie's horse, Sunflower. "I figure these paparazzi guys are like cattle, they travel in herds. We can keep it closed but that won't help Aubrey and Charlie's business."

"I say we keep it open for now." Sawyer didn't think the gate would keep out a determined reporter or photographer anyway. A fence never kept him out.

"What about Gina? Did the dude freak her out?" Jace toed a clod of dirt with his boot.

"Nah, she took it pretty well. But if this becomes a bigger situation where there's press camping outside her cabin she'll have to relocate."

Jace patted Sawyer's back. "That'll suck for you."

Sawyer flipped his cousin off. The truth hurt.

He didn't know how it had happened, but he'd done a complete 180 where Gina was concerned.

Cash, who pretended he wasn't amused by Sawyer and Jace's back-and-forth, said, "You have any luck with analyzing that picture?"

"I haven't heard back from my photographer friend yet. How about you? Have you gotten in touch with your FBI friend about the email?"

"Yeah, I just made contact. He's going to get to it when he can. I'll give him at least a couple days before I harangue him again."

Sawyer nodded. He couldn't ask for anything more than that, though he was anxious to get to the bottom of the strange, anonymous note.

The sun had started setting, streaking the sky in a palate of reds, oranges, and blues. There was nothing like a sunset on Dry Creek Ranch. The three of them stared up at the sky for a while, each lost in its beauty. It was times like this when the ranch stole his breath away. He'd seen a lot of magnificent places—Amalfi Coast, Mt. Fuji, Big Sur, Lake Louise, Pamukkale, Monteverde. But nothing stirred him the way the land of his ancestors did. His feelings for the ranch were deep and visceral. The soil, the trees, the hills, the creek, it was in his blood.

"Apparently your Gina"—Jace poked Sawyer in the shoulder—"has been brainstorming with Charlie and Aubrey on how to add to our side hustle here." He gazed in the direction of the old barn and the construction project that would soon house the overflow of the women's design business. "She thinks we should approach Jimmy Ray and Laney about opening a sarsaparilla stand on the ranch."

Cash nodded enthusiastically. "It's not a bad idea. Their sarsaparilla is the thing of legends."

Sawyer let out a long breath. "Not enough foot traffic. I'd hate to ask Jimmy Ray and Laney to be part of a losing proposition. I agree with Cash, their sarsaparilla is fantastic. A true original. But people aren't going to travel miles for a spectacular glass of root beer. At least I don't think they will. And a design studio, furniture store, and flower shop won't bring enough crowds to make it worth Jimmy Ray and Laney's while. What we need is a big draw, something that will make the ranch a destination."

"You think Macy's would be interested?"

Cash laughed at Jace's sarcasm.

"No, dipshit, something like a general store," Sawyer said. "And if we really wanted to be ambitious, a butcher shop that carried specialty cuts of our beef, just like Harris Ranch. Wasn't Harris Ranch your brilliant idea, Jace?" He knocked Jace's hat off his head.

Cash cocked his hip against the fence. "Harris Ranch is a big name, a big brand. No one has ever heard of Dalton beef. We've never been that kind of operation."

Grandpa Dalton had always sold his calves to large meat distributors, like Harris Ranch, who then slapped their own brand on the package. It's the way most cattlemen did business.

"We'd need to reinvent ourselves," Sawyer said. "In the long run, it could be more lucrative than the old way. And we could be our own destination draw for the Dry Creek Ranch roadside attraction."

Cash reached under his hat and scrubbed his hand through his hair. "Establishing ourselves like that would take a long time. We'd have to have some kind of marketing strategy, something that sets us apart from other meat companies. We're not organic. We're not grass-fed. So what's our claim to fame? I don't know, I just don't see it."

"We don't suck. That's our marketing strategy right there," Jace said.

Sawyer exchanged a glance with Cash and shook his head. "Yeah, that'll go over big. I can just see the billboards now. Big splashy letters: *Buy us because we don't suck.* Stick to law enforcement, dude."

"What I'm saying is how many of these folks with organic or grass-fed, or non-GMO labels have superior beef? I'm betting not many. Whereas our beef is fucking grain-fed delicious. We could go organic. I'm perfectly good with that. But I think we're overlooking our bestselling feature. Taste. Why not market that?"

"We're back to how again." Cash threw his hands up in the air. "Everyone says their product tastes better than the rest. How do you say it loud and effective enough to turn a butcher shop in the middle of nowhere into a destination? Marketing something like that would cost a fortune. A fortune we don't have."

"No, but we are related to one of the top PR agencies in the country." Sawyer didn't usually take advantage of his parents' position, but this was something for all of them. Even though his father had never taken to ranching, keeping Grandpa Dalton's legacy in the family was of paramount importance to him.

"And we just so happen to know a celebrity chef, too," Jace said.

"A fallen celebrity chef?" Sawyer was pretty sure that right now her endorsement would be the kiss of death. "I wouldn't count on Gina's influence."

"A butcher shop is certainly something to think about," Cash said. "But until we figure it out, I'm with Sawyer. It wouldn't be fair to ask Jimmy Ray and Laney to make that kind of investment. I know they'd do it if we asked. But it would be taking advantage."

The couple was getting on in age and had enough work running the coffee shop. And it wasn't as if they were desperate for money.

"Okay," Jace said. "But I like this idea of a butcher shop. If we can make more money going retail than selling our beef on the hoof we should go for it. There are all kinds of possibilities there, including mail order. I bet Kansas City Steak Company is making a killing."

Cash adjusted the brim of his hat. "Let's take it one step at a time."

Sawyer didn't blame Cash for being conservative, but he was on board with Jace. They were onto something, something that made sense. "I'll talk to my parents about it. They'll have some ideas. In the meantime, I like where this is going. It's a hell of lot better than turning the ranch into some kind of Disneyland sideshow."

The three of them pushed off the fence, ready to call it an evening.

"Hey, Jace, don't forget to talk to Tiffany."

"Will do."

They walked their separate ways. Sawyer would've paid a visit to Gina, but because Cash was her neighbor…he could do without the ribbing. He and his cousins generally stayed out of each other's social business. But now that Cash was married and Jace engaged, the two of them had relaxed that unspoken rule. And because he had no idea what he was doing with Gina— besides enjoying mind-blowing sex—he didn't want to face an interrogation by two skilled cops. Clearly, they had an inkling that something was going on, but Sawyer didn't feel the need to give them a front-row seat.

When he got home, he checked his email to find a message from Shooter. Call me, it said.

Sawyer found Shooter's number and hit *dial*. "Hey, you got something?"

"Maybe. It's hard to say without the original photo. But, yeah, I think it's been messed with. Whoever did it is good. There's none of the telltale signs. No warpage in the background and no patterns left behind by an amateurish cut-and-paste job. It's something about the way DeRose's body is turned. It's anatomically funky. I'm far from an anatomical scientist, but in my years of taking photos I've never seen a pose like this. There's something off about it. Her head isn't quite sitting right. And her skin's a little too blended. It could be her makeup, but it's usually a sign of fakery. Well-executed fakery, though. Usually I don't have to look twice to tell. But this one took a while."

Sawyer's pulse picked up. Now they were getting somewhere. "Is there a way to conclusively prove that the shot was photoshopped?"

"Not without the original. At least nothing that would hold up in court."

Sawyer didn't need it to hold up in the legal system, just in the court of public opinion. "It's going to be pretty damned near-impossible to get the

original." Sawyer didn't even know where it came from. Like all things on the internet, it started floating around with no credit line. "Is there anyone who's an expert I can send the copy to? Someone who'll write me out an affidavit that it's bogus?"

"There's a forensic guy who's well-known, testifies in copyright cases. I can't begin to tell you how many people think a photo on social media or on Pinterest is free for the taking so some moron can mangle or photoshop it for a meme. This guy has impeccable qualifications. But again, he'll want the original photo. And I don't even know if he takes on individual cases or just works with lawyers."

"What's his name?" Gina's lawyer could contact him. Sawyer was sure she had legions of them.

Shooter gave Sawyer his name. "Do a clip search on him. He testified for the *Times* when those two society chicks stole Lance's shot of Beyoncé and superimposed it on cheap T-shirts they then sold for a few hundred bucks apiece. Talk about nerve."

Sawyer vaguely remembered the case. "I'll do that. Thanks for looking at it for me, Shooter. Seriously, I owe you one hell of a solid."

"Buy me a drink next time we're in some shithole war zone, taking fire."

"You got it."

"I think your chef friend has a good case there. Something is definitely up with that photo. I'd be willing to put money on it."

"I'll contact this guy. At least now I've got more to go on."

As soon as he got off the phone he did a quick Google search and found an email address for the forensic photo expert. The guy worked for an image-analysis consulting firm in Boston. After taking a few notes, he called his mother.

"Well, if it isn't my long-lost son."

"I've been busy, Mom."

"Too busy for your mother?"

"Never too busy for you." He rolled his eyes.

"I heard you had a little excitement this morning."

"Nothing we couldn't handle. We're taking precautions." If you counted precautions as telling Tiffany to keep her trap shut. "Mom, do you know where that photo of Gina and Danny Clay originated?"

There was a long pause, then, "Sawyer, you know I can't talk about this with you. Why is it that you want to know?"

"I had a friend, a photographer buddy from the *Times*, take a look at a copy of the photo I found on the internet. He's certain it's a fake. But it would help to have the original. If we had it we could send it to this forensic

expert who is well-known for authenticating pictures. Maybe he could write a declaration or at least go on the record that the picture is bogus."

His mother didn't say anything, but he could hear her thinking on the other end of the line.

"Mom?"

"I really shouldn't be talking about this without Gina's permission. Do you have Gina's permission, Sawyer?"

"Yep. Gina's on board." Gina hadn't explicitly given him permission to discuss her case with his mother, but close enough. He was helping her, after all.

"We don't know where the photo originated. It was, of course, the first thing I looked for. We've hired someone to trace not only where the photo came from, but the timing of it. Unfortunately, so far no luck."

Sawyer found that peculiar. Typically, these types of pictures were sold to tabloid editors who wanted nothing more than to take credit for scooping their competition. It's how they sold newspapers.

"Well, do you want to contact this expert and see what he can do with a copy?" he asked. "It seems to me that if you can prove the photo is a fake you can clear Gina's name."

"I wish it was that simple. And since when have you taken a personal interest in one of my clients?"

Sawyer could hear the smile in his mother's voice. Wendy Dalton knew her son all too well. He didn't ever get involved with his parents' clients. Most of the time, they were insipid celebrities or unscrupulous corporations that no self-respecting journalist would have anything to do with.

"She's my neighbor, thanks to you, and we've become friends." Friends with benefits.

"Well, as I've explained to Gina, it is going to take more than proving a photograph is fake to resurrect her once-thriving career. Reporters are like sharks, dear. They circle when they taste blood in the water. You of all people should know that."

"What about Gina's ChefAid job? Wouldn't it go a long way to persuading them to keep her on as their brand ambassador?"

"These are all things your father and I are working on."

Sawyer pressed, "At least the expert opinion that the photo is a fake might convince Candace Clay that her husband didn't cheat on her."

"I'm not so sure the photo even matters," his mother said. "It appears Candace was speaking to a divorce lawyer before the news of Gina and Danny hit the World Wide Web."

"What? That's bizarre, don't you think?"

"Not particularly. Half of California is getting divorced. Why should the Clays' marital problems surprise me?"

"The timing, for one thing. The whole world believes that Danny did his wife wrong. And here she was planning to divorce him all along. You don't see anything strange in that?"

"For all we know, Danny's been having affairs on his wife for years. She was fed up with it, planning to leave him, then *boom*. Another affair. This one extremely public with a television rival."

"Rival?" That's not the way Gina described her and Candace's relationship. To hear it from her, there was no ill will between them until now. "Were they competitive?"

"Not according to Gina," his mother said. "But Gina is young, beautiful, and at the height of her career. Of course, she didn't see Candace as a professional threat. But who knows how Candace saw Gina?"

"How'd you find out about Candace talking to a divorce lawyer?" That was confidential stuff. A lawyer could be disbarred for divulging those kinds of privileged conversations between a client.

"Just like you, I have my sources."

"Reliable sources?"

His mother chuckled. "Very reliable. You think I'd be where I am today if they weren't reliable? Would you like to text me the contact information for your photo expert?"

"Sure. What else do you have up your sleeve? Last I looked, Gina only has three weeks to persuade the ChefAid people she's not a home-wrecker."

"You sound very concerned, darling." She was laughing at him.

"Don't read anything into, Mom. We're trying to run a ranch here, not to mention a new business. We can't do that if we have to batten down the hatches because we're being overrun by reporters from TMZ, now can we?"

"You sure that's it? For a second there, I got the impression that you were worried about Gina."

"You're clearly delusional, Mom."

She laughed. "Whatever you say, dear."

He told her about the butcher shop idea and asked her about marketing plans.

"It's a fabulous strategy, Sawyer. And nowadays you can do so much with social media. The ranch should have its own Twitter account, a Facebook page, and of course you should be posting lots of pictures of Dry Creek life on Instagram. Show the world what happy cows you have."

"I think the California Milk Advisory Board has already gone the happy cow route."

"Yes, and look how well it worked for them. What I'm trying to tell you, Sawyer, is that you don't need an expensive marketing firm. At least not at first. You can start spreading the word online."

As if he had time to be screwing around on Twitter. He could barely fit his writing into the day. But maybe they could hire someone, a kid even. "I'll talk to Jace and Cash about it."

"What's going on with the ranch next door? Last time we talked, you said there was a *for sale* sign up."

Sawyer sighed. "It sounds like Mitch Reynolds will probably buy the place and turn it into a hellhole. One of those golf-course communities for retirees."

"That would be a shame." Although Sawyer's mother was an urbanite to her core, she understood how much the ranch meant to him, Jace, and Cash and the importance of preserving Grandpa Dalton's way of life. Tough to do when your neighbor is a gated community of tract homes.

"Yep. Nothing we can do about it." He turned up the air-conditioner. The loft felt like a furnace today.

"Let me talk to your father about it. But I'm sorry, sweetheart."

Yep, they were all sorry. It was the end of an era.

Chapter 14

After getting off the phone with his mother, he decided to deliver the news about the photo to Gina in person. It was a flimsy excuse to go over to her cabin, but he managed to convince himself that a phone conversation wouldn't cut it. Even if it was getting late. He walked over, telling himself he needed the exercise. The truth was he didn't want Cash to see his Range Rover in Gina's driveway.

She answered the door in a pair of denim shorts and a tank top, no bra. It was all he could do not to pick her up and carry her to the bedroom.

"What's up?" She swung her arm across the threshold of the cabin, inviting him to come in. The TV was playing in the background and Sawyer wondered if she was watching the FoodFlicks Network.

He peeked around the corner. Not FoodFlicks, a *Law & Order* rerun.

"I talked to my friend about the photograph of you and Danny on the beach. He says he's ninety-nine percent sure it's a fake."

"I didn't need him to tell me that. I know it's a fake because I've never been on a beach with Danny Clay in my life."

"We've established that. This is so you can go to the press with proof." Except there was no proof without an expert's written assertion that the picture was phony. "The problem is we need the original photo to establish it's a fake. You wouldn't happen to know where the photo originated?"

Gina shook her head. He followed her into the living room where she turned off the TV.

"I first saw the photograph on TMZ's website. It was after I got frantic calls from both my agent and manager. Neither of them knows where it came from and they just assumed that someone shot the picture and sold it to the tabloids. The problem with that theory is there was no photo to

take because we were never there. Not together, anyway. Which leaves me with only one conclusion: Someone with a computer and some skill with Photoshop cooked it up."

Yep, that was apparent. But who? The only way to discover the culprit was to trace the photo to its originator.

"We need to find out how TMZ got its hands on the picture or if TMZ was even the first publication to print it," Sawyer said.

"Well, you're the newsman—how do we do that?"

Sawyer might be a newsman, but he didn't truck with Harvey Levin or any of the other reporters at TMZ. And even if he did, the likelihood of them giving up their source was next to nil. He sure the hell wouldn't do it. "Let me see what I can do." He'd have to reach out to friends who might have a connection with someone high up at TMZ. But if his mother couldn't find the original photo, he doubted he'd have any better luck.

"Thank you." She brushed his arm with her hand. "I appreciate all you've done." She sat on the sofa and tucked her legs under her butt.

"You're welcome." Sawyer purposely took one of the leather chairs. He didn't want her to think he'd come here for sex, because he hadn't.

They sat for a while, saying nothing, comfortable in each other's presence. The cabin had lost its musty odor, which had been replaced by a combination of Gina's fragrance—something floral but not overbearing—and fresh bread.

It smelled like a home.

"You want ice cream?" She unfolded her legs and perched at the edge of the sofa. "I'm playing around with that machine I bought and a couple of new flavors."

Hell yeah, he wanted ice cream. He got up and wandered into the kitchen. There were ingredients, mixing bowls, and assorted other cooking utensils spread across the counter. It was evident that Gina DeRose was used to people cleaning up after her.

She opened the freezer, pulled out a plastic tub, and dished him up enough ice cream to feed an entire bunkhouse of cowboys.

She caught him sniffing the bowl. "It's blackberry. The ones you saw me picking the other day."

He remembered. When he and Angie were kids, they used to pick and gorge on the berries until they stained their hands and face blue.

Sawyer dipped his spoon in the bowl and took a lick. It was creamy. Something between frozen custard and gelato. "Good," he said as he filled his mouth with another bite.

She served herself half a bowl. When she saw him comparing portions, she said, "This is my second helping of the night. Besides"—she eyed him up and down—"you have more places to put it."

He laughed because he was at least a foot taller than her. "I guess the machine's working out."

She nodded and licked the back of her spoon. "One good thing that's come out of this whole disaster is this." She pointed at her bowl.

"Ice cream?" he asked, puzzled.

"Cooking. I didn't realize how much I'd missed it. Ironic to star in a cooking show, yet never cook."

"Why's that?"

She gave a half shrug and hopped up on the counter. "Not enough time and I have a team who does it for me."

"It's too bad because you're really good at it." He took another big bite, waited until he swallowed, and said, "This is award-winning."

"Nah, it's basic."

"You mean it's not some strange, unappetizing flavor like beet or bacon or peanut butter curry. Because I hate that shit. It's for poseurs."

She laughed. "It's plain blackberry ice cream, using your garden-variety French vanilla base. Anyone can make it."

He took one of the barstools and straddled it backwards. "Why do you always do that? Why do you always have to belittle what you do?"

"I'm just honest."

He jabbed his spoon in the air. "I used to think it was false modesty, because someone who's gotten to where you are couldn't possibly think so little of her qualifications. Now…I don't know what to think. Is it that you don't really enjoy cooking, so you tell yourself you're not good at it?"

She put her bowl down and gave the question some consideration. "I love cooking more than just about anything else in the world. Growing up, the kitchen was the only place where I truly felt that I shined. But I was a kid. I wasn't being held up against the greatest chefs of our time."

"We already discussed how I think you measure up to every one of them," he said. "But never mind that. If you love to cook and people enjoy your food, isn't that enough?"

"Not according to my mother." She tried to laugh it off like it was a joke. But he could see right through her.

"You need to get over it, Gina. Your mother's obsession with perfection was her problem, not yours."

She hopped down, put the tub back in the freezer, and took the rest of her ice cream to the living room. A signal that discussing her mommy

issues was over, which was fine with him. No one would ever mistake Sawyer for a shrink.

"Let me ask you something," he said and resumed his spot in the chair. "If someone wanted to open a butcher shop and sell their own beef, what would be the best marketing strategy?"

She raised her brows. "Someone? Would that someone happen to be you and your cousins?"

"Yeah." He finished the last of his ice cream and seriously considered going back for seconds.

"A butcher shop on the ranch as part of the whole agrimall thing you guys are working on?" When he nodded, she said, "It's ambitious, but smart. Really, really smart."

"We were talking about your idea to get Jimmy Ray and Laney to open a sarsaparilla stand and I said there won't be enough foot traffic without an anchor to make it worth their while. But a butcher shop that sells Dalton beef could be that anchor."

"You're not big enough." She did that sexy leg-tuck thing on the sofa again and Sawyer had trouble staying on topic, even though he was pretty sure she'd just insulted him.

"Not yet," he said. "But we could be. We've got everything going for us that appeals to a gourmet market. We're family owned and operated—fourth generation. We've got a great story. And we've got quality beef."

"But no one knows you exist. In order for people to travel to buy your steaks, they have to think they're getting something special. Something they can't buy in the supermarket or at a big box store."

Sawyer didn't disagree. "How do we develop that image? How do we get the word out?"

"Restaurants. There's no better product placement. When someone goes to Chez Panisse and reads on the menu that the beef comes from Dry Creek Ranch, suddenly you've got cachet. Suddenly, people are driving from the Bay Area to Dry Creek to buy a roast, especially if they can't get Dry Creek Ranch beef at Safeway or Whole Foods."

How many times had he gone to a trendy restaurant and seen the appellation or name of the farm from which a particular ingredient came from highlighted on the menu? Niman Ranch pork or Capay Valley chard or Straus butter. How many times in restaurants had he mocked the gratuitous name-dropping, then in the supermarket faced a mile-long row of brands and chose the one he'd seen on a menu, assuming it must be the best?

"How do we get our beef in restaurants?"

"Me." She leaned back and threaded her hands behind her head. "I might be a pariah in TV land, but I still have some friends in the restaurant industry. I could make a few calls. And if I ever get my show back I could do some serious product placement, like dedicating a whole episode to beef braciole, using Dry Creek Ranch meat."

"You would do that for us?"

"For Aubrey and Charlie, sure." A teasing smile played on her lips. "But I still think you need something besides a butcher shop that will attract visitors. A store like Dean and DeLuca would be a sure thing."

The likelihood of a national store like that coming to Dry Creek Ranch was a pipe dream. But he knew what she meant. Something with enough name recognition to attract large crowds. Yet, it couldn't be something shoppers could find in any city shopping mall, otherwise they wouldn't make the trek to the Sierra foothills.

"You have any contacts with Dean and DeLuca?" he asked, half-jokingly.

"Nope. But give me a little time to think of another option where I might have an in."

She untucked her legs and stretched them across the ottoman. He flashed on how she'd wrapped those long, shapely legs around his waist and made himself shut the vision down. He wasn't here for a bootie call. If she insisted that would be one thing. But he'd come over to talk, not to tangle up the sheets.

"What if we started our own gourmet grocery store? We could focus on local goods. Olive oils, wine, produce, cheese—you know the drill."

She wagged her hand from side to side. "I'm not saying no. But something with name recognition would be better. Basically, you're talking about a fancy farm stand. With a good roadside billboard, you might attract people who are passing through. But I don't know that anyone would drive hours just for your farm stand."

Sawyer rubbed the back of his neck. "Since there are lots of them along California highways, it would have to be one hell of a farm stand, I guess."

"Exactly." She yawned, which should've been his cue to leave, but he wanted to loiter.

"I should go. Let you get some sleep," he said halfheartedly just to be polite, hoping she'd invite him to stay. The desire to linger was an anomaly for Sawyer, who usually couldn't get his boots on fast enough when leaving a woman's house. He wouldn't call it fear of commitment, just attention deficit disorder where members of the opposite sex were concerned.

"It's not even ten yet." She eyed his empty ice cream bowl. "You want something else to eat? Or I could open a bottle of wine."

"You have beer?" He didn't wait for her to answer, got up, checked her refrigerator, and found a six-pack of Firestone hiding behind a carton of Greek yogurt. He held up one of the beers, silently asking permission.

"Help yourself."

"You want one?" She nodded and he popped the caps off two bottles and brought them back to the living room.

There was a noise outside. It sounded like a critter scampering across the deck. He flicked on the porch light and peered outside the window.

"What?" she asked. "Did you hear something?"

Other than a swarm of gnats buzzing around the glow of the lantern, he saw nothing amiss. "It was probably a raccoon or an opossum." They had plenty of both on the ranch.

"Or another stalker with a camera." She got to her feet and joined him at the window.

"Jace said he'll talk to Tiffany about keeping her mouth shut."

"What good will that do? The horse is already out of the barn."

Probably, but he couldn't help but hope that their visitor was an isolated incident. "We'll see. If need be, we'll take evasive measures."

"No evasive measures," she said, standing so close he could feel her body heat. "This is your home and your business. It should always feel secure, not like a sideshow. If more reporters come, I'll leave."

"I don't want you to leave." The admission—the revelation itself—surprised the hell out of him and he immediately began to think of ways to rephrase what he'd just said, because he needed time to digest whatever this was he was feeling. "I mean, you shouldn't have to go. You came here because it's safe. I'll damn well make sure it stays that way."

"I'm not afraid of these people. I just don't want them creating a problem for your family."

"We can handle whatever comes up," he said, knowing full well that only weeks ago he would've seized on an opportunity like this to boot her all the way back to LA.

But somewhere along the way his attitude toward her had changed and it was damned inconvenient. Outside of his family, he didn't take on other people's problems unless it was for work. And those crusades tended to be about world crises, not how to shield a fallen celebrity chef from the paparazzi. But something significant had changed between them and it wasn't just fantastic sex.

"I'm sure you can. But I'm not that selfish."

"Yes, you are." He winked to show he was teasing, but wanted to steer them onto their usual course of needling each other. It was easier than

facing up to the fact that he might be falling for her. He wasn't ready to fall, especially for a woman who was so ill-suited for him.

"I talked to my mother earlier. I told her I was helping you and that you were on board with her sharing info with me." He held eye contact with her to make sure he hadn't overstepped. She nodded. "My mom says that Candace Clay had approached a divorce attorney before the scandal broke. Did she tell you that?"

"Yes, which shows you how obnoxiously phony showbiz is. According to everyone in television, they were the 'it' couple, so in love there were literally hearts flying out of their asses." Gina rolled her eyes. "I guess that was a load of horse manure."

Their public image might've been a complete facade, but it seemed to Sawyer that both Gina and his mother were missing the bigger point. "You don't think the timing is strange?"

Gina hitched her shoulders. "Maybe Danny's a huge player and Candace was sick of his infidelity long before the story about him and me broke. Who's to say?"

"Where's your computer?" Sawyer had an idea.

Gina got up and fetched her laptop from the bedroom. "Why?"

"I want to see something." He snatched it from her and opened a Google image search for Candace and Danny Clay, which returned pages of pictures.

Gina perched on the arm of his chair while he sifted through the photos. "What are you looking for?"

He jumped back on the internet and pulled up the notorious wide-lens shot of Gina and Danny on the beach. "Something that looks like this with Danny or Candace or both of them in it. I'm thinking this was shot somewhere tropical." He pointed at the palm trees in the background of the photo. Unfortunately, there were a hell of a lot of tropical beaches. "Just keep your eye out for something that has this background." He returned to his search.

"Why them?" Gina leaned in to get a better look at the screen. "Someone could've superimposed Danny and me onto a beer ad for all we know."

"You could be right, but it's a lot less work if one of you is already in the shot. When was the last time you visited a tropical beach?"

"Uh…never. I can't remember the last time I had a vacation, let alone one in Tahiti. And this doesn't look anything like Malibu." She motioned at the photograph of her and Danny that Sawyer had moved to the other half of the screen.

"Nope. That's why we're searching pictures of the Clays. Call it a hunch, but I'm betting they were recently somewhere that looks just like this."

And even if his premonition didn't pan out, it at least kept his hands busy—and off her. He was still reeling from their unprotected sex that morning. He couldn't remember being that irresponsible, not even in high school.

"Can we do this on the couch?" She wriggled her butt on the arm.

He put the laptop down on the coffee table, lifted her off her feet, held her a little longer than he should've, and dropped her in the center of the sofa. Sawyer took the end of the couch and went back to scrolling through pictures.

She scooted closer to him and rested her head against his shoulder.

"If you're tired I can do this," he said, trying to pretend that he wasn't affected by her nearness.

"No, I'm awake. You're just comfy. Like a big pillow." She yawned. "I don't see anything."

So far, the shots he'd found were mostly of the promotional variety. Some of them appeared to be screen grabs of past episodes of their show and there were a few pictures of the couple attending charity events.

From Candace's tight smiles and mannequin-like poses with Danny, Sawyer wasn't surprised that her marriage was on the rocks. Judging by the photos—Danny was all smiles and adoring glances at his wife—her husband hadn't gotten the memo.

Or he was an Academy Award–caliber actor.

Who could honestly say? Perhaps Danny was more comfortable around a camera than his wife. Perhaps Candace had had a bad case of food poisoning when the photo had been shot. Sometimes a photo wasn't worth a thousand words. Sometimes they were just snapshots of a single moment in time.

When Sawyer got tired of scanning publicity shots, he entered a set of new terms into the search engine. *Clays. Celebrity chefs. Vacation. Beach.*

The first page of photos depicted a lot of the same. Candace and Danny headshots, more pictures of the couple on the set of their show, and a collection of them posing with other celebrity chefs. The next page was filled with images of the couple at the South Beach Wine and Food Festival.

At least they were getting closer. There was actually sand in a few of the shots.

"They go every year." Gina burrowed her head under his arm and rested her cheek against his chest. He subconsciously wound a strand of her hair around his finger.

"Do you go too?"

"Sometimes. The last few years, I bailed, sending someone from my company instead. I hate those things. It's a lot of hobnobbing."

From the photos it looked like one big drunken party for the rich and bored. He scrolled down, just about to give up. That's when he saw it. A photograph of Danny and Candace on a strikingly familiar beach.

Gina sat up straight. "Oh my God, that's it. That's the picture."

The photograph depicted Danny sitting in the sand, wearing the same swim trunks as the ones in the photo with Gina. Same ear-splitting grin. Same sandy beach. Same palm trees. Same blue ocean water. The only difference was Candace sat next to Danny in an embroidered sundress.

"It's as if they erased her and stuck someone else's body into the picture with my head."

Sawyer moved the two photos side by side for a closer comparison. "That's exactly what someone did." The pictures were identical. Except in the second one, Candace had been replaced by a bikini-clad Gina.

"What does the caption on the photo say?"

He clicked to enlarge the picture, then moved his mouse to the visit box, which took him to a tourism page for Tulum, Mexico and a caption that said they were there two years ago, shooting an episode of their show on how to make ceviche.

They both looked at each other and then she squealed and threw her arms around his neck. "You're a genius, Sawyer Dalton. This will prove I'm not the skank everyone thinks I am."

"Hang on." He gently pulled her away. "This is only one piece of the puzzle. Before you go public, you need more. Like time stamps to show which photo came first. And motive. Otherwise this doesn't make any sense."

"I don't care whether it makes sense. That photo"—she jabbed her finger at the screen—"shows that the one of Danny and me is bullshit. Pure and simple. I'm going to post it on my website. Show the world that I've been falsely accused. This proves it."

Not quite. But he didn't want to burst her balloon. "Slow down, sweetheart. Let's do this the right way. First, let's call my mom. This is what you're paying her for and she'll know exactly how to proceed with this new information."

Gina reached for her phone on the coffee table and Sawyer covered her hand with his. His mother kept late hours, but it was closing in on midnight. "Why don't you wait until first thing tomorrow?"

It wasn't as if his mom could do anything with their information now anyway. And Sawyer wasn't convinced this was all they needed to clear Gina's name. The original photo was far from a smoking gun as far as he was concerned. But it was a start.

A good start.

He saved the picture to Gina's hard drive and emailed himself a copy. Glancing at his watch again, he knew he should go. But instead, he stayed rooted to the couch like an ancient oak tree.

"You want to spend the night?" she asked.

"No," he returned honestly. "But I can't seem to force myself to leave."

For once, she didn't have a smart refrain, just took his hand, tugged him off the sofa, and led him to her bedroom. He watched her undress, took off his own clothes, crawled under the top sheet, and curled himself around her.

When he woke the next morning, he found her tucked up against him with her head on his chest. It felt so right that a rush of warmth coursed through him. And that's when he knew that this was different than anything he'd ever felt for a woman before.

Dangerously different.

Chapter 15

A week had passed and there hadn't been any unwanted visitors hiding in Dry Creek Ranch's underbrush or flashing strobe lights. In other good news, Gina got her period. She should've been relieved, but instead experienced a tinge of regret. Not that she wanted to be pregnant. Children had never been part of her game plan.

But lately, her game plan seemed less clear than it always had. And to borrow a cliché, her biological clock was running out. Then there was Sawyer. Theoretically speaking, he was the exact kind of man she would want to be the father of her children. Smart, good, hardworking. Wonderful with kids.

She'd seen him with his niece and nephews. They couldn't get enough of him, climbing him as if he were a mountain. He'd hang them upside down until they erupted into fits of giggles and walked with them standing on his feet.

She loved watching the easy way he had with them, the easy way he'd lift Ellie out of her saddle after a day of riding or bait Grady's hook when they were fishing in the creek.

There was no doubt that Sawyer Dalton would be a wonderful father, even though it didn't appear to be in his game plan. At least not with her.

She started to call him to tell him there wouldn't be any babies in their future when her agent buzzed.

"Are you sitting down? Because you're not going to believe this."

Why did everyone say that? Gina preferred to stand while hearing bad news. And that catch in Robin's voice told Gina she was definitely in for bad news.

"What?"

"Candace Clay wants your *Now That's Italian!* time slot for her new show."

Light-headed, it turned out Gina really did need to sit down. "So they've canceled me for sure."

"No one is saying anything over there. It's like a goddamn library, it's so quiet. I only heard about Candace from Skyler Rome, who heard it from his agent, who also happens to represent Candace. We were at a charity event together and he had a couple of drinks too many, letting it slip."

"Candace has been a busy bee, hasn't she?" Gina had caught everyone on her team up on the Tulum photograph and the rumor that Candace had been seeking a divorce even before the controversy broke.

"Yes, she has. Word on the street is Danny is prepared to take her to the cleaners. So, I guess she's looking out for her future. I can't say I blame her."

"But it does seem sort of convenient, don't you think? It's not that I think she's behind ruining my life, but she's certainly using my downfall to better herself."

There was a long pause, then, "We're all opportunists, Gina. That's Hollywood."

Gina supposed her agent was right. Lord knew Gina had climbed over a few backs to get where she was. Now, it just seemed unscrupulous. Not because it was happening to her, but because it was a shitty way to live life, like dancing on someone's grave.

Watching the Daltons try to save their ranch using ingenuity and grit made all the Hollywood pushing and posturing feel shallow. And just plain dirty.

She blew out a breath. "What do we do now, Robin?"

"Not much we can do as long as no one from the network will deign to return my calls. What does Wendy Dalton say about exposing the original photo?"

"She's considering leaking it to the press, but wants to consult with a few media types to see how it will play. Wendy's afraid that it might look desperate. That the photo really doesn't prove much, even though I think it does." She would've pushed Wendy if not for the fact that Sawyer agreed with his mother's assessment. And Sawyer would know, being a member of the media.

"I trust her," Robin said. "Wendy is the best in the business. In the meantime, I say keep doing what you're doing. Stay low-profile."

Which probably meant no more trips to the kitchen store in Grass Valley. At least whatever talk Jace had had with Tiffany seemed to have done the trick. Last week's excitement with the lone camera guy appeared to be a

one-off. At least so far. She suspected that at some point, he'd either be back or he'd tell his friends.

Her secret location couldn't stay secret forever.

"I will," she said and signed off.

She started to make that phone call to Sawyer when she decided to walk over to his barn apartment instead. It was early enough that the temperature still hovered in the seventies and she wanted to stretch her legs.

But no one was home, though Sawyer's Range Rover was still in the driveway. He'd probably gone riding. At least once a week the men on Dry Creek Ranch spent the wee hours of the morning checking the fences that kept their cattle in before going off to their respective jobs.

Well, he'd have to wait to hear the good news.

She sighed and headed to Aubrey and Charlie's barn. Construction was finally done and the women were spreading out in their new digs. With the extra room, Charlie was able to do a few more displays in the shop. While Gina didn't know a darn thing about decorating or home decor, she enjoyed watching Charlie and Aubrey work their magic. They had so many beautiful pieces that it was a feast for the eyes.

She found the women, along with Sawyer, Jace, and Cash, in a meeting with a man she'd never seen before. A rangy cowboy who reminded her a little of Brad Pitt in his *Thelma & Louise* days. This man, though, had more crinkles around the eyes and brackets around the mouth. Sun damage or a hard life. Maybe both.

Nice-looking, just the same.

When she quietly tried to leave, Sawyer motioned that she should stay. It was awkward because she wasn't family. But she was nosy, so she took a seat at Aubrey's new pedestal conference table on one of the cowhide chairs. They were quickly introduced. No last names, just Gina and Ted.

The stranger glanced her way and tipped an imaginary hat, which sat on its crown on the table in front of him. There went keeping a low profile. But there didn't seem to be a spark of recognition in his hazel eyes. Not everyone watched the FoodFlicks Network or read the tabloids, she reminded herself. From his weathered hands, she could tell he worked hard and probably didn't have a lot of time to watch cooking shows on television.

"What would you need?" Cash asked.

"A studio and shop," he said and glanced around the gleaming new conference room where Aubrey's samples, catalogs, and fabric swatches had been organized on racks and wall boards. "Nothing as elaborate as this. Just a room where I can do my leatherwork and a small showroom

to display some of my saddles. I'd need good internet. Most of what I sell is off my website or custom."

"We could make that happen," Jace said.

Gina wanted to say something but held her tongue. It wasn't her place. But between building a flower shop and the saddlemaker's studio, the Daltons would go into hock. Despite Aubrey's contention that people shelled out a lot of money for saddles, Gina didn't see how either business could pull in enough sales to pay a decent rent, let alone make a new construction build-out fiscally worthwhile to the Daltons.

"How long do you think it would take?" Ted asked. "I was kind of hoping to be up and running before Christmas."

Sawyer glanced at Jace and Cash. "We're still trying to decide if we want to build from the ground up or go modular. Of course, either way we go it would have to be architecturally cohesive with the ranch. That might take some time."

"We can have you set up by early winter," Jace assured, sounding overanxious.

In Gina's opinion, it wasn't a good way to negotiate a lease. But again, she kept her mouth shut.

Sawyer tried to change the tenor of the conversation by getting right to the heart of the matter. "What were you thinking in terms of rent?"

"A triple-net lease. I couldn't afford to do anything more than fifteen-hundred a month and even that's a stretch."

At least the guy was offering to pay for common area maintenance and insurance on top of his base rent. But $1500 wasn't much. With the flower growers, the Daltons had their crop to fall back on if the girls stiffed them on the rent.

"How do you feel about letting lookie-loos watch you work?" Cash asked. "We're trying to set this whole thing up as an agritourism type of attraction. Everything we do here, including the furniture, is tied to the land, tied to the resources that come with ranching and farming."

"I've got no problem with that. In fact, I like it." There was that smile again. He wasn't nearly as good-looking as Sawyer, but one look at Ted the saddlemaker and the ladies of Dry Creek were going to wet their panties.

Sawyer shot her a look when she stared too long. Ordinarily, she would've told him to get over himself. But she sort of liked that he was being territorial. They'd never discussed their friendship or put any kind of label on it. But for the last seven days they'd spent the night together, splitting their time between the cabin and Sawyer's place. He'd made it

seem like it was in case any more tabloid reporters showed up. But she knew better.

They'd spent those nights talking even more than having sex, which was saying something. She'd never had this much sex in her life.

"If you're into it we can make this work," Jace told Ted. "But before we start building anything, we'll need a contract. Can we send something over later today?"

"We good on the price?" Ted rubbed his chin.

No, Gina thought they needed to negotiate for something higher. But Jace nodded.

"Then we got ourselves a deal." Ted shook everyone's hand at the table. When it came to Gina's turn, she reluctantly stuck out her hand. It was easier than explaining that she wasn't part of the deal and no one appeared to mind that she'd been included.

"So what's your role here?" he asked her. "You doing a farm-to-table restaurant as part of this project?"

Shit. He knew who she was.

Sawyer stepped in before she stumbled over her own tongue, so caught off guard by the question. "Gina's just visiting for a while. If you could keep that on the QT we'd really appreciate it. Otherwise she gets hounded by the press. The kind of press who peers through your blinds at night or chases you down the highway at high speed, if you know what I mean?"

Ted stood and swiped his hat off the table. "Never saw her before in my life." He winked and adjusted his Stetson on his head, then turned to the Daltons. "Looking forward to doing business with you. And by the way, everyone calls me Tuff. T-U-F-F. Not Ted."

"Tuff," Cash repeated and shook his hand. "We'll get that contract over to you. In the meantime, why don't you email us the kind of square footage you think you'll need. You can send it to Aubrey. She and Charlie are heading up this operation." He looked over at his wife with pride shining in his eyes.

Oh, to be loved like that. Gina couldn't even imagine it.

Tuff took off. At the sound of his truck engine they all started talking at once.

Jace stuck two fingers in his mouth and let out a whistle. "One at a time."

"Fifteen-hundred bucks a month ain't bad," Cash said.

Gina thought it was piss-poor. In LA, people were paying more than three dollars a square foot for crappy locations. West Hollywood and Beverly Hills were fetching as much as nine bucks. Dry Creek Ranch might not have the cachet of Beverly Hills, but the man was selling saddles, for goodness

sake. Between a storefront and a studio, she estimated Tuff would need at least a thousand square feet, minimum. Fifteen-hundred bucks a month was a steal, especially with common area maintenance and insurance.

"I'm going to add my two cents' here for what it's worth. Don't make the lease for any more than a year. Personally, I think you could get twice that rent."

Five pairs of eyes stared at her.

"If the project takes off, Ted…Tuff…will do well. Don't box yourself into a corner. The first year, fine. It's still an experiment. But after that, renegotiate."

"I think she's right," Sawyer said. "I liked him. I like what he does and how it'll fit in with what we're trying to do here. But let's stay fluid as far as the rent's concerned. Who knows where this thing will lead?"

"All right," Cash agreed. "A one-year lease for now. Then we'll reassess. We've got to come to terms on the build-out, especially if we're planning to have this done by winter. Do we want new construction or something already built? We'll also have to put in some kind of parking. A weedy lot isn't going to suffice, especially when the rain comes and we've got mud. There's also a separate road to consider. I'm not exactly thrilled about a parade of cars going up and down our driveway. This will all cost money. Money we don't have."

"We can do a gravel lot," Jace said. "I know a guy who can do it cheap. I think we hold off on a new road until we see what kind of traffic we get. As far as our storefronts, we build them ourselves. Use Jeb Guthrie to do the plumbing and Cole Electric to wire the places. Money? We get a loan."

Cash let out a heavy sigh. "I don't like borrowing against the land. Look how well that worked out for Randy Beals. How much do we stand to make from the cattle this year?"

Sawyer reached inside his pocket for his phone and did a quick search. "It should be good as long as these beef prices hold. But if we use the revenue for the business center we'll clean ourselves out. No reserves. I don't like that, either."

"Nope." Cash shook his head.

Jace leaned back in his chair and laced his hands behind his head. "Did you think this would be completely risk-free? Maybe Gina here could tell you how businesses work."

Sawyer laughed and elbowed his cousin in the ribs. "Listen to you. And here we all thought you were just a dumbass cowboy. Jace is right. No pain, no gain. Let's use the cattle money and build this thing as frugally as

possible. Worse comes to worst, we go belly-up and have to borrow a little money to get us through the next year. Just enough to make ends meet."

"Okay," Cash said. "Let's do this."

"I'll have Mike draw up plans." Aubrey scrawled a note on her legal pad.

Gina knew Mike was a local architect and Aubrey's former employer. Despite her going out on her own, the two still did business together.

"Make sure we get the friends and family discount," Cash said.

Aubrey reached over and kissed him on the mouth. "You got it."

"Does that mean this meeting's adjourned?" Charlie checked her watch. "I've got a client who needs furniture for a four-thousand-square-foot home in Tahoe in a few minutes. I'd like to get started pulling things before she gets here."

"Go." Jace kissed the top of her head. "Make us rich, baby."

There was so much love in the air, Gina could choke on it.

The room quickly cleared out, everyone having somewhere to be, leaving her and Sawyer alone.

"You're up early," Sawyer said. "I snuck out about five and you were still sound asleep."

"I have news. But first, what the hell kind of name is Tuff? He doesn't even spell it right."

Sawyer chuckled. "According to Cash, he used to ride the rodeo circuit. Tuff, Rope, Slim, Ty. Pretty par for the course. And if you ride seventeen-hundred-pound bulls for a living, spelling's probably not your strength."

"I don't know, he seemed like a pretty smart guy."

Sawyer hitched his brows, his blue eyes twinkling. "Why, because he knows who you are?"

"No, because he had you at fifteen-hundred dollars a month. You didn't even blink an eye. Just gave him what he wanted."

"He said that's all he could afford."

She folded her arms over her chest. "What did you expect him to say? 'I can do a lot more but you look like a sucker.'"

"That's not the way it works out here, Gina. We take a man at his word. It's not like the guy is a major leather manufacturer. He probably makes two saddles a year. But your advice on keeping the terms of the lease to one year has been noted. Now, what's your news?"

"I'm not pregnant," she blurted.

He was quiet for a long time. Almost stoic. "That's good."

The two words were simple enough but he'd sounded somewhat ambivalent. Though she'd probably imagined that and was hearing what

she wanted to hear. She told herself to stop overanalyzing things. Of course he was relieved, elated, liberated.

"Yep," she said. "And Candace Clay is in production on her new show and is trying to steal my time slot on FoodFlicks."

"How'd you find that out?" He pulled her out of the sleek cowhide chair, undoubtedly a Charlie creation. "Let's walk."

The temperature had more than likely climbed to a less-than comfortable ninety-something degrees. Hardly walking weather. But she followed him anyway. They took the route that led to the creek.

"My agent called. She was at a party with Skyler Rome and he let it slip. Candace and he share the same agent."

"How good is your time slot?"

"Pretty damn good. I started with the Saturday-night death slot. They thought I was just another dump-and-stir demonstration show and wouldn't rack up enough ratings to make it past my first thirteen-episode season. They were wrong. Now, I've got Sunday and Monday nights, considered prime FoodFlicks viewing time."

"How significant do you think it is that Candace is homing in on your territory? Or is this typical jostling for dominance? At newspapers and magazines everyone is trying to get their story on the front page or the cover. Seems like this is the same thing, no?"

She shrugged because he was right. It was dog-eat-dog in TV land. "It just feels like she's trying to steal my life."

"Given that she thinks you stole her husband, can you blame her?"

"I guess not." The bottom line was Gina didn't care whether Candace's motives were revenge or ambition. Either way, she was in serious jeopardy of losing her time slot. Hell, she'd probably lose her show altogether.

When they got to the creek, Sawyer sat on the flat head of a boulder and pulled her down into his lap. He wrapped his arms around her and they sat like that, swaying a little. There was a slight breeze coming from the west, tempering the heat.

"How do you know you're not pregnant?"

"The same way every woman knows." She glared at him.

"From peeing on a stick or because your period came?"

"The latter. But I'll take a home-pregnancy test if it'll make you feel better."

"Not necessary." He leaned down, picked up a stone, and flicked it with his wrist over the water. It skipped at least five times.

"How'd you do that?"

"Practice and mad skills." He sorted through a small pile, found a flat rock, handed it to her, and held her wrist. "Like this." He demonstrated a few times, then let go of her hand so she could try on her own.

She tossed the stone the way he'd shown her, but it made a loud *plop* and sunk to the bottom of the water. "You make it look easier than it is."

"I used to sit out here for hours with Angie, skipping stones. She was even better at it than I was. Jace was the best, but Angie came in a close second."

"No new news?"

"Still waiting for Cash's friend to trace that email." He leaned back and took her with him.

The air smelled green, like grass and sage and mulched leaves, with a trace of honey. The creek gurgled quietly, like a song. And for a few seconds Gina lost herself in the tranquility of nature and Sawyer's arms.

"Tuff. That thing he said about a restaurant. You interested?" He skipped another stone. This time it bounced across the surface all the way to the other side.

"I don't know the first thing about the hospitality industry." She tilted her head back and rested it against his chest. "Fresh out of culinary school I went the home-chef route and worked for the Hollywood elite, thanks to my father's contacts. And unlike Emeril, Gordon, Giada, and the slew of other celebrity chefs who opened restaurants, I went the prepared-food route. I steered away from frozen pizzas because Wolfgang had that market sewn up. But there was plenty of room for frozen Italian entrées. That's where I excel. Restaurants? Uh-uh."

"It seemed like a good idea when he brought it up. Our beef, the local bounty of produce, your cooking skills. You'd kill it."

"So next to wine country with Keller...Chiarello...Morimoto, I'd be a laughingstock."

He clasped her shoulders and forced her to turn around. "The hell you would."

She looked away and muttered, "I thought you couldn't wait to get rid of me."

"Ah, I see you're going for classic avoidance. Look, if you don't want to do it, don't think it's your thing, don't believe Dry Creek is the place for it, don't want to take the risk—I get it. I really do. But this other crap... you not being good enough...me wanting to be rid of you...it's bullshit, Gina. And you know it."

It wasn't bullshit, it was the God's honest truth. There's a reason she'd gone with frozen foods. Surrounded by mass-produced garbage that had

been around since man walked on the moon, it wasn't difficult to stand out. To be better than the rest. But a restaurant in Northern California, the food mecca of the country? Ha. It would be like a skating enthusiast competing in the winter Olympics.

She started to ask him if he was trying to benefit the ranch by riding on her famous—now infamous—coattails, but stopped herself. That was unfair. He'd never once taken advantage of her celebrity. Just the opposite, in fact. He'd shielded her from the public, helped her try to find the culprit who'd made up the lies about her, and believed her when most would've laughed her to kingdom come.

"I want my old life back." Because even if she didn't miss it now, she would. It was proof that contrary to Sadie DeRose's pronouncement that Gina would never amount to much, she was a rock star. "A new restaurant is a full-time job. I can't do that and run my other businesses and produce a thirteen-episode show a year. Not when Dry Creek Ranch is more than four-hundred miles away."

"I get it." Sawyer got to his feet, taking her with him. "Let's go. It's hot." He didn't wait for her, just walked away.

"Where are we going?" she called to his back.

"I'm going home. I have an article to write." The context of those two sentences were clear.

"Seriously? You're angry because I don't want to open a restaurant?"

He stopped and turned around. "No." There was a long pause. "Okay, I'm angry. But it's not because of the restaurant. I don't know why I'm angry, but I am. I'm going home to figure it out. I'll call you later."

She watched him follow the creek at a brisk pace, then started back to her own cabin. Halfway there, her phone vibrated inside her messenger bag. She'd turned it to silent during the meeting.

By the time she wrenched it loose from its compartment, the call had gone to voicemail, where it was marked *urgent*. Gina found a tree to stand under while she listened. Cell service on the ranch could be spotty but today her manager's voice came through loud and clear.

"I've tried calling you three times," she said in the message. "Call me as soon as you can. It's not good news."

Gina squeezed the bridge of her nose, feeling a headache coming on, then hit the *return* button on the phone.

Chapter 16

Sawyer found Cash sitting in his living room with the AC turned up when he got home.

"I let myself in when I realized no one was home. Your truck was still here, so I figured you were either taking your time walking home or you were with Gina." His mouth quirked to show that he knew that Sawyer had been spending a lot of time over at her place. It was impossible to keep anything a secret on the ranch. Or in all of Dry Creek, for that matter.

"What's up?"

"I'm not sure." Cash lost the grin and his expression turned sharp. "My buddy, Ken, got squirrelly all of a sudden."

"What do you mean?"

"He's not returning my calls, which isn't like him. The guy's solid, not flaky. Initially, I feared he had some kind of family emergency…something that took precedence over sending me a quick text that he was still working on tracing the email, or whatever. But I checked with another friend who says Ken's been at work every day this week. That everything seems fine."

"So what do you think's going on?"

"Don't know." Cash shook his head. "It isn't like him to say he's going to do something and then not do it. Even stranger is the radio silence. He knows Angela is my cousin. We worked cases together when she first went missing. Knew the toll it took on me. On our family. This isn't something he'd blow off."

"Maybe his supervisors told him he couldn't use Bureau resources."

"There's so much going on in that lab, no one knows what anyone else is doing. Ken spends his day in a cubicle the size of a shoebox, doing cyber searches. Most of it sleep-inducing. That's not it."

"Sounds like you might have a vague idea."

"Yeah, I think he found out something he doesn't want to share. Why? That right there is the million-dollar question."

"Or are you reading way too much into it? The guy could've just gotten busy."

"Maybe." But Cash wasn't buying it, Sawyer could tell. "If I don't hear anything in the next day or two, I'm taking a little trip. A little face-to-face time with Ken."

"You have time for that?" Sawyer walked to the fridge and grabbed two bottled waters and tossed one to Cash. His cousin spent the good part of the day driving across Northern California, investigating livestock thefts.

"I'll make time." Cash took a swig of the water and put the bottle down on Sawyer's coffee table.

"Speaking of...Aren't you working today?" It was after ten.

"Yep. I left the morning clear for the meeting with Tuff. At noon I have a cattlemen's lunch in Placer County." Placer was just next door to Mill County. When Grandpa Dalton was alive he sometimes went to the Placer cattlemen's lunches at the Auburn Fairgrounds. A few of those times, he'd taken his grandsons with him.

Sawyer took a sip of his water and eyed Cash over the rim of the bottle. "What are some of the things your friend Ken could've found that he wouldn't want to pass on to you?" Sawyer couldn't let it go.

He had his own ideas, like maybe Angie had been the victim of someone on the FBI's radar and agents didn't want to blow their case. Hell, for all he knew, Angie was involved in something illegal and was under investigation. But that didn't sound like his sister. She'd been caught up in some wacky causes but none of them were criminal. Perhaps Ken's reticence had something to do with the New Mexico commune. The timing was certainly suspect. Sawyer had gotten the email about the same time he'd been trying to unearth information about the farm. Or whatever the hell it was. Could be that the FBI was interested in the commune too. For all Sawyer knew the Bureau was dealing with another Branch Davidian situation.

"Why speculate?" Cash let out a sigh. "There's dozens of reasons. Let's see what I can find out."

It was a fancy way of Cash saying he didn't want to go there right now. But Sawyer was pretty sure they'd come up with the same possibilities.

None of them good.

"So what's the deal with you and Gina?" Cash unartfully steered the conversation away from Angie. "I see you sneaking over there a few nights a week and her driving over to your place the other nights."

Sawyer could've pleaded the Fifth. Cash would've let it go. All three of them tried hard to respect one another's space. Living in a fishbowl, you had to. But why? His cousin wasn't an idiot. He saw what he saw. Knew what he knew.

"I don't know." Sawyer shrugged. "I guess somewhere along the way we became more than friends."

"Is it serious?"

"Nah." How could it be? Gina wanted her old life and Sawyer didn't want any part of it. He was a writer and a rancher, not arm candy for a celebrity. The restaurant…it had been a stupid idea. She was too big for Dry Creek Ranch, even if she had wanted to be a restaurateur. Which clearly she didn't. "Just a summer thing. Passing the time until she goes home."

Cash held his gaze. "How's her situation coming? You figure out who's responsible for that picture…the texts?"

"Not yet. We found the original photo, though. The one that was photoshopped to make it look like Gina was in the picture. Now all she has to do is prove it."

"I imagine that won't be an easy feat. You got anything better?"

Sawyer let out a wry chuckle. "You mean the proverbial smoking gun? No, not yet. Working on it."

"You got two cops living next door. Yell if you need help. We'll put our heads together. Of course, if you don't want her to leave…" The corner of Cash's mouth turned up.

Sawyer ignored the insinuation because it was too close to the truth. He needed a good assignment, something that would take him on the road. Something that would clear his head and take his focus away from Gina.

"We could use the cabin, maybe rent it out to add to our Dry Creek Ranch roadside-attraction coffers."

Cash rubbed his hand down his chin. "Tuff mentioned looking for a place close by. He's sharing a bunkhouse with a bunch of cowboys. He'll need his own digs when he leaves wrangling behind."

Though Sawyer had been the one to bring it up, the idea of someone other than Gina living in Cash's old cabin bothered him. Boy, did he have to get a grip. He was like Travis with his first crush.

"I've gotta giddyup if I'm going to make it to that lunch." Cash got to his feet. "I'll let you know if I hear from Ken."

"If you wind up paying him a visit, can I tag along?"

Cash grabbed his hat off the rack by the staircase. "Don't think that would be a good idea. I can't even get the guy to return my calls. He sure as shit won't talk if you're there with me. I'll get it done. That's a promise."

He lifted his hand, waved it in the air, and ate up the stairs with that long stride of his.

Sawyer polished off his water, got another from the fridge, and booted up his laptop on the kitchen island. He promised he wouldn't let himself think about Gina until after he got his writing done.

Ten minutes later, he trolled Realtor.com to find the listing for Beals Ranch. Ten million dollars is how much Randy wanted for it. And Sawyer had no doubt that it was worth every cent. A contiguous, fully fenced, nearly flat thousand-acre working ranch, complete with barns, irrigation, corrals, equipment, three wells, and a couple of houses in Gold Country was rarer than the precious metal for which the region was named.

He flipped through the twenty-eight photos, starting with an aerial view of the ranch. It was beautiful land, guarded by the Sierra Nevada mountains. No doubt it was a developer's wet dream. Only sixty-five miles from Sacramento, ninety to Reno, and a hundred and fifty to San Francisco. Despite its proximity to large cities, it felt like a world away. And with nearby Grass Valley, Nevada City, and Auburn a person could get just about everything they needed, even Starbucks.

He closed down the real estate tab on his computer and returned to working on his article. It was due in a few days and he needed to flesh out a lot of what he'd already written. His editor at *Esquire* was already haranguing him about doing a piece on the staggering homicide rate in Central America, which would likely entail weeks of travel.

It used to be one of the best parts of his job. But now he was dreading it. He told himself it was because of Angie. He needed to stay close in case they broke the email riddle.

But deep down inside he knew it had more to do with Gina. She'd become a preoccupation. He had to keep reminding himself that they traveled in different lanes and he didn't see how their highways could ever converge.

Nope, she'd made it clear they both wanted two very different things. Time to stop fixating and get back to work. Get back to the things that mattered.

Chapter 17

Gina pressed her face against the glass of the small Cessna aircraft as the plane took off from Auburn Municipal Airport. She should've left the previous night in her car, but hadn't been up for the seven-hour drive to Los Angeles. And a commercial flight was out of the question.

At least she'd had the whole night to work the phones. And even though the chartered flight was an extravagance, she couldn't afford to put this off.

ChefAid had made it known it was ready to cut her loose.

She was getting pummeled from all sides and needed to put her boxing gloves on.

"Can I use my phone?" she asked the flight attendant, who sat in the seat behind the cockpit.

The young woman shrugged. "You're really not supposed to, but…"

That was all the permission Gina needed to put her cell on airplane mode and start calling her team. She wanted them all assembled at her Malibu headquarters in ninety minutes.

The two-story building not only housed the offices for her frozen food and houseware divisions, it also served as her set. A gleaming 1200-square-foot stage made to look like a well-appointed home kitchen. That is, if you had seven figures to blow on a home kitchen. The lighting and acoustics—the brainchild of two of the most renowned set designers in Los Angeles—cost more than most upscale kitchen remodels alone.

After this fiasco, who knew if she'd still need it.

Wendy Dalton was picking her up at the Santa Monica Airport so they could discuss strategy before Gina's meeting with her staff. She wanted all hands on deck.

If ChefAid wanted to pay her out for the remaining three years on her contract, there might not be anything she could do about it, according to her lawyer. But they were talking about dumping her without a cent in favor of a new face.

No way would she let someone dethrone her without a valiant fight. As long as she had three years left on her contract, she intended to make the bastards adhere to their agreement.

She used the sixty-minute flight to finish up her phone calls, texts, and emails. By the time they landed, she felt like she'd worked an eight-hour day.

Wendy met her at the curb in a silver Mercedes-Benz. Gina had packed light. Just a briefcase, her laptop, and purse. Between her office and home, she had everything she needed, except a car. If she had to, she'd hire a driver.

She stashed her things in Wendy's back seat and got up front.

"Good flight?"

"It was fast and productive."

"Good, because I've got news. Very interesting news. Fasten your seat belt, because we've got a war on our hands."

Wendy waited for Gina to buckle up and nosed into traffic. It was past rush hour and yet cars still crawled along Pacific Coast Highway like overfed snails. Gina hadn't missed LA's bottlenecks. She still hadn't figured out the roads in Dry Creek, but at least she was mostly alone on them while she got herself hopelessly lost.

"You ready for this?" Wendy asked as she headed for Malibu. "It's Candace Clay."

"What?" Gina turned sideways in her seat.

"That's who's trying to become the new spokeswoman for ChefAid. She's a real operator, that Candace."

"When I talked to Linda yesterday she said she didn't know who was in talks with them, only that it was another chef."

"At the time none of us knew. But these things never stay secret for long."

"Are you sure?" Candace Clay? As far as Gina knew, the Clays worked exclusively with the cookware company, Tramontina. If memory served her right, the Clays had their own line of nonstick pots and pans.

"Yep. My source on this is rock-solid. It sounds like Candace has become quite ambitious since that photo of you and her husband hit the internet. She's apparently trying to build an empire and using the publicity of Danny's affair to her benefit."

Gina messaged her temples, feeling another migraine coming on. "I can't believe this is happening. Next, she'll be coming for my soul."

"Let's not get carried away," Wendy said. The woman reminded Gina so much of her son. Both were no-nonsense, save-your-drama-for-your-mama, let's-get-it-done individuals.

It instantly gave her pangs of homesickness for Dry Creek Ranch. Funny, because she'd never thought of the ranch as her home. But she missed Sawyer. All night she'd wanted to call and commiserate with him that the enterprise she'd painstakingly built for herself through hard work and perseverance was being taken apart one piece at a time.

But since their creek-side disagreement, she no longer knew where she stood with him. He hadn't called or texted. And it had been the first time they'd slept apart in a week.

Now, though, wasn't the time to ponder what had crawled up Sawyer's ass to cause the distance. Not while her own ass was on the line.

"Should I try to move up the meeting with ChefAid?" It was a week away. Gina had hoped by then she could show she'd been the victim of a smear campaign. As soon as the public learned the truth, she'd be the hottest ticket in town.

"First, we should talk to Henry about your legal options. They may not be so quick to wiggle out of a contract with you if it means a lawsuit."

"He'll be at the meeting. We can have a private conference with him first thing."

"That's wise." Wendy's foot grew heavier on the pedal after they passed Pacific Palisades. It was a reverse commute and the traffic had lifted.

There were twenty people, including her manager, agent, and the publicist she hadn't fired, waiting when they arrived at DeRose Food Enterprises. Henry was running late.

"Just give me ten minutes to use the restroom and freshen up," Gina told her staff and turned to Darby, her assistant. "Did you have brunch delivered?"

"There's food and coffee in the conference room." Darby motioned for everyone to follow her through the double doors, leaving Gina with a little time alone.

She went to her office to drop off her briefcase and stood at the picture window, watching the waves crash on the shore. This morning, the Pacific looked as turbulent as her insides felt. She gathered her composure and hit the ladies' room before joining the rest of her team.

It was time to kick some ass and take back her life.

* * * *

Gina stretched out on her California king bed as a cool breeze wafted through her open French doors. The ocean lapped against the beach just outside her bedroom. She could smell a hint of furniture polish and the organic cleaning solution Jessica used to mop the floors. Everything sparkled with cleanliness.

It didn't matter how many times she dusted or knocked down the cobwebs at Dry Creek Ranch, the cabin always had a patina of grime. And yet, she'd come to admire—maybe even adore—the rugged ranch that had been her sanctuary for the last month.

And especially the people.

Here, she didn't have many friends. In the beginning, before *Now That's Italian!*, she'd had a handful of people with whom she socialized. But between the hours spent working and promoting her brand as well as ChefAid's, she'd been too busy to invest in those relationships. Now that she was a celebrity it was difficult letting new people in. She never knew if they wanted to be friends with Gina DeRose the person or Gina DeRose the FoodFlicks star.

Most of the people with whom she felt comfortable worked for her. But socializing with employees was a dicey proposition.

At Dry Creek Ranch, though, she was free to just be. And despite the scandal and the bad publicity, Charlie and Aubrey had welcomed her friendship with open arms.

She swung her legs over the bed and wandered into the kitchen for a bottle of sparkling water. Every room from her house had a view of the ocean. There were steps down to the beach and if it wasn't for the fact that she was supposed to be incognito she would've taken a stroll along the sandy strand to clear her head. But the tourists were out in full force.

And unlike in Dry Creek, where mostly everyone minded their own business, here the tourists were not only on the lookout for famous people, they went to great lengths to seek them out. They frequented all the usual celebrity spots: Jerry's Deli, the Ivy, Chateau Marmont, Runyon Canyon, even LAX. Hell, for a few bucks they could take a bus tour of the stars' homes.

Stalking at its finest.

Here, inside her house, she was safe from the prying eyes of the masses.

She'd gotten home around eight, after an exhausting day. Henry had drafted a letter to ChefAid, reminding the CEO that he was bound by the contract.

"We sound tough," he'd said in that Oklahoma drawl that his grandparents had brought to California with them during the Dust Bowl and had passed down to the next two generations. "But it's pissing in the wind."

According to the morals clause, ChefAid had the right to jettison Gina and hire Candace. Henry had written the letter anyway, letting them know that they couldn't can Gina without a very public legal battle.

"They'll pay you out to avoid the lawyers and the publicity. It's easier that way," Henry had told her.

At this point, she didn't know if she even cared anymore. The fighter in her should've been outraged by the unfairness of it all. But she was too tired. Tired of the scratching and the clawing and the jockeying to stay on top.

If only Sadie could see her now. Wouldn't her mother have the last laugh?

Her cell went off and Gina searched for where she'd last left the phone. She followed the ringing and found it on the charger stand in her kitchen. She glanced at the caller ID.

Sawyer.

Her heart stopped.

"Hello?"

"Why didn't you tell me you were going to LA? I would've given you a ride to the airport."

Charlie had shuttled her to Auburn. She could've driven herself, but was afraid to leave her car unattended in the lot for days. There was no telling how long she'd be here.

"I was under the impression you were mad at me...over the restaurant thing."

"I told you it wasn't the restaurant."

She took the phone with her into the living room and curled up on her white sofa. "Then what?"

There was a long pause. "Charlie told me that someone else is vying for your ChefAid gig."

"It's Candace. Your mom found out."

"Damn, the woman knows how to get even, doesn't she? Where are you and are you okay?"

"I'm home. And I'm fine." But she wasn't fine. She was hanging on by a thread. But she had too much pride to tell him—or anyone, for that matter. *Fake it till you make it* had always been her motto.

"I would've come with you, Gina, if you'd only told me."

"Everything was last minute, including the chartered flight. Besides, you weren't talking to me at the time."

"Ah, stop with the bullshit. I went home to get some work done. Don't turn it into something it's not."

She got off the couch, went outside onto the balcony, and stared out at the sea. It was nearly dark, shrouding the water in shadow. "You were angry when you left the creek. You said it yourself."

"I was frustrated, not angry."

"Frustrated over what? Because I don't want to open a restaurant on the ranch?"

"No," he said and remained silent until the quiet became awkward. "You want to know the truth? I'm falling for you and I don't like it. Besides the fact that I wasn't looking for a relationship, our lives don't mesh. Not even a little."

The words stunned her. Not the part about their lives not meshing. They didn't. He thought she was a pampered celebrity and she'd cop to that. She wasn't interested in changing who she was, not for a man. Not for anyone.

But he was falling for her.

She'd known he was attracted. He'd made that clear every night they slept together. She'd known he enjoyed their little game of wordplay. She'd even known that he genuinely liked her, despite his opinion that she was a spoiled brat. She'd known all of that.

But falling? As in the L word?

"What do you mean by falling?" She wanted him to clarify to make sure she wasn't misconstruing this conversation.

"Ah, for Christ's sake, Gina, what the fuck do you think I mean?"

Not the most poetic declaration, but her heart skipped like the flat stones Sawyer sailed across Dry Creek. Still, she was cautious. Other than her father, no one had ever loved her. Certainly not Sadie. And Sawyer? He was the finest man she'd ever known. She couldn't bear to even hope.

"What are you planning to do about this Candace situation?" he segued, either to give her an out on responding to his pronouncement or because he didn't want to talk about it anymore.

"My lawyer has written a letter to ChefAid, reminding them that they're contractually obligated to me. Whatever good that'll do." The evening chill bit through her thin loungewear and she hugged herself before deciding to go in, shutting the doors behind her.

"The woman isn't wasting any time capitalizing on her victimhood, is she? It gives a suspicious person license to wonder, doesn't it?"

"What are you saying?" She grabbed a light throw blanket and wrapped it around her like a shawl and curled up on the couch again. Just hearing Sawyer's voice went a long way to taking the sting out of the day.

"Someone set you up. Opportunity stands out as a good motive, don't you think?"

"Are you saying Candace is the one behind the picture, the texts, the gossip? Seems like a cheating husband is a humiliating way to enhance your career."

"In the beginning I would've agreed," Sawyer said. "But I'm starting to wonder. She definitely appears to want your life in a big way. Your time slot on FoodFlicks. Replacing you at ChefAid. Either it's payback because she believes you slept with her husband or she's one cunning woman."

"So you think this is all a publicity stunt to bolster Candace's career? Wow, it seems a little out there."

"Perhaps. Nothing wrong with considering all possibilities. When are you coming home? Or are you?" His voice trailed off, almost like he was holding his breath.

"I don't know yet. We're trying to decide whether to move up our meeting with ChefAid. It would help if I could prove that this whole thing with Danny is a hoax. He's still trying to call me, by the way. Did you ever get in touch with him?"

"Nope, he's not taking my calls. He probably knows I'm a reporter and thinks I'm using you to get a story. I'll keep trying."

"What about my manager? Could she reach out to him? Or Wendy?"

Sawyer appeared to be mulling it over and finally said, "Before we found the original picture, I would've said no. They're your employees, after all. If the press caught wind of it they would've thought you were setting up trysts with him through your staff. Now, though, you've got a legitimate reason to talk. Yeah, have one of them reach out to him. See where that goes. But Gina, don't trust him."

"I don't trust anyone." That was the truth. And wasn't that a sad statement about her life?

"You can trust me."

"Can I?" Or would he break her heart?

Besides the fact that I wasn't looking for a relationship, our lives don't mesh. Not even a little. His words reminded her that she couldn't rely on him. His infatuation with her was as fleeting as her stardom had been.

"Yes. I'll come if you want me to."

She'd never wanted anything more. But what was the point? He couldn't fight her battles for her and she didn't want him to. "I've got this. But thank you."

The moments stretched between them.

"Right," he finally said. "I'm around if you need me." He sounded disappointed or perhaps that was what she wanted to hear.

She didn't need a savior. *I can handle this myself.*

Worse comes to worst, she'd lose it all and rebuild. She'd done it once; she could do it again. Gina still had her business sense and a knack for predicting trends. No one could take that away from her.

"Thanks for calling, Sawyer." She started to tell him she missed him and stopped herself.

Our lives don't mesh.

"Yup" was all he said and clicked off.

She lay on the couch, conjuring his blue eyes. The ones that saw right through her. No one had ever read her the way he did. No one had ever called her out on her insecurities and told her that he believed in her.

"Why do you always do that? Why do you always have to belittle what you do?"

Focus, she demanded. Right now, she needed to focus on saving her business, not on Sawyer. Though his voice alone had given her a second wind to climb back to the top of the mountain and take her rightful place as queen.

She got her laptop from her office and began to furiously take notes. There were a thousand ideas floating around in her head.

If she lost her ambassadorship with ChefAid, she'd start her own appliance company. And when she was done, she'd bury the big guys. If she lost her show, she'd make a new one. Sell it to the DIY channel. Hell, screw cable. She'd go network. Look at Rachael Ray and Martha Stewart. Both had had their own syndicated talk shows.

This was exactly what she loved. Empire building. Once again, she would prove Sadie wrong. Show her dead mother that she was the daughter Sadie had always wanted.

A star.

"To hell with you, Mother." She ripped the throw blanket off, rolled it into a ball, and chucked it at the wall, tears streaming down her face. "I'll show you."

Her head continued to pound until she thought it would explode. In search of aspirin, she tore through two medicine cabinets like a wrecking ball.

"I live in a damn palace with every modern convenience. Yet, not one goddamn over-the-counter painkiller," she muttered to herself, before finally finding a bottle of Tylenol in the kitchen.

She washed down three tablets with water and wiped the snot from her nose. Her quiet tears had turned to wracking sobs.

Before Gina knew what she was doing, she reached for a mixing bowl. Next, the eggs and milk, which Jessica delivered every week from the farmers' market, removing the old. There was flour in the cupboard and vanilla beans from Madagascar.

She thought about Laney's chess pie and started with her crust. Flour, butter, salt, Crisco, and ice water. Home cooks were afraid of pastry dough, but it was easy as pie. She laughed to herself and swiped her hand across her cheek to wipe away a stray tear.

With the whir of the food processor, she started to feel better. And when it was time to hand-stir the filling, she'd become so lost in the task that her sadness had diminished. There was just this: The solitude of her kitchen and the warmth and comfort of making something from her heart.

An hour later, the pie came out of the oven, looking as beautiful as Laney's. Gina planned to bring it to work in the morning. Sustenance for the troops on a busy day. But she never got that chance.

At seven sharp there was a pounding on her door loud enough to wake Forest Lawn cemetery. She threw on a robe, padded across the white ash floors in her bare feet, and opened the front door only to have a dozen camera strobes flash in her face.

"Ms. DeRose, is it true you and Danny Clay plan to marry in the fall?"

"Are you two doing a cooking show together?"

"Does Candace know?"

Like the proverbial deer caught in the headlights, Gina stood in the doorway of her house, frozen. It was only later that she realized that whoever set her up wasn't done with her yet.

Chapter 18

Sawyer waited in a San Francisco Starbucks while Cash ambushed his friend, Ken, outside the Phillip Burton Federal Building on Golden Gate Avenue.

The coffee shop was the closest Cash would let Sawyer get to the courthouse. Even so, Sawyer was grateful for the concession.

Afterward, they were meeting Cash's parents, Aubrey, and Ellie for dinner. Cash had grown up in the West Portal neighborhood, eighteen miles away from the federal building. His dad—Sawyer's uncle—was a retired SFPD homicide lieutenant. Law enforcement ran through the family's blood as much as ranching.

Sawyer stared out the window, sipping his third cup of coffee, wondering what was taking so long. Cash had been gone nearly two hours.

He checked his phone in case Cash had tried to call or text. And while he was at it, he scrolled through his Gmail account for a message from Gina. He hadn't heard from her in days, not since they talked on the phone. According to his mother, Gina was holed up in a hotel because the paparazzi had made it impossible for her to stay in her own home.

Maybe she'd come back to Dry Creek Ranch, maybe she wouldn't. Sawyer told himself he was beyond caring. Unfortunately, he'd never been a good liar.

On a lark, he'd called that blogger friend of his who worked for *Eater* and left a message. Sawyer wanted to run a few things by him on the latest tabloid BS that Gina and Danny were engaged. What a joke. Why didn't these asshats check their facts?

He glanced at his watch again and peered outside at a group of tourists in shorts and freshly purchased fleeces from Fisherman's Wharf to keep them warm.

"The coldest winter I ever saw was the summer I spent in San Francisco." The quote had been attributed to Mark Twain, but no one knew if he'd actually said it. Regardless, there'd never been a truer statement. Even in August.

Occasionally, the sun would peek out from the overcast sky and heat the City by the Bay for a few hours. Then, back to the fog. It was as different from Los Angeles as the West Coast was to the East Coast.

Although Sawyer had been raised in Beverly Hills, he liked San Francisco better. The people were more interesting, the city was more diverse, and more important, it was closer to Dry Creek Ranch.

His phone dinged with a text and he quickly put down his coffee.

On my way, Cash had written. That was it. No hint of what he'd found out, which Sawyer assumed was nothing. Two hours of wasted time, though he'd managed to send his article off to his editor and had made deadline. At least by California time.

Six minutes later, Cash came through the door. He'd dressed for the city. No cowboy hat; just jeans, boots, and a windbreaker, tossed over his arm.

"Well, you get anything?" Sawyer stood, but Cash motioned for him to sit back down.

"I want to do this before we meet with my folks." He eyed Sawyer's coffee. "Hang on a second."

"You're fucking kidding me, right?"

Cash ignored him and joined the coffee queue behind a kid with purple hair and enough piercings to open his own earring shop. Sawyer would've given Cash his cup. Another sip and he'd swim home.

Cash returned with a frappuccino and Sawyer rolled his eyes.

"There's something to the email." He sat next to Sawyer at the counter. "Ken was tight-lipped at first...afraid someone might see us together. Maybe waylaying him outside the federal building wasn't such a good idea. Especially because I'm persona non grata around there."

"I would think you'd be a goddamn hero after what went down."

Cash had tried to save the Bureau's ass on a serial-murder case that had consumed the nation. The killer had targeted female joggers in the Presidio. Naturally, the Bureau's top brass wanted to tie up the case in a neat little bow as fast as possible. They didn't want a serial killer tainting a national treasure. Despite Cash's warning that they had the wrong guy, his bosses made an arrest anyway.

The problem was Cash was right. The guy they'd nabbed was a scumbag to be sure—an ex-con with a rap sheet for sexual assault—but not responsible for the Presidio killings.

Cash shrugged. "It doesn't matter anyway. What Ken learned is classified."

Ah, jeez. It was just as Sawyer suspected. Whoever Angie had gotten caught up with was being investigated by the feds. What the hell had his sister gotten herself into?

"Is she alive? Please tell me he at least told you that much."

Cash blew out a breath. "He wouldn't go there. But what I was able to wheedle out of him was that the email address is a burner used by the US Marshals Service."

"How do they fit in?" Sawyer asked, perplexed. Marshals provided security in the federal courts, transported criminals, apprehended fugitives, forfeited assets, and performed tactical operations. What on God's earth did they have to do with Angie?

"So it wasn't Angie reaching out, it was someone from the US Marshals Service with a wrong email address?" He tried not to sound flip but it didn't make a whole hell of a lot of sense.

"I may be wrong here but, yeah, I suspect it was her." He pinned Sawyer with a look, waiting for him to catch on.

"WITSEC?" Sawyer exhaled, because the US Marshals Service also relocated witnesses in important federal cases. He tried to wrap his head around the implications. "You think she's been in the Witness Protection Program all these years?"

"Not all of them, not if you believe she was on that Taos commune two years ago. But she may be in WITSEC now. It's the only thing I can come up with that would involve the marshals. And when I asked Ken point-blank, he got real squirrelly."

"Classified. That's what he told you?"

"Yep." Cash tilted his head to the side. "WITSEC is about as classified as you can get, short of national security."

"Holy shit." Sawyer scrubbed his hand over his eyes. "What about the first three years she was missing?"

Cash shrugged. "Don't know. Clearly, she was involved in something she shouldn't have been. Something dangerous."

"You make it sound as if she was running around with the mob. This is Angela. The same Angela who spent a year in Japan, protesting the annual dolphin hunt in Taiji. The same Angela who chained herself to a Shell oil

drilling rig in New Zealand. The same Angela who thinks she can change the world. Not Sammy 'the Bull' Gravano."

"WITSEC isn't just for gangsters, Sawyer. These protest groups may seem benign, even heroic, but some of them are breaking the law. Some are even committing acts of domestic terrorism. The feds take that shit seriously."

"So Angela turned state's evidence against the followers of the Dalai Lama?" Sawyer didn't know why he was reacting with such vitriol and sarcasm. If Cash was right, he should be thanking his lucky stars that his sister was alive.

Safe.

"Don't kill the messenger." Cash took a sip of his Frapuccino, put the cup down, and hitched his shoulders. "I don't even know for sure that this is the case. It's only a theory."

"How can we confirm it?" Sawyer had sources on the Senate Judiciary Committee. He didn't like to use his influence as a journalist for personal reasons, thought it was unethical. But for the sake of his family he would. He would move mountains if it meant getting his sister back.

"I'll make a few calls. Ken's a mid-level analyst. I doubt he even knows the full story. More than likely he set off alarm bells when he traced the email to the marshals and was told to keep his nose out of it. There are higher-ups who owe me favors. Let's see what strings I can pull."

Sawyer started to say "thank you" and stopped himself. Cash had been right to complain the last time Sawyer had thanked his cousin. This is what the Daltons did. They looked out for one another.

Cowboy strong.

"This is good news." Sawyer chucked Cash on the shoulder. His findings filled Sawyer with so much hope that he'd nearly wrapped his cousin in a bear hug. But not in the middle of a Starbucks.

"We don't know that yet," Cash cautioned. "This is merely speculation. But we're on the right track. I feel it in my bones."

Cash had always had good instincts. That's why he'd been such a successful agent in the FBI. And now, a badass investigator for the Bureau of Livestock Identification.

"How soon until we know more?"

"I'll do my best, Sawyer. But greasing the right wheels takes time. In the meantime, let's not tell my folks. My dad'll go apeshit and start making a lot of noise. This needs to be done quietly, with discretion."

Sawyer nodded. "Until we know more, I won't say anything to my folks, either. I don't want to dare to hope yet."

"And even if it's true, Sawyer, the likelihood of a big, happy family reunion is next to nil. For her own safety, she may have to stay lost to us forever."

The answers could be bittersweet for sure. But Sawyer could only focus on one thing at a time. Right now, proof of life would be a major victory.

* * * *

The next day, Sawyer returned to Dry Creek Ranch. Cash, Aubrey, and Ellie stayed behind to take advantage of summer vacation and spend a few more days in the city. His aunt and uncle wanted to take Ellie to the zoo and to Alcatraz.

He'd been invited to stay but had declined, yearning to get home and begin hunting down the US Marshals' lead. Cash wasn't the only one with friends.

He pressed his back against the lumbar support of his leather seat to soothe the ache from sleeping on his aunt and uncle's sofa sleeper. All night, a metal bar had pressed against his vertebrae. He'd offered to get a hotel room but his family wouldn't hear of it. And it wasn't as if he hadn't slept in lots worse places. Besides, it had been a fun evening. They'd all stayed up late, playing a rousing game of Texas Hold'em, eating popcorn, and sipping his uncle's killer martinis. Ellie, of course, had stuck with grape juice.

It was a damned good visit.

But as he drove through the Dry Creek Ranch gate, his mouth ticked up and he got that feeling he always did when he saw his family's land stretched out before him. It was pretty damned awe-inspiring and it made a man happy to be home.

As he passed Gina's cabin, he slowed. Her BMW was parked where she'd last left it before leaving to go back to Los Angeles.

At his own home, he decided against parking in the garage and cut his engine in the driveway. Later, he might head to the coffee shop for dinner. Or raid Jace's refrigerator.

He grabbed his duffel from the back seat and climbed the stairs to his apartment. A gush of cool air and loud music hit him as soon as he walked inside.

He dropped his bag on the floor and followed the smell of browning onions. In the kitchen he found Gina at the stove with her back to him, dancing to a Rolling Stones song. Her hips swayed back and forth while he stood silently watching her, mesmerized.

As if sensing someone was there, she turned and jumped when she saw him. "Way to scare the shit out of me, Dalton."

"I see you're back in my kitchen." His eyes moved over her, taking in the clingy T-shirt and cutoffs.

"I'm making short ribs. Your beef, my recipe."

"What about LA? ChefAid?" She appeared to be in a good mood, which seemed odd given her situation. He'd kept up. There was nothing to celebrate.

"I couldn't take it anymore. Damned reporters found my hotel and chased me to work every day."

He noted she hadn't answered the real question. "Are you out of a job?"

"I own the frigging company, Sawyer."

"What about the rest of it?"

"ChefAid dumped me...or at least it's in the midst of dumping me. The company's signing Candace."

"And you know this how?"

She teared up, trying to pretend it was from the onions. "They told my lawyer and canceled our meeting next week. I'm only guessing about Candace. But, come on. It's got to be her. As far as my show, I don't know yet. FoodFlicks isn't returning my agent's calls. So, you tell me."

He cocked his hip against the counter. "You have a plan?"

"Yep," she said, trying to hold it together. But she was cracking. He could see the fission marks all over her face.

"Rebuild," she continued. "Make a new pilot. I was sick of the Italian shtick anyway. Ancestry.com says there's not a lick of Italian in me. Adopted, remember?"

He nodded. "Have you given up on proving that the story about you and Clay is a sham?"

"What the hell's the point? My reputation is in the toilet, my revenues are in the toilet, and I hate these people. I hate them, Sawyer. I hate them so much." She pressed her face against the wall and her body heaved with silent tears.

He pushed off the counter and pulled her into his arms. "Don't cry."

"Easy for you to say." She wiped her nose on the front of his shirt. "Everything I did...all the hard work...gone."

"You ever hear the saying 'There is nothing stronger than a broken woman who has rebuilt herself'?" His lips hovered over her hair. "You'll come back bigger and better."

"Maybe. Or maybe that was my one shot, my fifteen minutes, and now it's over. For good."

"Nah, you're too talented. And, Gina?" He gently grasped her chin and lifted her face so their eyes met. "The truth will eventually come out. You'll be vindicated."

"Yeah, when I'm like ninety." She sniffled.

He ripped a paper towel from the holder and held it to her nose. "Blow." She tilted her head and gave him a look.

He laughed. "I guess that came out...uh...not right."

Gina took the towel from him and wiped her watery eyes and then her nose. "You're a good friend, Sawyer Dalton."

For some inexplicable reason the word *friend* stuck in his craw. They were more than goddamn friends. To prove it, he covered her mouth with his and kissed her until he lost control. He hadn't realized how much he'd missed her until now.

She was into it too, kissing him back with a fervor that belied mere friendship. Her hands slipped into his back pockets and pulled him closer until they were grinding into each other, hungrily.

He angled her head and took the kiss deeper as he touched her breasts through her T-shirt. Her nipples hardened through the soft fabric and a growl escaped his mouth. God, he wanted her. He wanted her so much he could feel himself straining against the fly of his jeans.

She ran her fingers over the stubble on his chin. It was more tender than sexual, but the gesture made him hot just the same.

"You want to take this to the bedroom?" He started backing her out of the kitchen.

"Mm-hmm." She moved her hands under his shirt, lightly touching his stomach and he shuddered in a breath.

They didn't waste any time once they got to his room, tearing off their boots, shoes, and clothing. He pushed her down onto the bed and fell on top of her. She felt so good, everything about her. Her soft, damp skin. The hot pull of her mouth. The way she arched under him, silently begging for more.

She grabbed his hips and pulled him harder against her, crushing her breasts against his chest. He kissed his way down her neck to her chest, then, one at a time, rolled her nipples between his lips.

Her head thrashed against the pillow as she grabbed fistfuls of the top sheet while he spread her legs wide with his knee.

"You ready for me?" He touched her and found her already wet. "Oh, yeah, baby," he whispered in her ear, his chest expanding at the knowledge that he could do this to her. That he could make her so damned aroused.

He slid open the nightstand drawer and blindly searched for a condom. When he had it on, he entered her in one hard thrust. She called out, moaning his name in satisfaction, then thrusting up to meet him stroke for stroke.

He thought about her dancing in the kitchen, her body moving to the beat of the music. Her ass shaking and he nearly came.

"Let's slow it down for a second." He held her hips still while he moved slowly inside of her.

"Don't want to." She shook his hands away and tried to roll him under her, but he wouldn't let her.

"I want to make it last. I want it to be good for you." He kissed her neck. She turned her head to the side to give him better access. "I…"

"What?" he whispered.

"Nothing. It's just so good."

The best he'd ever had. Because of her, because of the way he felt about her.

With one hand, he held her arms above her head and began to thrust harder, simultaneously working her with his fingers. She squirmed against him, panting and trying to break her hands free. He let them loose and she gripped his shoulders, bucking wildly against him.

"Oh, Sawyer…Sawyer."

He kept kissing her. Her face, her lips, her throat.

"I'm—I'm—" She shuddered before she could get the words out. Her breathing quickened and her muscles clenched, and Sawyer felt her climax.

He bent her knees up so that her feet were flat on the bed and went deeper. Harder. Within a few seconds he was lost in the euphoric feeling of his own release.

He collapsed on top of her. Though completely sated, he wished their lovemaking had lasted longer. But once enveloped inside her warmth, he'd been unable to hold back. Sawyer was surprised he'd made it as long as he had.

He rolled her on top of him to save her from his weight and cushioned her head against his chest. They just lay that way. It was different than any time with her before or with anyone, for that matter. It felt permanent. Right.

"I can hear your heartbeat," she said.

He hitched his brows and his mouth curved into a half-smile. "Good thing. I'd hate to be dead."

She traced a line down his chest with her finger. "Thank you, I needed that."

And just like that the spell was broken. He rolled to the other side of the bed, angry. "Glad I could oblige." Maybe next time he could get her a blowup doll.

He hung his legs off the bed, crossed the room to the bathroom, got rid of the condom, and took a quick shower. Afterward, he found Gina in the kitchen, stirring her short ribs.

His phone rang and he was thankful for the distraction, because he had been about to say something to Gina that he probably would've regretted. Something to the tune of "I'm not your fuck buddy."

Chapter 19

Conflicted didn't even begin to describe the way Sawyer twisted Gina into knots. She was falling so deep for him, she was drowning. With everything else going on in her life, she couldn't deal with any more noise.

Then why the hell did you sleep with him?

Because he made her feel things she'd never felt before. Like she was more than her fictional TV persona. More than someone who was constantly trying to prove herself to the universe. More than the loser deep down inside she'd always feared she was.

But she couldn't let herself fall in love with him. When the time came to give her heart to someone, she would have to be back on top. Not needy and in a position of weakness.

Sawyer turned off the music, took his call into the bedroom, and shut the door. The only sounds in the house were the hum of the air-conditioner and the gurgle of the short rib juices in the Dutch oven.

She couldn't hear Sawyer's telephone conversation and assumed it had something to do with his work or the ranch. Alone with her thoughts, she thought about what he'd said.

"There is nothing stronger than a broken woman who has rebuilt herself."

She rolled the quote around in her head. She'd never heard it before, but glommed onto it like an anthem.

It would be tough to win back an audience with the rumors still swirling, especially while the beloved Candace played the victim. But eventually, people would realize that she hadn't run off into the sunset with Danny Clay and that the man was conspicuously absent from her life.

Little by little they'd forget. By then, Gina would have her house in order. A new pilot to sell to the networks and new brands to represent. This time, she wanted her names on the products and licensing rights.

Lord knew she had the money to make all these things happen. She just had to work hard and have patience. But she couldn't do that from the ranch, even if the idea of leaving hollowed out her insides.

Tomorrow, she planned to talk to Wendy about getting the paparazzi off her back. She'd even be willing to hold a press conference if it meant she could be rid of the hacks and live in peace.

Sawyer returned to the kitchen, breaking into her thoughts.

"That was Paolo Renato from *Eater*." He waited to see if she recognized the name. When she nodded—everyone in her world knew Paolo Renato— he continued, "There's a rumor that Danny Clay set the whole thing up when he found out his wife was divorcing him. Apparently, she'd always been jealous of your success and Danny wanted to stick the knife in. Humiliate her in public. But it backfired, because he's out of a job and it's a PR nightmare. FoodFlicks wants nothing to do with him. Paolo says he can't corroborate the story, but it's spreading through the food industry faster than a California wildfire.

"It explains the texts and the dick pic. How easy. He uses one of those fake-message apps to make it look like you two are having a text conversation, then, through one of his minions, leaks it to the press."

"Danny?" She couldn't believe it. He'd seemed as surprised as her when the story had first broken. "Is Paolo working on nailing it down?"

"Everyone is, according to Renato. For the tabloids this new revelation would give the story a second news cycle. For the mainstream media this is legitimate news. A celebrity capsizing an innocent person's career is no joke. I'd like to help Paolo get it first. *Eater* is reputable."

"Are you kidding? It's one of the few food publications that's read by both the general public and the industry. It would go a long way to absolving me. But how? Unless Danny confesses, I don't see any way of verifying that it was him."

"I sent Renato the duplicate photo of Candace and Danny," Sawyer said. "Made him promise our conversation was off the record. You need to call my mom. Tell her that I talked to Paolo and that he wants the story."

"I will. But Sawyer, do you think it's strange that Danny would put himself at such risk like that? Why would he make himself look like a cheater? How would that buy him anything?"

"Revenge against Candace for divorcing him. You're younger, more successful. He wanted to mortify her in the public eye." Sawyer hitched his

shoulders. "Hell, cops say marriage alone is a motive for murder. Twenty-five to life has never been much of a career starter. Yet, people kill their spouses all the time. He was probably so blinded by rage he didn't think about the consequences."

She supposed he was right but what an awful extreme to go to. And to take Gina with him. That was the part that angered her the most.

"I'll call your mom. Thank you for contacting Paolo."

He didn't respond. After sex he'd grown distant. She started to ask him about it when his phone rang again.

He answered and handed her the phone. "Speak of the devil."

She gave him a quizzical look and took his cell from him. It was Wendy. Gina told her about Sawyer's latest revelation and put the phone on speaker. They all talked at once.

"I'm hearing the same thing," Wendy said. "But at this juncture it's just idle gossip, nothing to work with."

"What about holding a press conference? I could say I don't know who fabricated the story, but it's not true. Show the original photo of Candace and Danny on the beach. Tell them that regardless of whether they believe me or not, Danny and I are not engaged, dating, or otherwise involved."

"We could've done that weeks ago, Gina. Until we can give a corroborated version of the true story, what does it buy you? Nothing. It only draws more attention to the negative story."

Gina looked at Sawyer to see if he agreed with his mother. Poker face. He either approved of Wendy's advice or didn't want to get in the middle.

"Okay, but I can't stay here forever. The rest of my business is flailing without me."

"Give me a couple of days to see if I can at least calm things down here as far as the media situation, throw them the Danny rumor. Let them chase him for a while," Wendy said.

"I'll start packing." This time, Gina knew she'd be leaving for good.

* * * *

The next day, Gina hiked across the ranch to Aubrey and Charlie's store and studio. A month ago, she'd despised the place: the dust, the ticks, the cows, and the log cabin.

She still wouldn't call herself a country girl, but Dry Creek Ranch had come to hold a special place in her heart. Even the cabin had grown on her, or at least it had lost some of its creepiness. The view outside her window might not be the Pacific Ocean, but the creek and endless skyline

of mountain peaks were breathtaking. And the peacefulness of the ranch had wrapped itself around her like a soft blanket. But it was the people, most of all, that, she'd come to love.

One in particular.

She stopped to catch her breath and leaned against a tree trunk, knowing that she'd broken her self-imposed rule. She'd let Sawyer in too deep and now he was embedded in her soul. She tried to fool herself into believing that a 500-mile separation wasn't that far and they could still see each other. But intellectually she knew they were doomed—like all her relationships. There wasn't space in her life for a full-time man, nor did she have the emotional wherewithal to make the room.

She pushed herself off the tree, emphatic that the two of them weren't meant to be and kept walking until she reached the old barn. Charlie was busy showing two women a farm table made from reclaimed barn wood. Gina quickly ducked into Aubrey's office, sight unseen.

Aubrey waved, pointed to the phone cradled between her ear and shoulder, and made the crazy sign with her finger.

"Laney, calm down. She's right here." Aubrey handed the phone to Gina and mouthed "Good luck."

"What's going on?" Gina asked on full alert, afraid that the paparazzi had discovered her hiding place and had descended on the coffee shop.

"I need you to get your tiny butt down here. Jimmy Ray has the flu and I've got a party of thirty-eight due at one o'clock. It's Tiffany's birthday lunch and I ain't canceling it."

"You want me to cook?" Gina asked, confused. Why did everyone assume that the title "chef" meant she'd worked in a restaurant kitchen?

Her first job out of culinary school had been in the kitchen of Steven Spielberg and Kate Capshaw's home, making healthful meals for their family. It had been a plum job, because in LA it wasn't what you knew, it was who you knew.

She'd gone straight from the Spielberg home to FoodFlicks, never once interning under a restaurant chef or even flipping burgers at a fast-food joint.

"Yes, I want you to cook," Laney trilled on the other end of the phone. "I'm up shit's creek here without a paddle. Now get movin', young'un."

"Laney, I can't—" There was a dial tone before she could finish her sentence. Gina turned to Aubrey. "She hung up on me."

Aubrey laughed. "Of course she did. She didn't want to give you a chance to say no."

"I don't want to leave her in the lurch, but…"

"You're a world-famous chef, not a short-order cook." Aubrey took the phone from Gina and hit instant redial.

Gina wrestled it away and pressed the *end call* button before anyone picked up. "I'll do it." She could handle thirty-eight people. She'd done dinner parties for the Spielbergs dozens of times, though it had been years. It was like riding a bike, she told herself. Besides, it would be her last hurrah in Dry Creek.

"You're sure? You certainly don't have to."

"No big deal."

She went home, found her floppy hat and sunglasses, and managed to get to downtown Dry Creek without getting lost. There was a parking space in front of the coffee shop. Instead of going through the front entrance, she slipped through the alley and pounded on the back door.

Laney answered, took one look at Gina's getup, and rolled her eyes. "No one's gonna see ya in the kitchen, girl."

"I had to get here first." She squeezed past Laney's ample bosom and came inside. "You're welcome."

She looked around the small kitchen, which was hot as hell. It was a far cry from the gleaming stainless-steel restaurant kitchens of her chef friends. Absent the overwhelming smell of cooking oil, it was spick-and-span, she'd give it that.

"Where's the menu and my mise en place?"

Laney found one of the restaurant's greasy menus and shoved it in Gina's hand. "I don't know what that last thing is."

Gina stared down at the menu. "Not this. What are we making for the luncheon?"

"Everything in there." Laney nudged her head at the menu.

Gina blinked her eyes a few times, trying to understand. "Are you saying this isn't prix fixe?"

"Now why would we do that? Not everybody likes the same thing."

"So these thirty-eight guests can order anything in here?" She shook the menu, which easily weighed two pounds, in Laney's face.

Laney put her hands on her hips and stared down her nose at Gina. "Just like everyone else in the restaurant."

"Oh my God." Gina rushed to the order window and peeked into the dining room. There were a few diners mopping up the last of their eggs. "Who cooked for them?"

"Jimmy Ray did. But I sent him home before he collapsed and made everyone else sick."

Just to make sure she wasn't mistaken, Gina's eyes moved to the front door where the sign still said *open*. "You're not closing for this lunch, are you?"

"Pfft, you may be a high-ass rich girl from the city, but I've got bills to pay. Hell no, we're not closing for lunch."

Gina squeezed the bridge of her nose. "Laney, do you expect me to pick up where Jimmy Ray left off?" Again she waved the menu in Laney's face. "I don't even know his recipes."

"JoJo and I will help you."

Gina pivoted around to find a guy missing his front tooth who had more tattoos than all the inmates in San Quentin put together. He was in a white apron, grinning. She assumed he was JoJo.

What had she gotten herself into?

She took off her ridiculous disguise, found another apron hanging from a pegboard near the deep fryers, and quickly put it on. She scooped her hair up and twisted it on top of her head in a knot.

Laney handed her a hairnet. When Gina balked, Laney sent her a disapproving glare. "You want the health department to write me up?"

She complied.

"JoJo, you start the mise en place." He stared at her blankly. "Ah, for Christ's sake! Chop and peel the vegetables, get out the spices, set up the ingredients, and put them all"—Gina glanced around until she landed on a steel prep table—"there."

"You talking about the fixin's?" He went to the large side-by-side refrigerator and started pulling out an assortment of ingredient bins.

"Yes. Thank you, JoJo."

He continued to organize and Laney poured fresh peanut oil into the fryers. The front door chimed, signaling that the lunch crowd had begun streaming in.

Time to get busy.

She worked for an hour, covered in a layer of sweat, filling orders. Mostly sandwiches, burgers, and melts with the occasional salad. Nothing terribly complicated.

When she tried to garnish each plate, Laney swept them away and tsked. "This ain't the Four Seasons."

Gina had been doubtful about JoJo but he manned the fry station like a champ while she dredged pieces of chicken through her own batter. If anyone had noticed that it wasn't Jimmy Ray's secret recipe they hadn't complained. At least there were vats of his waffle batter in the fridge.

A little before one o'clock, Laney pushed ten four-tops together and taped a piece of notebook paper in the center that said *reserved*. Soon after, members of Tiffany's party began trickling in with colorful gift bags. Every so often, Gina discreetly popped her head in the dining room to gauge the crowd size.

Full house.

Dry Creek needed another damn restaurant. She used her arm to wipe the sweat from her face and went to work on four "Jaspers," steak sandwiches with sides of fries and frosty mugs of homemade sarsaparilla. According to Laney, the special was named for Sawyer's grandfather.

"We need more fries, JoJo." Only one hour working together and already they were like a well-oiled machine.

She threw four steaks on the grill and caramelized rings of onions, going on instinct. Until someone cried foul, she was winging it. To take the time to go through Jimmy Ray's recipes would back them up at least an hour.

She flipped a tuna melt, let it turn to a golden brown, plated it with a scoop of Laney's potato salad, and called "order up."

Laney bustled into the kitchen with her notepad in hand. "Whoo-wee!" She pressed a hand against her lower back. "We're busy today. Ten chicken and waffles, eight chicken-fried steaks, six Caesar salads with chicken, four Cobbs, three patty melts, three tuna melts, two soups, and two Jaspers for the Tiffany party." She hung the order from a clip on the wall behind the griddle.

"Shit." Getting everything out at the same time was going to be a bitch. "You hear that, JoJo?"

"Yep." JoJo wasn't much for words, but he could fry like nobody's business.

"How we doing on the rest of the crowd?"

"So far, so good." Laney grabbed up two of the Jaspers, settled them into the crook of her arm, and went for the other two. "Maria's got us covered at the front of the house. I'll come back and help y'all with Tiff's order."

Gina made up more batter for the chicken-fried steak and went back to dredging chicken. While those were on the skillet, she'd work on the salads, which would take a little time.

When Laney returned, Gina was putting the finishing touches on the Cobbs.

"Oh, hell no." Laney stood over the salads, disgusted. "That looks like a museum exhibit, not like a lunch entrée. Put some more food on that plate, girl. Last I looked lettuce didn't cost that much."

"It's a deconstructed Cobb." Gina let out a huff.

"More like anemic." Laney scooped up handfuls of romaine and dumped them on the plate, ruining Gina's presentation. "You want to starve my customers?"

"For damn's sake, at least put a little care into it." Gina rearranged the lettuce leaves, added more boiled eggs, grilled chicken, bacon, and blue cheese. "That enough for you? Finish here while I grill the steaks for the Jaspers."

Out of the corner of her eye, Gina saw Laney retrieve two store-bought salad dressing bottles from the cooler and yelled, "Don't you dare." She swiped the bottles out of Laney's hands. "Watch the steaks. I'll make dressing. Where do you keep the anchovies?"

Laney sniffed. "At the Whole Foods in Roseville."

"Seriously?" Gina threw her arms up in the air. "How do you have Caesar salad on the menu and no anchovies?"

"This is cattle country. We don't do surf, just turf."

"Whatever." Gina rolled her eyes and found a blender on the appliance shelf. Within minutes, she'd gathered up the ingredients to make a mustard shallot vinaigrette for the Cobb and a classic Caesar dressing, sans the anchovies.

As soon as the dressings were done, she diced up some sourdough bread to make croutons for the Caesar.

"How are the steaks doing?"

"Done." Laney took the meat off the grill and sandwiched them inside toasted French rolls slathered with Jimmy Ray's secret sauce. Probably A1 and Worcestershire, if Gina had to guess.

"JoJo, how's things at the fryer?"

"Good," he grunted, filling a basket with frozen potato slices.

"We've got to pick up the pace, people." Gina would be damned if everything didn't go out to Tiffany's table at the same time.

She went into overdrive, first filling the waffle makers with batter, then slapping a couple of burger patties onto the skillet. Meanwhile, Laney focused on the tuna melts and ladled creamy tomato soup that Jimmy Ray had made the night before from a giant pot on the stove. Within minutes, Gina loaded Laney and Maria up with plates and everyone in Tiffany's party got their food on time.

Another rush of diners came through the door and Gina started the process all over again. Finally, at three, business let up. JoJo went outside to smoke a cigarette while Gina set up a new mise en place for the dinner service.

The time went by so quickly that Gina didn't even notice the change in light outside as the afternoon turned to dusk. She'd been so pumped full of adrenaline that she'd barely taken a break, let alone looked out the window.

It was madness but addictive.

"We did it!" She high-fived JoJo, Laney, and Maria, who'd stayed for a second shift.

Laney and Jimmy Ray ran a skeleton crew. Most of the time, Laney handled the front of the house by herself.

"You did it." Laney took off her apron, balled it up, and threw it in a hamper near the back door. Then she reached up and grabbed a bottle of whiskey off the top shelf of the appliance rack and poured them each a shot. "What Jimmy Ray don't know won't hurt him." Apparently it was his private stash.

"*Salute.*" Gina threw back the brown liquid and shuddered as it burned her throat.

After the others left, she stayed to help Laney put the dining room back into some semblance of order for the next day. "You think Jimmy Ray will be better by tomorrow? If not…I could help out again."

"Nah, if he's not up to it I'm closing the restaurant. It'll be the first time since Jimmy Ray had his bypass surgery. To be honest, I could use the break." Laney sagged onto a stool behind the counter, kicked off her clogs, and rubbed her feet.

"You done good, skinny girl." Laney opened the cash register, pulled out a wad of bills, and stuffed them into Gina's hand.

"What're you doing?" Gina tried to give the money back but Laney wouldn't take it.

"You work, you get paid, child."

"I did it as a favor, not for money." This time, Gina attempted to shove the bills into the pocket of Laney's dress, but the woman slapped her hand away. "Oh for goodness sake, I'm rich, Laney."

"Makes no difference to me. Like I said, you work, you get paid."

"Fine, I'll just throw the money on the floor. Good night." She placed the bills next to the cash register and this time used the front door.

She was halfway to the ranch when she remembered that she'd left her floppy hat and sunglasses at the coffee shop. Oh well, it was time to get a new disguise.

Chapter 20

That evening, Sawyer was sitting on Jace's front porch, drinking a beer, when they saw a yellow Lamborghini coming up the road.

"Who the hell's that?" Jace looked at his watch. "Too late to be one of Charlie's customers. Besides, she's at a Chamber of Commerce meeting. And Aubrey's still in San Francisco with Cash."

Sawyer took another swig from his bottle. "Sweet ride."

Jace hitched his shoulders. "Kind of douchey, if you ask me."

Yeah, Sawyer could see that. The car was a little loud. And the driver was stirring up enough dust to choke every living thing on the ranch.

Jace got to his feet and stood at the railing, shielding his eyes against the sun. "We should probably start locking the gate in the evening."

Sawyer nodded and finished his beer as they both watched the sports car wend its way up the road to the ranch house. Brakes screeched when the driver spotted them and the passenger-side window came down.

"You lost?" Jace hollered.

"Not sure. I'm looking for Gina DeRose. She's staying on the Dry Creek Ranch. That's what the gate said off Dry Creek Road. Is there a resort around here by the same name?"

Sawyer and Jace exchanged glances, then Jace said, "Nope."

The guy sat there, waiting for Jace to say more, but he didn't. Sawyer smothered a laugh. His cousin could be a real son of a gun.

"Then this is the only Dry Creek Ranch?" the driver finally said.

"Yep."

When it was clear it was all he was going to get, the man got out of his car and approached the porch. That's when Sawyer got a good look and instantly recognized him. Medium height, medium build, medium shoe size.

It had probably not been his dick in the picture.

"Is this where Gina DeRose is staying?" Danny Clay flipped up his designer sunglasses.

Jace started to respond but Sawyer stuck out his arm.

"Why do you want to know?" Sawyer asked.

That seemed to throw their uninvited guest off. "I have business with her."

"No, you don't. Want to try again?"

Danny appeared flummoxed. "Are you a friend of Gina's?"

"Yes, and you're on private property."

"I need to talk to her. It's imperative."

"Okay. Tell me what you've got to say and I'll pass the information along."

"It's of a personal nature." Danny squinted up at Sawyer with the sun in his eyes.

"Sorry, that's the best I can do."

Danny took a look around, first at the house. Then he turned in a circle, taking in the pasture, the horse barn, and the mountain range in the distance. "What is this place?"

"Cattle ranch."

"Is there a hotel around here?"

"A few," Sawyer said. "Want directions?"

"Not until I talk to Gina."

"We already went over that." Sawyer leaned against the rail, crossing his arms over his chest. "Who told you she was here?"

Danny contemplated the question, giving Sawyer the sense he was deliberating on how much information to disclose. "A tabloid photographer. He said he'd been here and that a couple of cowboys roughed him up. At the time I thought he was using the term *cowboy* figuratively."

"Nope," Jace said.

"Are you friends with this photographer?"

Danny gave a mirthless laugh. "No, my wife—soon to be ex-wife—is."

That caught Sawyer's attention. "And she sent him here to take pictures of Gina?"

"That's what I need to talk to her about."

Sawyer had absolutely no reason to believe him. If the rumors were correct, Danny was a vindictive son of a bitch, who'd had no qualms destroying Gina's career just so he could get even with his wife. But something about the defeated way he was standing there, like a boy who'd just lost his dog, made Sawyer willing to listen to the man's story. Then he could kick Danny's ass all the way back to Los Angeles.

"Why don't you come up on the porch, have a cold one, and tell me what this business is you have with Gina?"

"You're not going to tell me where she is, are you?"

"Not in this lifetime, buddy."

Jace went inside the house, brought out a couple more beers, and pulled over one of the rocking chairs. "Take a load off," he told Danny, using his sheriff's voice, which pretty much translated to "Sit your ass down."

Danny hesitated at first, pacing in front of his car. But when the realization finally sunk in that this was his best—and only—option, he reluctantly climbed the stairs. "I would really rather say what I have to say to Gina herself."

"We got that, Danny."

Danny hadn't registered even an iota of surprise that Sawyer had used his name.

Fucking famous people.

If he'd come to confess and apologize, it was best that it went through Sawyer. He would only beat Danny up. Gina would kill him.

Jace handed him one of the brews and motioned to the rocker. Danny kept looking around as if he'd driven to the ends of the earth and now it was about to swallow him whole. He had trouble getting the cap off his beer. Jace took the bottle from him, placed the edge of the cap on the top of the porch railing, held the neck, and slammed the bottle down until it popped off.

"Here you go."

The Daltons weren't anything if they weren't hospitable.

Sawyer didn't push. He'd learned from being a reporter that silence was the best way to get someone to talk. Long spells of quiet made people uncomfortable so much so that they filled the gaps by spilling their guts.

So the three of them just sat there for a while, staring off into the distance. It was a beautiful evening. Warm, but not hot. Jace had lit one of those bug candles from Charlie's shop to keep the mosquitos away. The sun was still another few hours away from setting, leaving the sky a cloudless dark blue and the fields bathed in sunlight.

"You mind if I use your bathroom? The last time I stopped was Harris Ranch."

"Sure," Jace said. "Inside, through the hallway to the right."

"You want me to take a walk?" Jace asked when Danny was gone.

"You can stick around. The asshole's going to confess to making up the whole bullshit story about him and Gina as part of a warped plot to get back at his wife for divorcing him."

"And you know this how?"

"I don't for sure, but that's what I suspect is going to happen. If he does, I'd like you to be here. You'll make a good witness when my mom takes it public."

Jace leaned back in his chair, propping his boots on the railing. "Then Gina will be able to go home...resume her life." He looked at Sawyer and bobbed his chin. "You going to be okay with that?"

"Yep."

"Liar."

"Of the worse kind."

Jace chuckled. "You try asking her to stay?"

"In a roundabout way." He blew out a breath.

"What the hell does that mean?"

"I told her she should open a restaurant on the ranch...be our anchor."

Jace let out a whistle and shook his head. "That sounds like a business proposition to me. Real romantic, asshole."

Sawyer didn't bother coming clean with Jace about telling Gina that he was falling for her. Why belabor his humiliation? "She can't be Gina DeRose in Dry Creek Ranch, Jace. Her life is in Los Angeles. Her life is being on television."

"So? Your life is traveling to the ends of the earth and writing stories about it. If you want her bad enough, you make it work."

"That's the thing, Jace. She's a one-woman rodeo."

Before Jace could respond, Danny came outside. He sagged into the rocking chair and took a long pull on his beer.

"My wife set us up."

* * * *

For the second time that day, Danny told his story while Gina sat in Jace and Charlie's living room, listening raptly. At first, she hadn't believed him. But he had a sworn statement from Candace's assistant, who knew everything. She'd been afraid of getting caught in the middle of the sham and had come clean to Danny.

Furthermore, Danny had managed to hack into Candace's computer and had found that she'd been corresponding with a reporter from TMZ and had been the source of the pictures and the texts.

"Why me?" Gina asked. Of all the women to throw under the bus, why had Candace chosen Gina?

"She wanted everything you had," Danny said. "Jesus, if you could hear her whine about how you had used your father's name to claw your way to the top. She hated how FoodFlicks favored you over its other stars, how ChefAid had chosen you as brand ambassador because of your youth and beauty. She called you a no-talent, convincing herself that your success was based on your connections and looks instead of merit. Her jealousy of you kept her awake at night. It was sickening."

Gina had been clueless about Candace's animosity. Every interaction she'd ever had with the woman had been cordial, even friendly. Turns out, Candace Clay was a colossal phony.

As far as Gina's success, it had been hard-won. Her father's name had certainly gotten her foot in the door. She didn't take that for granted. But if her ratings had fallen, FoodFlicks would've canceled her show without hesitation. ChefAid had partnered with her because she was a trusted name in the business—her frozen food line and kitchenware were top sellers—not because an appliance company needed sex appeal to hawk stoves and dishwashers.

"Why you, then? Why the divorce?" It was a personal question that under ordinary circumstances Gina wouldn't have dared asked. But because the divorce was the impetus for Candace to concoct Gina's downfall, it seemed only fair that she get answers.

Danny's expression grew sheepish as he fiddled with a loose thread on the hem of his polo shirt. "I wasn't exactly an exemplary husband." He paused as three pairs of searching eyes bore a hole through him. "Candace's best friend and I have been carrying on an affair for years."

Everyone knew that Candace's best friend was Valerie DeWalt, whose cookbooks were legendary. Valerie was a regular fixture on the Clays' TV show.

"Candace found out at Christmas. As soon as our divorce is final, Valerie and I are getting married. This is Candace's payback."

"What I don't understand is why didn't Candace just expose you and Valerie. Okay, she hated my guts. But it seems like a lot of trouble and risk to punish me for your infidelity. What if she'd been caught?"

"She has been caught," Jace interjected.

"Not soon enough to repair the damage she's done." Gina pinned Danny with a stare, waiting for him to answer her question. Everything Candace had done seemed so outrageous, so conniving that it was hard to believe.

"This wasn't just about payback. It was a carefully orchestrated plan to win public sympathy and drum up enough publicity for her to become

the new it girl…to be you and grab everything she could, including being the new face of ChefAid."

Gina had never thought of herself as an it girl. In fact, she resented the label. An it girl implied that she was a flash in the pan, someone who wouldn't last. To hell with that. She planned to have the same staying power as Julia Child or Martha Stewart.

"It was really quite genius from a publicity standpoint," Danny continued. "Not only did she ruin me but she got a complete career makeover in the process. Because let's face it, before all this, she and I were second-string players. Our show had become tired, unable to compete with the likes of you and the other young FoodFlicks stars.

"We were no longer getting invitations to host specials or judge the competition shows. It was just a matter of time before we were has-beens. Or maybe we already were." He let out a bitter laugh. "The thing is, I'd like to continue to have a career, even if it's an off-season show at six o'clock in the morning. After Candace gets through with me, I'll need the salary."

Gina didn't know if the public would forgive him. Although he hadn't cheated with Gina, he'd been unfaithful in his marriage to a woman who had a significant following. Their show might've been limping along in the ratings, but Candace had been one of FoodFlicks' pioneers.

Not her problem, she reminded herself. She had her own career to rescue.

"How do we get this out into the world?" she asked Sawyer.

Sawyer stood up, walked behind the couch, and put his hand on Gina's shoulder, then turned to Danny. "Are you willing to go public with everything you've told us, including your relationship with Candace's best friend?"

Danny didn't hesitate. "Yes."

"Why?" Jace asked.

Gina had the same question. From where she was sitting Danny still looked like a major POS. What did going public buy him?

"The truth: I don't want her to win."

Wow, and to think these two people once took vows to cherish each other until death did them part. Yet another reason not to surrender to love, Gina thought.

"We could talk to Paolo at *Eater*." Sawyer came around the couch and sat next to Gina.

"Before we do anything, I want to loop your mom in on this."

"Wendy Dalton's your mother? That explains a lot."

Sawyer shot Danny a look and Danny waved him off. "I only meant that Candace had done her research. Everyone in the industry knew that Gina had hired Dalton and Associates to manage the crisis. Candace must've

traced Wendy to you and the ranch and made an educated guess that it was where Gina had gone to lie low. Then sent that wormy photographer to check it out and drum up more trouble."

So it hadn't been Tiffany who'd blown the whistle after all.

"How did you wind up talking to the photographer?" Sawyer asked.

"He approached me and threatened to divulge Gina's hideout if I didn't pay him five-thousand dollars." He addressed Gina: "I tried to contact you about it but you wouldn't take my calls."

"Did you pay him?" Jace asked.

"No, but I told him I'd have him arrested for blackmail. Frankly, I don't think he feared my threat."

It was another piece of the puzzle. They still had the man's memory card and could use the pictures to prove that he'd been to the ranch. It wouldn't take too much work to connect him to Candace. More damning evidence against her.

Sawyer asked Danny to retell the entire story. This time while Sawyer taped it on his phone. An hour later he sent the recording to his mother and sent Danny to the nearest motel.

It had been one crazy day.

"I can't imagine that this won't clear you," Sawyer said as he walked her home. "When the news breaks about what a scheming liar Candace is, ChefAid will rescind their offer to her and come running back to you. You could probably jack them up for more money."

Gina laughed, though none of it was funny. "I don't know about that." She wasn't even sure she still wanted to represent a company that had so easily dumped her after she'd put her heart and soul into promoting its products. From now on, she planned to be more discriminating about the brands she represented.

She thought about today, slinging hash at the coffee shop and her gut told her that in a similar situation Laney would've stood by her. The Daltons sure had. They had never once wavered in their loyalty. The knowledge of that put a lump in her throat.

"This will be a big story. Probably even bigger than the original story."

"You would know." She flashed a weak smile. The idea of facing the press all over again, even if it was to absolve herself, was exhausting. If she could take a long nap while the true story came out and wake up when it was over, she would.

"You going home soon, huh?"

She wondered if she'd heard regret in his voice or had she'd imagined it? Gina remembered his earlier words.

"Besides the fact that I wasn't looking for a relationship, our lives don't mesh. Not even a little."

She quickly replied, "Yes. I'll need to be hands-on to clean up the mess Candace made."

They'd arrived at the cabin and loitered on the front porch. She wanted so badly for him to come inside. To stay the night.

"I don't know how I can ever thank you for…Danny. The questions, the recording, the way you handled it. If it had been left to me I would've driven to Candace's house and strangled her."

Sawyer's lips curved up. "Probably not a good idea. Jace would've had to arrest you."

Under the porch light, they held each other's gaze, then he looked away. The break in contact left her bereft and a sudden wave of loneliness wrapped around her like a shroud of gray.

Was this what life was like before Sawyer?

She forced herself to believe that as soon as she got back to her old surroundings and buried herself in work, the melancholy would dissipate.

"I guess this is it." He shoved his hands in the pockets of his jeans and rocked on his heels.

The air was still, not even a light breeze. There was only the sound of the creek and the stridulating of crickets while she deliberated on whether to beg him to come inside. One last time together before saying good-bye.

But she could see in his deep blue eyes that he'd already cut the cord and that she'd only humiliate herself.

"I'm falling for you and I don't like it," he'd told her.

Well, she didn't like falling, either. She abhorred the vulnerable way it made her feel. It was easier to be alone, to have only herself to disappoint.

"I guess so," she responded and started to say she hoped they'd stay in touch but stopped herself. She didn't want to go through this each and every time they saw each other.

"You left a bunch of cooking stuff at my house. I could bring it by in the morning, leave it on your porch."

"Consider it my gift to you. Something to go with your mother's All-Clad pots."

He gave an imperceptible nod. "Safe travels then."

She watched him cross the field in the dark, her heart breaking a little piece at a time, and went inside.

Chapter 21

It was exactly how Sawyer predicted it would be. Even the *Los Angeles Times* had picked up the story about Candace Clay's revenge publicity hoax. It was all the morning shows could talk about.

Candace would probably never work again. If she had any hope of redeeming herself, she'd take a page out of the Wendy Dalton playbook and announce that she was checking herself into rehab and later write an apologetic autobiography.

The public had done a 180 on Gina and she was getting offers far and wide.

Purina wanted her to have her own dog food line, *Saturday Night Live* asked her to host and ChefAid had come crawling back with their tail tucked between their legs. Sawyer had no idea whether Gina had agreed to take the company back, but she could probably demand her price.

As far as her show, she was in negotiations for two more seasons and was the top contender to host a new FoodFlicks reality show: Home cooks competing to make the best dish out of random pantry staples or some such nonsense.

Sawyer had ascertained all of this information from his mother. It had been two weeks and he hadn't heard a word from Gina.

"Why don't you call her?" Cash had offered as if Sawyer hadn't thought of it himself. At least a dozen times he'd started to dial her number and hung up before her phone rang.

She was a star again, which was all she'd ever wanted. And he was free to continue his nomad's life as a reporter. Different lanes, he reminded himself.

"Wake up." Jace snapped his finger in Sawyer's face. "Where'd you go?"

"I was just thinking about my new assignment," Sawyer lied. "What? What did I miss?"

"Rumor is Randy's got another buyer, someone other than Mitch." Jace hung his arms over the corral fence railing while Cash threw a couple of flakes of hay to the horses. It was Sunday and they could linger over their morning ritual. "Word is that Mitch tried to lowball him and in the eleventh hour someone else swooped in."

"Must've been another developer to sell that fast." Sawyer assumed it was a company from Sacramento or the Bay Area, which might be even worse. Mitch was at least local and would probably make mild concessions on the scope of the project to appease the neighbors.

"I was at the coffee shop yesterday and no one seemed to know anything about it," Cash said.

Sawyer nudged his head at Jace. "Who's your source?"

"Charlie knows the real estate agent. She's bought a couple of pieces from the store and told Charlie there was someone else, someone with deep pockets. That's all I've got. But isn't it a public record?"

Nodding, Sawyer leaned against the side of the barn. "But not until it closes escrow and even then the buyer could've used an obscure company name." He shrugged. "But how long can it stay secret in this town? I suspect that within the next couple of days everyone will be talking about it."

He puffed out a breath in the still air. The sale should've set him off, but his mind was elsewhere these days.

"If it was Mitch, the whole world would've known about it by now." Cash wiped his hands on his jeans and joined them at the fence. "The sumbitch would've gloated. If not him, Mercedes would've screamed it from the rooftop of Reynolds Construction. I've never met a more devoted secretary. You'd think the woman was his mother. Or lover."

"No one will be gloating when the project comes up on the city council agenda and I go to the meeting and object to it. I'll get every damn neighbor to come with me."

The folks around here would walk through fire for Jace, Sawyer had no doubt about that. Jace wasn't just the sheriff, he was a friend to everyone in the county. But even so, he was no match for the machine.

"As soon as we find out we'll come up with a plan," Sawyer said. "Until then there's not a whole lot we can do about it."

Jace gave Sawyer a once-over. "You look like shit." Sawyer hadn't been sleeping well. "Charlie says Gina's back on top, kicking ass and taking names."

"They've been talking?" A wave of jealousy hit him, which was ridiculous. He was happy Gina and Charlie were friends. Aubrey too. The three women

had gotten tight while Gina lived on the ranch. He would've lost respect for Gina if she'd thrown them over once she'd reclaimed her supernova status.

"Emailing, I think. Last I heard, they were all going to Vegas for a pre-wedding bachelorette deal later this month." Jace lifted a brow. "I take it you haven't heard from her."

Sawyer gave a nonchalant toss of his head. "It was better to just end it. Who needs the fucking friend zone?"

Sawyer watched his two cousins weighing his words. Clearly, he wasn't fooling them.

"Did she say she just wanted to stay friends?" Cash studied him.

She hadn't said anything—that was the damn problem. "More or less."

"More or less? Speak English, writer boy." Jace poked Sawyer in the shoulder. "You screwed it up, didn't you?"

Yeah, probably. He should've pushed, should've been more forthcoming about his feelings. But it wouldn't have made any difference. "Can we talk about something else, for God's sake?"

"Remember what you told me when I was limping around, crying in my coffee over Charlie?"

"Or me, when I couldn't get my shit together about Aubrey?" Cash pinned Sawyer with a look. "You told me to cowboy the hell up. Right back atcha, partner."

"Yeah, yeah. Seriously, I don't want to talk about this anymore." Sawyer pulled his sunglasses out of his front pocket and put them on. "Cash, did you get ahold of anyone else about Angie and the US Marshals Service situation?"

They'd briefed Jace on everything they'd learned thus far. Like them, Jace's lips were sealed until they knew more.

"Still working on it," Cash said, but there was a hesitance in his voice. He knew something. Sawyer had dealt with enough itchy sources to know when someone was holding back.

"You've got something, don't you?"

Cash tipped his head. "Not ready to talk about it yet."

Sawyer started to press, but Jace held up his hand. "Let Cash do his thing."

Okay, Sawyer got it. It was like when he roughed out the first draft of an article with an editor looking over his shoulder, asking a lot of stupid questions before he'd had the chance to flesh out the story. Cash would talk when he had the full picture, not partial facts.

"I'm going home." He waved his hat in the air and started across the field.

Soon, the days would go from being oppressively hot to pleasantly warm. Jace's wedding would be here. Then they'd move the cattle down from the hills before the first freeze.

Before all of that, he'd travel to Central America for his magazine story, an assignment he'd been dragging his feet on accepting. If he didn't sign the contract that had been sitting on his desk for weeks, *Esquire* would find someone else to do the piece.

He'd sign, scan, and send it as soon as he got home, he decided. There was nothing pressing to keep him here. And a set of new surroundings would do him good.

Keep the memories at bay.

On the way to his loft, he took a detour to Charlie's. She was behind the barn, refinishing an old beadboard hutch on a drop cloth underneath a market umbrella.

She took the bandanna tied around her head and wiped the perspiration off her face.

"Hey, what brings you by?"

"Just to say hi."

"I'd give you a hug but I'm disgusting."

"What are you planning to do with that?" He pointed at the antique cabinet.

"Right now, just clean it up, maybe give it a fresh coat of chalk paint. Why? You interested?" She smiled, teasingly.

He cleared a tree stump that Charlie had been using as a table to hold her tools and took a seat. On the dead grass sat an upside-down clawfoot tub. He supposed it was next in the queue for some tender loving care. "How's business?"

"Good. A woman who's opening a bed-and-breakfast near the American River dropped eight-thousand dollars here yesterday. She's thinking of hiring Aubrey to do some design work."

"Nice."

They let the silence stretch while she went back to sanding and he finally said what he came for. "How's Gina doing?"

She stopped and wiped her face again. "I was wondering how long it would take you to get to that. Other than the fact that she's being pulled in a thousand different directions, she seems okay. More tense than she was when she was here."

Tense is what he would expect from a woman who ran a multimillion-dollar business. "I'm glad everything worked out for her." He rose. "Take it easy, Charlie. Stay out of the heat."

He started to walk away when she called him back. "It's none of my business, but you two seemed good together."

Funny, he thought his and Gina's short-lived fling had been fairly covert, even if his nosy cousins had been watching from the sidelines. Apparently their women were keeping tabs on his love life—or lack thereof—too.

"Not that good," he said and went home.

* * * *

Sawyer opened his front door the next morning to find Cash standing there.

"You going somewhere?"

"Thought I'd stroll over to the horse barn." It wasn't like he was getting anything done in the apartment. For the last hour he'd been attempting to make a pot of coffee. The first time, he'd forgotten to add beans and had had to start from scratch. On the second try, he forgot to refill the well with water. If he didn't screw his head on straight he was liable to leave the house without his clothes on.

Just to be sure, he looked down to see if he had buttoned his fly.

"Can I come in?" Cash waited for Sawyer to move away from the entrance.

"Yeah, sure." Sawyer shook his head as if to clear it of its cobwebs and motioned for Cash to follow him upstairs. "What's up?"

Cash went to the kitchen and helped himself to a mug of Sawyer's third-time's-the-charm coffee. "Let's sit in the front room."

At first, Sawyer assumed Cash had come to give him shit about Gina the same way he'd done when his cousin had dragged his feet with Aubrey. She'd almost moved to Las Vegas. But this was different. Gina was already gone, back to the world she'd come from.

But Cash's body language spoke volumes. His cousin's lips were pressed in a grim line and his back was ramrod straight. It reminded Sawyer of Cash's FBI days. He wasn't here to talk about Sawyer's relationship issues.

Angie.

For a second he froze, afraid to hear whatever Cash had come to say.

The only explanation for his sister's uncharacteristic radio silence all these years was that she was dead. At least it was the only explanation that made sense. On an intellectual level Sawyer had always known that. He just hadn't wanted to believe it. Even the New Mexico lead seemed hinky, as if someone had made the whole thing up to throw him off course.

He took a bracing breath. "Just say it."

"Sit." Cash took the big leather chair, sipped his coffee, and put the cup down on the coffee table.

Sawyer wanted to stand. He actually wanted to run, find a quiet place, and bury his head in the sand. He took the sofa, squeezing the armrest until his fingers went numb.

"She's alive."

Sawyer's ears roared and he wasn't sure he'd heard Cash right. "What?"

"Angela's alive, Sawyer. I don't know where she is or even how long she's been there, but she's safe. At least for now."

"WITSEC?" When Cash nodded, Sawyer steadied himself. He was finding it difficult to breathe. Angie was alive. All these years and she was alive. He had so many questions swirling around in his head that he didn't know where to start. "What is she involved in, Cash? Who—what—is she up against?"

Cash scrubbed his hand down his face. For the first time since he'd arrived, Sawyer noted how tired his cousin looked. He'd been sitting on this for a while, probably gathering enough information to give Sawyer a comprehensive picture. Or at least as comprehensive as he could.

"Everything is still pretty sketchy, Sawyer. I'm lucky to have gotten what I did."

Luck had nothing to do with it. Before Cash had been terminated, he'd been on the FBI's fast track. He'd not only been a terrific agent; he'd had lots of friends. Friends in high places. Sawyer suspected one of those friends had helped Cash put some of the pieces of Angie's disappearance together.

"All I know is that she got caught up with the wrong people. People, who on the face of it appeared to be do-gooders, but were anything but. Arms dealers is what I've been able to glean, though there's been no official confirmation."

"The commune in Taos?"

Clay leaned forward and put his hands on his knees. "Yeah, that's part of it."

"Why didn't she call?" Sawyer stood up and began pacing. "You were a fed. You could've helped her."

"Best I can come up with is that she got in over her head and didn't want to get us involved. Didn't want us to face any danger."

Sawyer's head snapped back. "She wasn't working with these people, was she?"

"No, I don't think so. According to my source, she legitimately thought these yahoos were trying to feed the world and stumbled across something she shouldn't have. That's where things get hazy. No one will tell me who

these people are or what Angie found. But somehow she went to the ATF or they came to her and she's been an informant ever since. I'm speculating here, but I'm betting this commune…farm…was the group's headquarters and Angie went to spy. Someone must've made her and that's when she had to go underground."

Sawyer tried to absorb what Cash was telling him. Arms dealers. Informant. Underground. He had more questions than answers.

"Why didn't she contact us, Cash? All these years and she couldn't pick up the goddamn phone? We could've kept her safe."

Cash leaned his head against the chair and squeezed the bridge of his nose. "I don't have the answer to that. But keep her safe? Sawyer, we don't have a clue what she was up against. For all intents and purposes she was an undercover agent for the federal government, infiltrating a dangerous organization. You ever think that perhaps she was trying to keep us safe?"

Angie would've gone to the ends of the earth to protect her family…her friends. There was no question of that.

Sawyer's emotions were all over the map. Relief, fear, even anger. He wanted his sister back. He wanted his family to be whole again.

"When can we see her?"

Cash rubbed his eyes with the heels of his hands. The room was so quiet, Sawyer could hear the pounding of his own pulse. He sat again, knowing the answer before Cash even muttered the words, "Maybe never."

Those were the rules of WITSEC. No contact with former associates. Sawyer had covered stories about the program, which for the most part was shrouded in secrecy. All anyone really knew was that a witness was moved to an undisclosed location, given a new identity and history, and was forbidden from staying in touch with or revisiting anyone or anything from his or her prior life.

"Is that what your people told you?"

"They didn't tell me much, Sawyer. As far as they're concerned, Angela Dalton no longer exists."

It was a tactful way of saying that although Angie was alive, she may as well be dead to her family.

"I assume at some point she'll have to testify." Sawyer crossed his legs and then uncrossed them. He was having trouble sitting still. "If there's a conviction, will she be able to resurface?"

"I don't know. It'll depend on what kind of crime organization this is. Is it a situation where if you chop off the head of the snake, you kill the heart? Or are we looking at something with long-reaching tentacles? I wish I had

the answers, Sawyer. Believe me, I tried to get them. I called in every favor owed to me. This was the best I could do."

Sawyer sank deeper into the couch. "What you did…what you got… she's alive, Cash. Angie is alive."

"She's alive. And if she follows the rules she'll stay safe. Let's not mess that up."

He wouldn't. Sawyer loved his sister too much to risk her security…her life. "But I have to tell my folks. I have to let them know that she's all right."

"Yep. Agreed. I called them already. My folks too. Yours are flying in. My parents will pick them up at Sacramento International. They'll be here in a few hours." Cash's eyes wandered to the clock on the wall. "I figure it'll be easier to break the news of Angie while we're all under the same roof."

"What about Jace?"

"I called him. He's on his way too."

Sawyer nodded. It was a lot to parse. He stared out the window off into the distance, thinking about Angie. Did she live in a big city or a rural town? Did she have a job? Friends? A man?

"You okay?" Cash rose and Sawyer got to his feet as well.

"Yeah. Just need a little time for it to sink in."

"I've got to put in some time on the job before everyone gets here. You want to do this here?"

Sawyer absently nodded.

After Cash left, Sawyer walked around the apartment in a fog. He remained that way until his entire family descended.

The kids stayed at Jace's house, but everyone else gathered in Sawyer's living room. Aubrey and Charlie put drinks and snacks out.

"Don't hold us in suspense," Jed announced.

Shifting in his seat, Dan leaned closer to his brother and tilted his head to the side. "I assume we're here about the ranch. I also assume it's an emergency, otherwise this wouldn't have been so last-minute."

"It's not about the ranch, Dad, it's about Angela."

A hush fell over the room and Sawyer saw his parents visibly flinch. Wendy clutched Dan's hand while her other hand gripped the sofa armrest.

Sawyer cut a look to Cash, giving him a silent go-ahead to relay his information.

"She's alive."

Wendy made a noise deep in her throat and covered her mouth. Dan started shaking. Someone said something, but Sawyer was too consumed with watching his parents to distinguish who or even what they'd said. Maybe it had been "Thank God."

Cash let the story unfold in his no-frills, just-the-facts way. When he finished, the room exploded in questions.

"When can we see her?" Tears streamed down Wendy's face.

Jed closed his eyes. Being a former cop, he knew, of course.

"Maybe never, I'm afraid." Cash explained the rules and workings of WITSEC.

"We'll hire around-the-clock security," Sawyer's dad argued. "I want my daughter home and whoever these thugs are to be brought to justice."

"Dad, we have no idea what the backstory is on this or even how deep Angie's in...what she's up against." Sawyer took a deep breath. "But for the first time in five years we have proof that she's alive and safe, which is more than we had yesterday."

"And for that I'm very thankful, son. But this is—"

"Torture," Wendy finished. "It's pure torture knowing that she's out there somewhere and we can't see or talk to her."

Sawyer pulled Wendy in for a hug. "I know, Mom. But this is good news. You know Angie. Wherever she is, whatever she's doing, she's happy. Remember how you used to call her Sunny."

"My sunny delight." Wendy sniffled.

"That's right. Because no one was ever more optimistic than Ange. She was saving the world one cause at a time." A laugh caught in his throat.

"There's nothing to say that she'll be in WITSEC forever," Jace offered.

"These things are always fluid," Cash seconded. "In the meantime, I've been assured that she's fine...secure. I don't know about you, but for me that's a giant weight off."

There was a chorus of agreement.

After the shock wore off, a calm spread through the room and then a sort of jubilation. For all the consternation over Angie's WITSEC situation, they'd finally solved the mystery. Just knowing that she'd survived these past five years was something to celebrate.

For dinner there was an impromptu cookout at Jace's. Many steaks, burgers, beer, and wine were consumed over more conversation about Angie as they speculated about her situation. When they'd worn out every possible scenario, they skipped to talking about the ranch's new venture.

"I love the idea of the butcher shop." Wendy topped off her glass of Cabernet. "Your grandfather would've adored it."

"It'll take some time for us to get there, but it's definitely in the hopper for the future." Jace got up from the table. "Anyone want seconds before I shut down the grill?"

"I'm stuffed." Jed also got up, hooked his arm around Jace's neck, and helped him with cleanup.

"Anyone talk to Randy?" Dan asked.

"Yeah." Jace tossed a couple of empty beer bottles into the trash bin. "He got an offer from a Sacramento developer. Apparently, Mitch is trying to raise funds so he could beat the other guy's offer. Randy was straight with me...says he's going to go with the highest bidder. If Mitch doesn't come through in the next couple of days, Randy says he'll seal the deal with the folks from Sacramento."

Dan grabbed another beer from the mini-fridge. "How much are they offering?"

"Don't know, but I'm guessing it's close to asking. Randy wants what we want. Someone who'll use the ranch for agriculture. But no one with cattle was interested and at the end of the day it's business."

"On our way out tomorrow, I plan to stop by and say hello," Dan said. "I know this is killing him. All Randy ever wanted to do was ranch. Even when we were kids. Poor son of a gun."

The conversation turned to Charlie's store and Aubrey's design firm and ultimately Jace's upcoming wedding. Afterward, Sawyer's mom asked him to take a walk.

He intentionally avoided the direction of Gina's old cabin and they followed the creek to the horse barn.

"Big day, huh?"

"The only thing that would've made it better is to have shared it with Angie." Wendy took Sawyer's hand. "But tonight I will sleep. Do you know how long it's been? I haven't made it through a night since the day Angie disappeared." She made a fist with both their hands and put it against her heart. "Oh, Sawyer, it's a miracle. And you, Cash, and Jace worked so hard to find her. I'm so proud of you."

She stopped and reached up to stroke his face. "Now tell me what's wrong. You look tired...worn out. I don't think that has anything to do with your sister. You've been moping around all night...looking blue."

"No, I haven't."

"Sawyer." She put her hands on her hips and cocked her head to one side. "I'm your mother and a mother always knows."

Precisely. That's why he didn't want to have this conversation with her.

"I'm fine, Mom."

"Is that why you call me every couple of days to ask about Gina? Is that why she calls me, pretends to act like it's business and then proceeds to interrogate me about you? It's ridiculous, Sawyer. It's so obvious that the

two of you care about each other. If we've learned anything from Angela it's that time is too short to waste. If I could take back all the silly lectures, the criticisms, the yelling matches to spend even one more day with your sister, like I am with you now, I'd do it in a heartbeat."

She paused and wrapped her arms around herself. "I'm going to let you in on a little secret. Despite Gina's facade, she not as self-assured as she likes people to think. For all her tough talk, she's not as strong as you."

"She's stronger than you think, Mom." Most people would've folded under the pressure Gina had been under. No matter how many times circumstances knocked her down, she'd gotten up again. Hell, the woman was Tyson Fury.

"Not like you, my beautiful boy." Wendy reached up on tiptoes, pulled his head down, and kissed him on the forehead. "If you want her, Sawyer, you've got to fight for her. Otherwise, she'll let fear rule her and bury herself in the Gina DeRose persona she's created for herself. Don't let your fear do the same. You might miss out on something really special."

They walked back to his loft, the sun setting low in a paint-streaked sky. No more words about Gina passed between them, just small talk. Sawyer's dad met them at the loft and they spent the rest of the evening watching a movie together.

Afterward, Sawyer gave them his bedroom and took the couch. In the morning, they ate breakfast together. Cash's parents came up just long enough to say good-bye before loading Wendy and Dan's overnight bags in the car.

"We'll stop by Randy's on the way to the airport and wish him our best," Dan said.

Sawyer went outside with them and waved good-bye from the driveway, then came upstairs and lingered over a second cup of coffee.

For lack of nothing else to do, he shuffled through the *Esquire* contract on his desk, picked up a pen, then put it back down. For the rest of the morning, he paced and checked his phone over and over again.

At lunchtime he started to make a sandwich, decided he wasn't hungry, and returned the sliced beef, cheese, and mayo to the refrigerator.

About one, he realized this wasn't going to work. If he stayed home, walking the floor, he'd go stark, raving mad. He swiped his keys off the hall tree and jumped in his Range Rover.

The next thing he knew he was on Interstate 5, following the signs to Los Angeles.

Chapter 22

"Tell ChefAid I'm not interested." Gina sat at her desk, turning down the third counteroffer since Tuesday from the company that had been so willing to ditch her when the chips were down. The CEO at ChefAid kept sweetening the pot and Gina kept saying "No."

"This one seems too good to pass up," Linda said.

After the *Times* piece hit newsstands, her manager had been juggling offers faster than a circus clown. The story, "A Hollywood Horror Tale for the Ages," gave a blow-by-blow of how Candace had attempted to torpedo Gina's empire to enhance her own career. There was nothing like a phoenix rising from the ashes to excite exploitive corporate executives. They all wanted to hitch their wagons to Gina's renewed stardom.

"Don't care how good it is. Tell them to go fu—Just tell them to go away, that we're not interested."

"What is Robin doing about FoodFlicks?"

"We're still working on it. If I sign for another season it won't be for *Now That's Italian!* I want a fresh start, something different."

The sad truth was ever since she'd returned to LA, she'd been miserable. She tried to tell herself that it was a simple case of ennui, that she needed to shake things up. But how could someone suffer from boredom when they'd been doing nothing substantive for the last six weeks? Unless, of course, she counted cooking. She'd done a lot of that.

She closed her eyes for a second and tried to summon the zen of working in Sawyer's kitchen. But all she saw was Sawyer. There he was, all six-two feet of him with his thumbs hitched in the pockets of his Levi's, a smile playing on his lips, looking like he could handle the world.

Her heart folded in half.

She missed him so much it hurt. The only other time she'd ever felt this alone was when her father died.

Her mother's death had brought great regret. Gina wished she could've been the daughter Sadie had wanted. She had grieved her mother's passing and even now, missed her. But the loss of Sadie hadn't left a gaping hole in her the size of the Grand Canyon.

Not like it had with Sawyer.

"Gina…Gina." Linda's voice snapped Gina back to business. "What do you want to do about the dog food offer?"

"I don't even have a dog. It's ridiculous." She swiped her hand in the air and waved away the offer.

"I suppose you want me to tell Supplycrafters that we're not interested too."

"Not yet."

Linda lifted her hands, palms up, perplexed. "You're turning down ChefAid but considering Supplycrafters They don't even manufacture food equipment for the home cook. It's all industrial…for restaurants."

"They didn't treat me like a leper. Besides, I have friends in Dry Creek who could use new fryers for their coffee shop. Maybe we could wangle a deal."

"I'm sure if you signed on the dotted line you could get your friends a professional-grade oven and a dishwasher too. Even a walk-in refrigerator." Linda laughed. "You'd be better off buying them as gifts. Otherwise, you're tying yourself to a company that's off-brand. We should entertain the GE offer if you want to continue the home-appliance route."

"That's the thing, I want a change." The problem was she had no idea what that change looked like. It just didn't resemble anything in her past or current portfolio.

"Then we should take one of the single-serve coffee deals. I vote for the one George Clooney does…Nespresso." Linda waggled her brows and Gina laughed.

"Put that one on the to-be-considered pile along with Supplycrafters I want to examine all my options before I make any decisions."

"Why don't I send Darby out for lunch and we can eat while we start sorting through the pile and eliminating the ones you definitely don't want."

"Like RollAuto?" Gina shook her head, befuddled. What in the world did car parts have to do with food?

"Don't worry, I crossed that off the list." Linda made her way to the credenza and pulled out a stack of takeout menus. "What are you hungry for?"

"I'm not."

"You need to eat, Gina. You didn't touch breakfast and Darby got your favorite muffins from La Farine."

"I put on a few pounds while I was on the lam." Homemade ice cream, berry pie, strawberry shortcake, and all the other goodies she'd made while at the ranch. "I'm trying to lose them before we start taping a pilot for the new show."

"Why? The weight looked good on you." The subtext of that was Gina didn't look so good now. In the last two weeks she'd shed a few pounds.

She tried to tell herself that she was too busy picking up the pieces to eat. But honestly, she simply didn't have an appetite. For the first time in her adult life, she was questioning her choices. Questioning whether this was where she wanted to be. All her life she'd clawed and climbed to be famous, successful, rich.

But what had it gotten her?

A beautiful home in Malibu where the rooms were empty. A cooking show that ironically didn't allow her to cook. A business empire that prospered or failed at the whim of her popularity. And legions of fans who would turn on her in an instant.

No family or friends who were loyal to the bitter end. No one she could cry to when the day went wrong. No one to celebrate when the day went right.

No one who loved her.

Here, she was truly alone.

Until now, she'd never noticed the absence of relationships in her life. Never missed not having someone to come home to. She'd been too busy trying to take the world by storm. But since leaving Dry Creek Ranch… leaving Sawyer…the emptiness had made her feel hollower than the show business she pretended to love.

"You know what, Linda, I think I'll go out to lunch." She pressed the intercom on her desk and asked Darby to come to her office.

A few minutes later, Darby popped her head through the doorway. "What can I do for you?"

"Could you book me a charter flight? I'd like to leave as soon as possible."

"I'll get right on it."

The look of shock on Linda's face was priceless. "What about all these offers?" She bobbed her head at the clutter of contracts and paperwork strewn across the conference table. "I thought—weren't we planning to sort through them? And where are you going?"

"I suddenly have a yen for chicken and waffles."

She slung her purse over her shoulder and left the building. Four hours later she was preparing for takeoff.

* * * *

Sawyer pulled into the parking lot of a law office along PCH near Malibu. Gina lived somewhere around here but he didn't have the address. And in general, celebrities were unlisted. He had no reason to believe Gina would be any different.

He searched for the location of her office building and studio on his phone, figuring he'd have better luck finding one of those. But it was late, past nine, and he doubted she'd still be there.

He'd driven straight through from Dry Creek Ranch, stopping only once at a rest area to take a leak. Even with a traffic backup in the valley, he'd made excellent time.

Contemplating the wisdom of calling his mother for the address, he decided it would be better to phone Gina herself. Give her a heads-up because who knew what kind of security she had?

Plus, just showing up without any notice might not be the best strategy.

He took a deep breath and punched in her number, girding himself. There was a good chance she'd tell him to go home. If she did, he'd have to go to plan B, because he wasn't leaving until she heard him out.

"Where are you?" she answered, surprising him.

"In a parking lot on Pacific Coast Highway, not far from your house. I think. What's the address and I'll come over."

There was a long pause. She was going to tell him not to come. He'd insist that they at least meet at a restaurant. What he had to say wouldn't take long.

"The problem is I'm not there," she finally said. "I'm here."

"Where's here?"

"Your barn loft apartment. I've been waiting for you for hours."

He scrubbed his hand down his face, surprised.

"Okay, I'll turn around and come home." He'd fly if it wasn't for the fact that he had his Range Rover.

It took a few minutes, but it dawned on him to ask why. Why was she in Dry Creek?

But before he could ask she said, "Charlie said you were here this morning. Your car's gone. Did you just get to LA?"

"About an hour ago, if you count the valley. How about you?"

"I flew in this afternoon."

"Why?"

"The same thing could be asked of you...Unless you were visiting your parents."

"No, they were just in Dry Creek."

"Charlie told me they left this morning. She told me about Angela too. Oh, Sawyer, you found her."

"Not quite. But we know she's alive. It's a long story. I'll tell you everything when I get there. Is that why you came? Because of Angie?"

"No, I only found out about her after I got here. But it's incredible, Sawyer. You must be so relieved."

"I am. More on that later. But I need to talk to you. Really talk. So why'd you make the trip?" As far as he knew, she'd taken everything she owned with her when she'd left, including his goddamn heart.

"Same reason—I need to talk to you too. In person. But don't come home tonight. It's too much driving. I'll worry that you'll fall asleep at the wheel. Wanna stay at my place? I can give you the door code to get in."

"Sure." He didn't bother to write anything down when she rattled off the numbers.

"Sawyer?"

"Hmm?"

"Uh...I'll tell you when you get here."

He grabbed something to eat at an all-night diner, tanked up on coffee, and was home just before dawn the next day.

Gina's Louis Vuitton luggage was scattered across his entryway. This time, he managed not to trip over anything and a smile bloomed in his chest. His little pain in the ass was back. What he wouldn't do to make it permanent?

She was still fast asleep, her hair fanned across his pillow while the early-morning light made a soft halo around her face. It took all his willpower not to brush a kiss across her lips. But he didn't want to wake her.

He quietly went to the kitchen, where he made a pot of coffee. While he poured himself a mug, she came out of the bedroom.

"You're here." She blinked up at him, trying to clear the sleep from her eyes. "I thought you were going to stay overnight in LA...come back today."

"Change of plan."

They both stood there awkwardly when he decided to take the bull by the horns.

"This isn't going to work for me."

She looked down at herself. "Me staying here and sleeping in your bed?"

"No, you not sleeping in my bed."

He ate up the distance between them with two long strides, took her arm, led her to the living room sofa, and without any fanfare laid it out for her. "I'm in love with you." He waited a beat for that to sink in and continued, "If you're not in love me, then we don't have much to talk about. But if you feel even half of what I feel we need to figure out how to make this work. LA's where your company is…where you make your television show. I get that. So I'll split my time between here and there."

She stared at him with her mouth agape, saying nothing.

"Gina?"

"I thought you were trying to fight this thing you and I have for each other." She waved her hand between them. "I think your exact words were, 'I'm falling for you and I don't like it.'"

He scrubbed his hand over his unshaven face. God, had he actually said that? For a professional wordsmith he had no game. "At the time I said it I was scared shitless. Now, I'm scared shitless of losing you." He took in a deep breath. "These last two weeks have been hell, Gina. I'm so crazy in love with you that I can't sleep. Can't eat. Can't work. Can't think of anything but you."

She leaned into him and stared into his eyes. "I came to tell you the same thing."

"Yeah?" His heart did a two-step. He got up, lifted her, and sat down with her in his lap. "So you and I…we're a thing now, right?"

"I think we've been a thing for a while and we didn't want to admit it to ourselves. We're kind of stupid that way."

He chuckled. "You know us cowpokes. We're dumber than dirt."

"Nope. Smartest man I ever met." She laid her head on his chest and burrowed in.

"Look, I know it'll be difficult having me live here and you in LA. Maybe once we get this ranch project up to speed I can move to Los Angeles. In the meantime, I'll come as much as possible."

"You'll hate that." She traced his lips with her finger. "The ranch is where you belong."

"Not if it means being without you." He'd go to the ends of the earth if it meant being with her.

"Uh-uh." She shook her head. "That won't work for me."

His mouth grazed her ear. "You have a better suggestion?"

"I do. I came to walk it through with you."

"Start walking."

"I move here. Live with you in this excellent loft apartment, where I have unlimited access to your kitchen."

He did a double take. It was the last solution he expected. "What about your show? Your business?"

"I've spent a lot of nights thinking about just that. My future. Because you...this ranch...have changed me in ways I never thought possible. The last couple of weeks without you have been miserable. I want a whole new direction, Sawyer. I want to cook again. I want to have friends...family. I want my time in Dry Creek to be my forever."

She took a deep breath and pushed forward. "I can run everything from here, including the frozen food and kitchenware divisions. Our processing plants are in the Central Valley, so I'm actually closer here. The housewares are made overseas and are distributed out of New York, Chicago, and Los Angeles. I have good people for that and am only a plane ride away if they need me. These days, with a computer and high-speed internet, you can run a business from anywhere."

While it sounded doable, he was surprised. How long until she missed the bright lights of LA and all the bennies that came with it? "What about your show?"

There was a long pause, then, "I'm not sure I want to do it anymore."

He lifted her chin with his finger. "Why? I got the impression the show was important to you...that being on television propelled everything else." And being a television celebrity was wrapped up in her self-worth, which Sawyer didn't think was altogether healthy.

"It certainly made the brand. But that's not why I did it. My whole life I felt like I had something to prove, something to show Sadie DeRose that she hadn't made a mistake by adopting me. She'd wanted to be a movie star, so I followed in her footsteps, doing the closest thing I knew how. I may not have been a leading lady on the silver screen, but television launched me into homes across the nation. Soon, I was a household name and face. I was famous. I was what my mother had always wanted her—and then me—to be."

"And now?"

"I don't need it to define me anymore. I guess it took me thirty-seven years to figure out that I was so busy trying to prove myself to my mother that I forgot to live for myself and do the things that truly make me happy."

He liked what he was hearing. Not because it benefited him, but because Gina had grown. So had he. Sawyer supposed love did that to a person.

"So what makes you happy, Gina DeRose? Besides me, of course." His mouth split into a smile.

"Having a man who loves me, even when I've been falsely accused, on the brink of a professional meltdown, and stripped of everything."

Sawyer waggled his eyebrows. "Especially when you've been stripped of everything."

She laughed. "You've got a one-track mind, Dalton."

"Yep." His hands inched up her camisole and she slapped it away.

"I was just about to get to the best part."

He kissed her belly and tilted his head up to look at her. "This isn't the best part?"

"I want to do the restaurant."

Taken aback, Sawyer stopped kissing her. Gina was full of surprises today. "Here?"

"At Dry Creek Ranch." A smile spread across her face, transforming her from gorgeous to radiant. "A steak house that would feature the ranch's beef. It could be the anchor. We could also do the country store. Chock-full of my products, of course. And the butcher shop, a Dalton beef exclusive retailer. Or we could go nationwide—your choice."

Damn, he liked the sound of that. All of it. But it had to be real.

"You seriously want to do this…a restaurant? What made you change your mind? Because, Gina, I don't want you to do anything you don't really want to do. We'll find our anchor. You do what makes you happy, not what you think will make me happy."

"You make me happy." She reached up, pulled his head down, and covered his mouth with hers. When they finished kissing, she said, "Cooking makes me happy. Feeding people makes me happy. And someone once told me I had to stop being so critical of myself. That I had to start believing in myself. I'd say opening a destination restaurant is a good step in that direction, don't you?" She took a deep breath. "I won't lie. I'm scared to death. Scared I'll fail…become a laughingstock. But I'll never know if I don't try, will I?"

"Only if it's what you want."

"It's what I want. And you, Sawyer Dalton, is who I want."

He held her so close he could hear the beating of her heart. "Right back atcha, baby."

"Shall we take a walk and tell everyone?"

"Soon." He lifted her off the couch. "First, I want you all to myself."

She stared into his eyes and his pulse picked up, doing that two-step again. Forty-two days ago, Gina DeRose had taken over his house and now she owned his heart.

"How soon can you move your stuff here?" He carried her inside the bedroom.

She touched her hand to his chest. "Soon as I can hire movers. Do I get dibs on the closet?"

"As long as I get dibs on you." He started to undress her. "At some point, though, we'll have to discuss your choice in luggage."

She rolled her eyes. "Oh shut up, Sawyer Dalton, and kiss me."

"Will kiss for food." He laid her gently on the bed and came up alongside her.

"You'll get plenty of both. Now love me, cowboy."

"With pleasure." And with that, Sawyer did what he was told.

Epilogue

Six months later

"There." Gina pointed to the space where her new ovens would go, then turned to the far wall. "That's where I'm putting the grills and griddles."

As the new brand ambassador for Supplycrafters she was getting all her restaurant equipment free. In return, the appliances would be featured in her new FoodFlicks reality show, *Restaurant Chronicles*, which would document the start-up of DeRose Steak House.

Only two more months until they started taping. Two months after that, the restaurant's soft opening.

Sawyer turned in a wide circle. "Wow, it's huge. You think we can actually fill this place?"

"I don't think it, I know it. We're booked solid the first month. The local hotels are going to love us."

The sound of electric tools floated through the space. Since September, there'd been nonstop construction. First, the flower shop and Tuff's saddlery went in and now they were finishing the build-out of a small sarsaparilla and pie stand next to the restaurant. Laney came nearly every day to boss around the workers.

The complex, a series of rustic buildings that mimicked Charlie and Aubrey's old barn and a group of landscaped trails with benches and picnic tables, had a bird's-eye view of the creek, the mountains, and the cattle pastures. The parking lot, cordoned off with a low split-rail fence and hitching posts, also mirrored a Western theme.

A general store and butcher shop was next in line. And who knew what would come after that?

Gina's steak house announcement and the national press it received had been good for publicity. So far, they had a stack of applications from companies that wanted to set up shop on Dry Creek Ranch, including a proposal to put in six EVgo charging stations for electric cars.

Sawyer liked that venture the best. While road-weary travelers juiced up, they'd spend time eating and shopping.

Cha-ching.

Gina spray-painted a series of *X*'s on the wall.

"What's that for?"

"I changed my mind about the location of the walk-in cooler. I want it to go here."

While she'd put Aubrey in charge of designing the dining room, she was micromanaging the hell out of the configuration of her kitchen.

"You're driving the contractors crazy, you know that, right?"

"I want everything to be perfect." She gazed up at him, her eyes twinkling.

"It will be." He bent down to taste her lips and let the kiss linger. "Because you're perfect. But if we don't get going, we'll be late."

"You're the one making out with me in my restaurant." She squeezed his butt and kissed him one more time before grabbing her purse off one of the sawhorses. Then she led the way outside.

In Sawyer's Range Rover, they took the new paved lane that bypassed their homes and emptied out at Dry Creek Road about two miles from the ranch gate. The new entrance would be used by diners and shoppers, while the old gate was solely for family. In the end, everyone had decided that privacy was worth the cost of a separate road.

Sawyer snuck a quick glance at his watch. "They'll all beat us there."

"Sorry."

He reached over and squeezed her knee. "Nothing to apologize for." The fact was, he didn't know how she managed to organize her time so well. Between getting a new restaurant off the ground, prepping for a new television show, and juggling her other business interests, she still made plenty of quality time for them.

"I still can't believe it," she said. "Do you think your parents are crazy?"

Sawyer laughed. "*Crazy* doesn't begin to describe it. But definitely crazy in a good way. I just wish my grandfather was alive, but I know he's looking down, smiling his ass off."

He hung a left at Beals Ranch, drove through the gate, and continued up the private gravel road. A collection of vehicles was parked in front of

the ranch house, his mother's Mercedes standing out among the pickup trucks and his aunt and uncle's SUV.

He and Gina let themselves into the house to be greeted by his entire family. Even Travis, Grady, and Ellie were there.

The place looked bare without the Bealses' furniture. Someone had dragged in an old picnic table and two benches. Aubrey, so pregnant she looked ready to burst, sat on a folding chair. Cash stood over her, his hand on her shoulder. While Charlie was nowhere near as round as Aubrey, she too had started to show. Sawyer figured Jace had knocked her up on their honeymoon.

"We ready to do this?" Sawyer's dad held up a bottle of Dom Pérignon.

"Oh, Dan." His mother searched the kitchen counter. "I forgot the flutes. We have no glasses."

Uncle Jed laughed. "I could probably scrounge up a few Solo cups in my trunk."

He started to go out to his SUV but Jace stopped him. "Let's just pass around the bottle."

"Works for me," Jed said, though Cash's mom pulled a face.

Sawyer's dad popped the cork and held the bottle in the air. "To our family. May this new venture of ours flourish and may my late father, Jasper Dalton, smile down on his legacy." Dan tilted his head toward the ceiling. "Pop, we know you're up there, looking down, proud as hell of your grandsons."

Dan swiveled around and found Jace. "Son, more than anything, we wish your folks and baby brother could be here too. We loved them and miss them every day. But we know they'd be especially proud of you and Charlie." He zoomed in on Charlie's belly, then glanced across the room to Aubrey and smiled "Well done, kiddos. Sawyer and Gina, we expect someday soon you'll be next. To more Daltons and to Dry Creek Ranch!"

"Hear, hear," everyone shouted.

Jed grabbed the bottle from Dan and again raised it. "To my brother and Wendy. Without them this couldn't have happened."

There was another raucous round of "Hear, hears."

Cash turned to Jace. "Do you have the sign?"

"Right here." Jace held up a large package wrapped in brown paper. "Let's do it!"

On cue, everyone followed Jace outside, got into their respective vehicles and drove the mile to the ranch gate, where they parked on the dirt shoulder.

One by one, they filed out of their trucks and SUVs and gathered around the entrance. Jace climbed on top of the cab of his Ford. Cash got in the

bed and handed him up the package. With a pocketknife, Jace made quick work of the wrapping. Down came the iron Beals Ranch logo that hung from the wooden crossbeam of the gate and up went a beautifully carved Dry Creek Ranch sign with the Dalton brand.

Gina snapped a few pictures with her phone. "I'll post it to social media."

Jed hauled out the opened bottle of champagne and they took turns passing it around. When everyone had had a sip, even the kids, Sawyer smashed the bottle against the gatepost to christen their new property.

Somehow, his parents had cobbled together a sizable down payment to purchase Beals Ranch and Randy had made good on his promise to give the Daltons first dibs. The hope was that the restaurant, Aubrey and Charlie's business, and the rent from their new tenants would keep them afloat. With the extra land, they also planned to increase their cow-calf operation.

Worse came to worst, they could always develop a piece of the land with a few ranchettes and put them on the market. Not ideal, but a hell of a lot better than a gated golf-course community.

In the meantime, they had a renter for the Beals old ranch house and a nearby winery had signed a lease to plant a section of the property in Barbera grapes, though the bulk of the land would be used for livestock.

"This is a good day," Dan said, beaming. "Damn, would my father be strutting right now."

Sawyer pulled Gina closer and wrapped her in a one-armed hug. He wanted to share all the joy he was feeling with her. She gazed up at him, love shining in her eyes.

"This is amazing," she said, staring out at miles of pastureland. "We're going to kick so much ass here."

Sawyer chuckled. "You think?"

"I know."

Cash cleared his throat. "Let's go back to the house. I've got a surprise."

The kids hopped off of Jace's tailgate. "What is it, Uncle Cash?" Grady shouted.

"You'll see when we get there."

Sawyer scooped up the glass from the champagne bottle and tossed it in the back of his Range Rover. Together, the whole family caravanned up the hill again.

Gina reached for Sawyer's hand and threaded her fingers through his. "What do you think the surprise is?"

"Beats the hell out of me. Maybe Aubrey is having twins."

Gina poked him in the side and he laughed. When they arrived at the house, they stayed inside Sawyer's truck until everyone had gone inside.

"Have I told you today how much I love you?" He pulled Gina over the console into his lap.

"Probably." She pressed her lips against his. "But you can tell me again. I never tire of hearing you say it."

"Later, when we get home," he said and winked. "Not only will I tell you but I'll show you. First, let's see what Cash has up his sleeve."

He lifted her out of the driver's side because he couldn't take his hands off her, then twirled her around in the air. His dad was right: It was a good day. Strike that, it was a monumental day. He was living the dream. The ranch expansion and he had the woman he loved, all in one awesome package.

Inside, Cash set his laptop on the table and motioned for Sawyer to join Wendy and Dan on the bench. Jace and Cash's parents hovered close so they could see the screen.

Sawyer turned the computer to avoid glare from the sun. "What are we looking at besides a blank screen?"

"Be patient and you shall see." Cash played around with the FaceTime app.

A few seconds later, a woman appeared on the screen and Sawyer's mother screamed.

Angie.

His beautiful sister beamed at them and it was like a slice of sunshine.

Gone was her long blond hair. It had been cut into a shoulder-length bob that made her appear older and more conservative. Otherwise, she looked exactly as she had five years ago. The same Dalton blue eyes as the rest of them and that impish smile that always made his parents cave whenever she was in trouble.

"Hi, everyone." She gave a jerky wave and Sawyer noted that her eyes were wet.

His too. He reached out and touched the screen as if could feel her face.

"They're only giving me a few minutes," she continued. "I just wanted everyone to know that I'm fine, that I'm safe, and that I love you."

Sawyer's mother began to sob.

"When can you come home, Angie?" Sawyer's voice cracked.

She shrugged and flashed a sheepish grin. But this time the smile didn't quite reach her eyes. "Someday, I hope. I miss you all like crazy. But I'm good. I have a nice job, a cute place to live, friends. Really, it's all good." She stopped to catch her breath. "Mom, Dad, don't cry. Think of it as I'm away on a long vacation."

"Can we come see you?" Sawyer knew it was against WITSEC rules, but so was FaceTiming. Cash had obviously pulled strings. Maybe the feds would make an exception for a visit too.

"Nah." Angie tried to smile again. "Let's see what happens, okay? Enough about me, I'm dying to hear about you." She searched the dining room for the kids and the moment she spotted them, waved. "Hi, Ellie, I haven't met you yet. You're so pretty. You look just like your daddy. And Grady, the last time I saw you, you were just four years old. My goodness, you've grown. You too, Travis. You're almost as tall as Jace." Angie surveyed the room again. "Where's Gina?"

Gina moved closer to the camera. "I'm here. It's lovely to finally meet you, Angela."

"I love your show. Cash says you're opening a restaurant at the ranch and that my brother is crazy about you."

"I'm crazy about him too," Gina said in a soft voice and swiped at her eyes. "I'm glad you're safe, Angie. Sawyer has missed you so. Well, I don't want to take away time from everyone else." She rose and joined Charlie and Aubrey in the living room. Sawyer knew it was to give them privacy.

Wendy and Dan spent the remaining time telling Angie how much they loved and missed her, how her disappearance had left them brokenhearted. How relieved they were that she was alive and well.

Seeing her like this—so close up—but knowing she was likely thousands of miles away was maddening. The big family milestones—the births of the new Dalton babies, Travis's high school graduation, their parents' fortieth anniversary—she would miss them all.

"As soon as you can, come home, Angie. I want you at my wedding."

Everyone around the table gaped at him. There hadn't been a marriage proposal yet, let alone an announcement.

Hell with it. If Angela couldn't come home, she could at least be part of the most important day of his life.

"Gina, come back in here for a sec," he called to the other room.

She rushed in, Aubrey and Charlie on her heels. Sawyer positioned the computer screen so Angie could see better, then tugged Gina closer.

"Let's do this, baby, let's get hitched." He got down on one knee. "Gina DeRose, will you make me the happiest man alive by marrying me and being my wife?"

There was a collective round of "ahs."

Normally, he wouldn't have turned something so momentous as a proposal into a public spectacle. He'd really intended to pop the question

in private. Just Gina and him, somewhere on the ranch. Maybe down by the creek where he'd taught her how to skip stones.

But as long as Angie couldn't see him walk down the aisle and celebrate his wedding day, they would at least have this. Even if it was only on FaceTime. Even if he had to propose in front of a large audience.

He grabbed the foil left over from the Dom Pérignon bottle and wrapped it around Gina's finger. "Don't say no." He squeezed her hand. "You'll break my sister's heart."

Gina laughed as she swiped tears from her eyes. "Yes, I will marry you. And what the heck took you so long?"

The room erupted in laughter.

"Been a little busy. But I promise it was worth the wait. You won't ever be sorry, Gina DeRose," he said and got a little choked up. "Because I won't ever stop loving you."

"Me neither." Gina peered up at him through long lashes and for a long time they stared into each other's eyes. "I've waited for you my whole life and I'm never letting you go, Sawyer Dalton."

"I'm so happy for you both," Angie called from the screen, her eyes watery. "They're telling me I have to go now. Take good care of my big brother, Gina." And just like that she was gone.

A hush fell over the room. No one seemed to know whether to mourn or celebrate. The silence seemed to go on forever, filling the room with melancholia.

Suddenly, Wendy rose and gathered Sawyer and Gina in her arms. "We have a wedding to plan."

Everyone began talking at once, wishing the couple congratulations, slapping Sawyer on the back, and hugging Gina.

"I presume you'll want it on the ranch," Wendy continued. Both he and Gina nodded, because where else would they have it?

"Charlie's barn," Gina blurted. "I mean, if that's okay."

"Are you kidding? We'd love nothing more," Charlie said. "We'll move all the furniture to the back offices and anywhere else we can find space."

"We can use the restaurant too." Gina clapped her hands together. "Dinner in the steak house and dancing in the barn. The ceremony under the stars." She drew back. "What do you think, Sawyer?"

"As long as I get you, we can throw whatever kind of party you want." He pulled her into his arms, pressed his lips against her ear, and whispered, "A real ring soon and a proposal that isn't in front of everyone. Something romantic."

"I love you, Sawyer. And I can't wait to be your wife. I'm glad you included Angie. It was a lovely thing to do." She stroked his face. "Are you okay?"

It was a mixed bag. His sister should be in the bosom of her family, celebrating their new acquisition. But six months ago he didn't even know if she was still alive. So when he looked at it like that—hell, yeah he was okay.

And the real silver lining was he'd just gotten engaged to the love of his life. "Better than okay, baby. This weekend, we do this right." He held up her hand and gave her ring finger a squeeze. He'd book a room at the St. Francis and take her to the diamond district.

Before he could say more, Aubrey, Charlie, Wendy, and his aunt whisked her away for wedding talk.

Cash came over and rested his hand on Sawyer's shoulder. "Congratulations."

"Thanks and thanks for greasing whatever wheels necessary to set that call up with Angie. It meant the world to us, Cash. I only wish…" he trailed off. Cash had done all he could.

"Who knows"—the edges of Cash's mouth kicked up—"maybe Angie will be able to make it to the wedding after all? Stranger things have happened." Cash winked and sauntered away to talk to Jace.

Sawyer looked after him, wondering if that was wishful thinking or if Cash was actually trying to tell him something.

Son of a gun.

Sawyer broke into a wide grin.

"What are you smiling about?" Gina sidled up beside him.

"Just happy is all. What do you say we blow this gin joint and celebrate in private?"

"I'd say let's do it."

A rush of cold air hit them as they walked outside, hand in hand. The snowcapped mountains were shrouded in fog, making them look like magic clouds. The grass was green and wet and smelled like fresh-cut hay.

From the front yard he could hear the gurgle of the creek that divided the two ranches and wondered how long it would take before they started calling Beals Ranch Dry Creek Ranch.

Perhaps they never would and that was okay. A tradition upheld.

Next month, the cows would start calving and Gina's restaurant would open in June.

Sawyer wrapped his arms around Gina and turned her so they could both behold the beauty of the land and their future together.

It was going to be a good year. A very good year.

Printed in the United States
by Baker & Taylor Publisher Services